For Carmen

"Fantasy is the impossible made probable. Science fiction
is the improbable made possible."

— Rod Serling

Science-in-fiction is the possible made believable.

PART ONE

Grand Captiva

1

DINO

Bang! A door opened. Bright fluorescent lights. Footsteps at his side. A whiff of disinfectant invading his nostrils, sweet, pungent, sickening.

Dino Stampa woke with a start. For a split second, he didn't know where he was. He stared at a sleek rail at the foot end of the bed, the wall opposite a pale funeral-home green, radiating clinical coldness. He touched his temples, trying to ease the throbbing pain. Something tugged at his arm. He was hooked up to an IV; it felt like being chained to a pole on wheels. What the hell was going on?

Then it all came back slowly, vague and indistinct.

Emergency... The hospital...

But where was Cat?

Dino tried to put the pieces back together in his foggy brain. His mind reeled backwards.

The previous day had been just like any other day. After work, Dino had driven over to his girlfriend's house. Cat worked as a nurse at Lee County Hospital and often was on late shifts, but not on that day. They both looked forward to one of those rare evenings spent together, decelerating. Peaceful, relaxing, cozy—at home.

As Dino scrambled out of his over-chilled car, the ambient air felt oppressive—the summer weather pattern was establishing itself early in southwest Florida.

The aroma of Italian herbs and garlic dangled in the air as he entered. He glanced toward the dining table, where dinner was waiting. Mia, Cat's six-year-old daughter, greeted him

3

with a sheepish smile, her large, dark eyes shining with anticipation. "I brought you something," Dino said, conjuring up a box of raspberry-chocolate ice cream, her absolute favorite.

Dino didn't have any children, but he loved Mia as if she were his own. At one point, Cat had confided to him that he treated Mia better than her real dad did. He had shrugged at the time, his head hot with embarrassment, warmth radiating throughout his body.

"How was your day?" Cat said after she gave him a peck on his cheek.

Dino pulled her closer and gave her a long kiss. "You look gorgeous."

Cat waved his compliment off with a hand, her blonde ponytail swerving to the side. Typical Cat. Always controlled, matter-of-fact. She wouldn't openly display her affection for others, but underneath the self-protecting carapace she was the most caring, loving person he had ever known.

They sat.

"Nice tomatoes," Dino said, his mouth stuffed with salad. "You aren't having any?"

Cat shook her head. "Dino, you know I don't like tomatoes." She picked daintily at the grilled chicken cutlet on her plate.

"Mia, salad?"

She grimaced at him but said nothing. Not a great fan of veggies either.

"They're the ones from the farmers market," Cat said. "You know, from Miguel, that friendly Mexican guy."

"Oh, yeah, Miguel." He nodded, shoving another tomato into his mouth. "These are outstanding. Natural flavor made in Florida. Unlike some of those pale, tasteless tomatoes grown in greenhouses up north."

Dino sat up in the hospital bed, trying to remember what happened next but quickly lay down again. His memory was sketchy, fragmented like a scrappy phone conversation caused by a poor signal. He was exhausted, as if he'd pulled an all-nighter.

There was a blank, but then he remembered having collapsed on the bedroom floor halfway between the bathroom and the bed, feeling sick. At some point, Cat had fumbled around with his arm, mounting the cuff of her blood pressure monitor on his upper arm. "Oh my God," she had muttered.

There was another long lapse of memory. He remembered hearing car doors slamming shut, tires squealing, a siren wailing. An ambulance, probably. Then... nothing.

Where is Cat? Dino thought. *Is she safe?* He tried to reach for his cell phone but could not find it on the console next to him. Where was everybody? As he struggled to figure out what happened, his head sank into the pillow, and he drifted back into the oblivion of sleep.

***

Several hours later, a young man in a white coat appeared at Dino's bedside.

"I'm Dr. Snowhill. How are we doing this morning, Dino?" He pronounced it *Dye-no*.

Dino weakly shook the proffered hand. "Actually, it's *Dee-no*. Italian name, makes me a lot younger at heart. I'm not too bad, thanks, except I'm still wired up to this damn bag. What happened?"

"You were in pretty bad shape last night." Dr. Snowhill sat down in the visitor chair. His eyes looked tired, and he hadn't shaved. "We brought you back from the near dead."

"What's wrong? What did I do that I shouldn't have done?" Dino sounded flustered.

"You tell me. We don't know exactly—you just stopped breathing. When we brought you back from a coma-like state, you were agitated and confused." Snowhill knit his brows and lowered his voice. "Do you take drugs, recreational drugs?"

Drugs. Dino flinched, his mind roiling. He had a sudden piercing memory of his younger brother, Tony, who'd died some ten years ago in a speeding accident after taking party drugs. Pure horror.

"Look, I know what drugs can do to people. I don't go near them, ever. Why do you ask?"

"Because you exhibited classical symptoms of an opioid overdose. Have you taken any medication in the past few days? Any painkillers?"

"Nothing. No drugs, not even an aspirin. Didn't put anything on my skin. Didn't eat anything suspicious. No seafood, no nothing—" Dino sat up in bed. "Doc, could this be food poisoning, or an allergy? I remember now that I was sick as a dog last night. Vomited all over everywhere."

"I can't rule out food poisoning, but it's unlikely. It wasn't an allergic reaction."

"What about Cat and her daughter, Mia? Are they okay?"

"No worries. They're fine. She brought you here last night, under the wire. We just talked a while ago. She'll come by later." He stood up. "We need to draw blood one more time. A lab tech will come by shortly."

"What for? My cholesterol levels are fine—"

"Look, Dino, this is serious. We had to give you Narcan when you came in. I'm not sure how you were even still alive when you got here, but that Narcan probably saved your life. Narcan is... how shall I explain—"

"It's naloxone. An opioid receptor antagonist."

Dr. Snowhill gave an approving nod, a knowing smile on his face. "What do you do for a living?"

"I'm a biochemist with a small contract company in Fort Myers—*Rainbow BioLabs.* We do analytical work, mostly for the government."

"Air, water... soil analyses, I guess?"

"Yeah, mostly pesticide residues, air pollution, toxic chemicals on food, but we also do occasional blood tests for small clinics and hospitals."

"So, you're familiar with the problem." Snowhill squinted, leaned forward, his expression dead serious. "Dino, what's going on here? You took an opioid, right? Why don't you just tell us what it was? It'll show up in your blood and urine anyway."

"Because I didn't take one. I swear I didn't. I don't know what caused this, but it was *not* an opioid."

Snowhill's expression signaled he wasn't buying Dino's story. "You had to have taken something. You had all the symptoms of opioid overdose. What did you take? Heroin, fentanyl, oxycodone? Look, we just want to help you."

"*Goddamnit*, don't patronize me. I didn't take any opioids." As soon as Dino said it, he regretted his outburst. He knew he had a short fuse, but usually his hothead cooled down equally fast. "When can I go home?"

"Not until we get the results of your blood and urine analyses. We'll talk then."

Snowhill crossed his arms and stared at Dino for a few seconds. His pinched face expressed annoyance, but he reached out his hand and gave Dino a pat on the arm. "Get well soon."

"Thanks." Dino felt bad enough without having to deal with some arrogant doctor accusing him of using drugs.

Snowhill's pager beeped, and he buzzed out the door, mumbling an apology.

Dino lay in bed, searching his muddled brain for an explanation of his near-death experience. Fighting back his memories of Tony's death. *Drugs*—what a ridiculous accusation.

Cat... He missed her. Working at LCH, she couldn't be far away. He wondered what she'd say when he told her about the doctor's suspicions.

He felt his stomach knot up as he remembered what the doctor had said—that her level-headed, swift action last night had saved his life.

2

CAT

Catherine Gillespie exhaled loudly, releasing the tension she had kept pent-up all day.

She had briefly visited Dino at the ward during her break. "Good news, Cat," he had said. "I'm out of here shortly." But Dr. Snowhill had told her that they were still waiting for test results before he would release Dino.

She rubbed her stiff neck, tried to relax her strained shoulder muscles. Dino and his carefree, even reckless, behavior... What had he done this time?

Cat knew that she tended to burden herself with too much responsibility, acting overly protective, but she couldn't help it. Dino pushed the limits at times, and he needed someone like her, someone with a cool head, someone who'd think before acting.

Sometimes she wondered how she managed to balance her demanding job and her personal life—taking care of Mia, working overtime, pulling double shifts. She was fortunate to have met Dino not long ago. He was a bastion of calm that brought stability to her life—most of the time. Not now.

The doctor had said that it must have been opioid overdosing.

Opioid overdosing? Dino?

The ER nurse had told her about three cases with strange opioid overdose symptoms that had been admitted in the past few days. One of them had died last night. "Wonder if that's what your friend had," the ER nurse said casually. Cat had blown her off, but now that she thought about it, Dino's mysterious symptoms last night fit right into the picture. Shallow breathing, racing pulse, blood pressure at rock bottom, pin-point pupils. It just didn't make sense.

Cat shook her head. She knew Dino hadn't been in touch with any prescription opioid drug, let alone an illegal drug—or at least she thought she knew that. No, he wouldn't, not after his brother.

But the most puzzling thing she'd learned from the ER nurse was that, despite enormous efforts by the experts at the analytical lab, the nature of the mysterious opioid drug had remained elusive. All tests for the most commonly known opioids had turned out to be negative. Nothing. All the typical symptoms of opioid OD, yet no trace of any opioid in their system.

She understood why the doctors and staff at LCH called these strange cases "phantom opioid" poisonings. And now Dino...

***

By the time Cat reached Dino's room, he was dressed and engaged in a somewhat testy conversation with Dr. Snowhill.

"I came to tell you that the results of your tests were negative and you could go home, but I see that you're already dressed and on your way out of here." Snowhill looked disgusted.

"Yeah, and the reason the results were negative was because I haven't been using opioids. I told you that."

"We still don't know what caused your respiratory depression. You nearly died, Dino."

"Well, we're not going to figure it out laying around here. I'm out of here."

"Your discharge papers will be at the front desk. Let us know if you have any further problems."

"Sure thing," Dino said dismissively.

After the doctor left, Cat grabbed Dino by his arms, throwing him an appraising glance.

"Dino, what's the matter with you? Why were you so angry with Dr. Snowhill? Goading each other?"

"Because he wouldn't believe me when I told him I'm not taking drugs and then my lab tests showed no signs of opioids in my system, and he still won't give it up."

"Hey, listen, you don't know what's going on here. Apparently, we've had several cases of patients with opioid overdose symptoms in the past few days. They haven't been able to find any trace of a known opioid in any of those patients, but one of them died last night. *That could have been you.*"

He didn't say anything. He just pulled Cat close to him and held her there and then they made their way out of the hospital.

3

MIGUEL

Miguel Castro was no coward, but staring into the muzzle of a gun at five o'clock in the morning chilled him to the bone.

The 25-pound box he held slipped from his left hand and hit the ground with a thud. He tried to grab it—too late. The lid flew open and three large, shiny red tomatoes tumbled out. Miguel watched in horror as they rolled in slow motion down the driveway and stopped at the feet of the man with the gun.

Miguel stretched his arms toward the man, his wrists flexed, palms open in a conciliatory gesture, and stammered something, but his throat constricted, making his words unintelligible. The dim light spilling out of his open garage was enough to reveal a wiry man with mean, narrow eyes and a haggard face. Miguel had never seen this guy before.

An instant twinge of panic seized him. His mind raced. What could this man possibly want? Miguel carried only a few bucks in his pockets. He sold fruit and vegetables for a living at a couple of farmers markets in Southwest Florida. He didn't live in a well-heeled neighborhood. His ramshackle house certainly didn't look as if it contained anything of value. Maria, his wife, and the kids were still asleep.

"*¿Qué quiere?*" Miguel asked, his voice strained.

"Cut the crap," the guy said with a husky voice. "Where are they?"

Miguel's mind was spinning. *They?* Was Gun Man talking about his family? No way he would let the attacker get anywhere close to them.

The neighborhood looked ghostly in the pale moonlight. A dead, ominous silence filled the air, the tension palpable.

Even the cicadas had stopped chirping. The pleasant, warm predawn Florida morning suddenly felt muggy and oppressive. Miguel wiped the sweat from his forehead and ran his hand through his thick, black hair.

He took a deep breath and shrugged. "What you talking about? What do you want?"

"Don't give me that shit, man," Gun Man hissed. He was still holding the gun in his left hand, arm outstretched, leveling the weapon at Miguel's chest. "You know exactly what I want." With a flash of his white sneaker, he squashed one of the tomatoes at his feet, slowly swiveling his foot sideways several times as though he were grinding a cigarette butt under his heel. A small rivulet of red juice trickled down the driveway.

A million thoughts swirled through Miguel's mind. He was out of his depth, his anxiety flitting into a wave of anger. Like a cornered animal, he was determined to fight.

"*No tengo idea de qué estás hablando,*" Miguel fired off in his native language. It was true, he had no clue what the man wanted.

"Why don't you speak English, like everybody else, buddy?" The mugger took a few steps closer and brandished his firearm. "Do you really want me to jog your memory?"

Miguel thought he saw a light go on across the street. Could he stall this guy? Maybe someone—anyone—would come out or drive by. Yelling for help was out of the question. For a split second he considered pulling his cell phone from his pocket but abandoned the idea immediately. The gun was pointed right at his stomach.

"The ones that you pilfered from us," Gun Man continued. "Where are they?"

"*Pilfered?*" Miguel cocked his head. "I don't understand…"

"You're such a fucking idiot. The ones you stole some days ago. The friggin' Grand Captivas. We know you took 'em. You know what they are… I want them back. Now."

"You talking about *tomates*?" Miguel's eyes widened in disbelief. "I picked them up at the farm, as always, and took them out for delivery." He swallowed. "And then... I sold them."

"You sold them?"

"*Sí!*" Miguel was both annoyed and clueless. "That's what I always do. That's my job." The fruit and veggies he sold at the farmers market were always fresh. Why would he still have tomatoes from almost a week ago?

That's when his brain registered the *plop* of the silencer. A second later a sharp pang exploded in his left leg. Miguel went down heavily on the ground, his face contorted with pain. He cursed and leaned on his right elbow. Blood oozed from the wound onto his pants, and seeped down the driveway, mixing with the red splashes of the smushed tomato. Seconds later, a second shot, this time to his upper body, threw him fully to the ground.

Then darkness...

4

DINO

Wing News, the local channel for Southwest Florida, had the story on the *Late News*, a report of a near-fatal shooting in Sementina Springs. Miguel Castro, thirty-nine, had been shot at his home before daybreak. The motive for the shooting was unclear. The small house where the man lived with his family had not been burglarized, but the garage where he kept his truck had been turned upside down. The victim had been hospitalized, but he was no longer in critical condition. The police were intensifying their efforts to identify the perpetrator.

"That's him," Dino yelled, pointing to the TV screen.

Cat turned down the volume. "Poor man. Miguel's always been so friendly. Why would anyone…"

"We bought tomatoes from him the other day, right?"

She nodded. "The day before you were rushed to the ER."

Dino's thoughts strayed back to that morning at the Farmers Market.

"Tomates—muy sabrosos," Miguel, the short man with the moon face and the stubbly chin had said. "Very tasty."

"I bet they are. What are these?" Cat asked, pointing to a pile of shiny red, seemingly succulent, ripe tomatoes.

The vendor pointed to a small placard that read, *GRAND CAPTIVA*. "New variety, try it." He cut a tomato in half and offered the juicy slices to them. As some of the pulp trickled down his fingers onto his chapped hand, Dino noticed the man's dirty fingernails and raised his hand.

"No thanks, not now," he said, smiling.

The impressive signboard attached at the top of his stall said, GREEN, RED & SUSTAINABLE, INC.—SEMENTINA SPRINGS. When he'd heard the name of this company the first time, he'd wondered, slightly amused, whether the three words were the actual last names of the founding partners—like those of a typical law firm—or simply referred to the produce they sold.

Dino had peered again at the Grand Captivas. "Are they fresh?" He realized immediately that was the silliest question one could ask a vendor at a farmers market. Or the waiter at a seafood restaurant, for that matter.

Miguel's pudgy face cracked into a smile. "Everything is fresh." His hand made a sweeping gesture encompassing the entire display of vegetables.

As they walked back to their car, Cat was carrying a bulging white plastic bag.

"I still can't believe someone shot him," Cat said. "One is no longer safe *anywhere* nowadays."

"In most cases it's a personal thing," Dino said. "People who know each other. Revenge, jealousy, settling an old score, what have you."

"Or drugs."

Dino nodded. "Speaking of drugs," he said, "you said you had several cases of opioid overdose at the hospital, right?"

"Allegedly." She talked fast now, gesticulating as she often did when she became agitated. "They call them phantom opioid poisonings because the symptoms resemble those of opioid OD. But they couldn't find the culprit. Really strange. Dino, your case was just one of a dozen. My gosh, I'm still jittery."

Dino leaned forward. A sudden idea had struck him. "You think I could help them out? At the lab we have state-of-the-art analytical equipment." He thought of the brand-new analyzers, the excellent technical staff, their year-long experience with toxic substances. "I mean, this is serious. I'm concerned about more people getting sick or dying. This must be stopped."

Cat uttered an impish laugh. "That's okay, Dino. At LCH we have an outstanding clinical-chemical service lab. We're a bit short-staffed, but those guys know what they're doing." She gently touched his arm. "Thanks anyway."

Dino shrugged. "Okay. Why don't you keep your ears open and let me know. Just in case."

Unable to ID a toxic chemical in a blood sample? Hard to believe. He was sure he would be able to track it down if given the chance. Which, on top, would be much more challenging than the usual routine work he was assigned to accomplish. Except his moody boss wouldn't approve of it.

Dino decided not to breathe a word about this to the old, querulous tyrant.

5

DINO

The next day, Dino was back at work. Usually an early riser, he came in late.

Rainbow BioLabs, LLC—Biomedical Analytics was located in a recently renovated two-story building in downtown Fort Myers. Dino entered through the glass door and strode right up to the receptionist behind a stylish counter that looked like the front desk of a luxury hotel in the Emirates. He wiped his forehead with his sleeve. The oppressive heat had barely receded overnight.

"Morning, Jess. Got anything for me?" He put his palm on the granite countertop. It felt cool to the touch, smooth like an alabaster vase.

Jessica handed him some mail and a couple of phone messages. "You should return these calls, please." As she gazed at the clock on the wall, her pointed expression said it all.

He was late. He got it.

"The boss wanted me to remind you that the analytical report for Tallahassee is overdue." Jessica peeked toward the office area. "He was quite upset, actually, when he didn't find you yesterday."

"Come on," Dino said aloud, "I had a medical emergency the night before and was rushed to the hospital. He can't blame me this time. It certainly wasn't my fault." He still felt a bit dizzy, but a lot better than the day before.

Jessica shot him a doubtful look, reached for her coffee mug, and refocused her attention on the computer.

Dino tossed the mail on a side table in his crammed, tiny office and cranked up the A/C. A stale, musty odor lingered in

17

the air. He absent-mindedly ran his hand over a dried coffee stain on the pebble-grained surface of his desk, trying to figure out what was at the top of his to-do list.

Jason Goodlette, aka The Boss, busted into his office without knocking.

"Dino—I looked for you all day yesterday," Goodlette said, somewhat out of breath. He could be intimidating with his tall figure, broad shoulders and massive chest. By the sound of his deep, thunderous voice, it was clear he was upset.

Dino looked up at Goodlette—early fifties, but he appeared younger, clean-shaven, hair dyed a dark brown, combed back.

"Morning, Jason," Dino said. "Had a medical emergency, but I'm back. I informed Jess, though—"

"Well, she didn't tell me," Goodlette snarled. "Listen—where's the government project report? You're way over deadline. I've reminded you before."

No asking after his health. "You'll have it tomorrow morning. It'll be on your desk when you come in."

"It better be."

"Sure, no sweat. I'm almost done. Why all this flurry?"

"Flurry? There's a reason we have deadlines. In fact, the government... are you listening to me at all, Dino?"

Dino wasn't. Through the open door he had spotted Brian, his head technician, who displayed a wide grin.

"Tomorrow morning, then," Goodlette snorted and left the room, muttering something to himself. He turned as he left. "Oh, another thing. Earlier last week, same story. I needed you for something and couldn't find you. Away for the entire day. You moonlighting or what?"

"Dental appointment," Dino said, opening his mouth and touching his incisors for emphasis.

Goodlette looked up at the ceiling and shook his head as he left the room.

Awkward, but Dino could care less. Always the same story. Goodlette pressured everybody for reports, then when he got them, they sat on his desk for a week before he even looked at them. Annoying. To be fair though, Jason Goodlette also had a pleasant side. He was generous with his employees and gave out fat end-of-the-year bonuses.

Two weeks ago, he had treated the whole gang to dinner at the best restaurant in town.

The government project report was almost finished, but it needed some editing. It would take him half a day, at most.

Dino leafed through the stack of sheets he'd just printed out. Tallahassee had commissioned a detailed investigation on possible contamination of tomatoes with pesticide residues. Because tomato farming was an essential part of Florida's agribusiness, protecting the plants was an important economic goal. Too many potential enemies, like insects, weeds, and diseases, were trying to harm tomatoes; chemicals—pesticides—were therefore used extensively.

Monitoring those residues was not unusual, but the point with this particular project was that they wanted to include organically-grown tomatoes in Southwest Florida. Tomatoes grown without the use of conventional pesticides.

The study had been triggered by unconfirmed rumors that some of the tomato farmers in certain rural areas had utilized pesticides, despite their produce being labeled "organic." If this turned out to be true, they could be sued. On the other hand, if the rumors turned out to be false, then litigation for reputational damage could follow.

Initially, Dino hadn't been thrilled about the project—another boring routine task—but such chemical analyses were his bread and butter. His team of technicians was trained to use the latest analytical methods to find small residues, even tiny traces, of herbicides, insecticides, and other potentially toxic compounds on food products.

Dino tapped his pen against his hand and stared into the

distance, lost in thought, then gathered himself and glanced at the report. Once again, the results of this latest test were negative and unspectacular.

He stared at the computer screen. Although the samples they had analyzed stemmed from several tomato farms in the area, he focused his attention on one particular company that was famous for producing a large variety of first-class tomatoes and distributing them throughout the country—*Green, Red & Sustainable, Inc.,* better known to locals as *GR&S,* with headquarters in Sementina Springs, in the southern interior of the Florida peninsula. Their corporate philosophy was "organic" production—no pesticides.

The results were crystal-clear. The randomly sampled GR&S tomatoes appeared to be clean, GR&S fully living up to its reputation and trademark.

Not that he had expected to find anything exceptional, let alone alarming, and yet...

Then it hit him like a bolt of lightning.

Pesticides... He knew that high doses of certain widely used insecticides could elicit symptoms in people that were only too familiar to him—nausea, rashes, itching, dizziness, pinpoint pupils, among others. And respiratory depression.

Dino gritted his teeth. His suspicion was unsubstantiated, maybe a bit far-fetched, and yet it seemed obvious...

Maybe he was chasing shadows, but he didn't care. All Dino wanted was to get to the bottom of what'd caused his emergency.

Later in the afternoon, he called Dr. Snowhill.

"Sorry, I was an ass. Have you found out anything more about my recent near demise?"

"We still can't give you a definite answer." The doctor sounded breathless, his voice carrying a stressed undertone. "As I told you at the hospital, your blood and urine were clean for all commonly known opioids. We didn't find anything. We still don't know what caused you to stop breathing."

Dino didn't listen to the doctor's explanations. He nodded with a grim determination. What Snowhill had said confirmed his sneaking suspicion. It was more than obvious they didn't find opioid drugs in his system—*because he hadn't ingested any.* Simple as that, whether Snowhill believed him or not.

It was clearly something else.

The tomatoes they had purchased at the farmers market were organic tomatoes. Miguel had told them it was a new variety they should try. *Grand Captiva*—the name stuck because Captiva was their favorite island; every once in a while they would drive up there for a Sunday morning brunch and some live guitar music, and a stroll on the sandy beach.

The next step would be to have a closer look at those Grand Captivas.

6

DINO

Early the next morning, with Cat and Mia still asleep, Dino secured the remaining tomatoes from the batch they had bought to run a chemical analysis on them for a panel of pesticides.

He walked to the window in the breakfast nook and looked through the transparent plastic bag at the three mid-sized, round, smooth-skinned, impeccable red tomatoes. Organically grown. In the morning light that spilled in through the slats of the blinds, they looked innocent, friendly, inviting. But in his current mood he would bet heavily that they were covered with a nasty, invisible, thin layer of poison—pesticides. He couldn't wait to take the tomatoes to his lab and subject them to a merciless inspection and a meticulous analysis. He had all the tools of the trade.

He drained the last of his coffee, grabbed the plastic bag, and reached for his car keys. He had alerted Brian the day before that a high-priority task might be coming up and that Brian should work it into his busy schedule somehow.

As Dino stepped into the lab, Brian was waiting for him. He stood by the door, his white lab coat unbuttoned, stroking his bald head. Brian was his most experienced technician; a bit slow at times, stolid, but a math and statistics genius—more accurate than any digital calculator. He nodded as he listened to Dino's instructions on how to check for pesticide residues.

The purring sound of a robotic autoanalyzer filled the room, the common monotonous background melody of their busy analytical lab.

"You'll have the results in a couple days," Brian said quickly before Dino could come up with one of his stereotypical phrases about the urgency of the tests.

As Dino started to leave, Brian came up to him, averting his eyes. He cleared his throat. "Jess told me you were in the hospital? That right?" Brian said, empathetic as ever.

"Yup. But I'm fine now."

"What happened? I don't want to be nosy, but I was really worried."

"Oh, just a few scratches, that's all." Dino waved it off with his hand.

Brian nodded. "This last-minute, ultra-urgent analysis," he said slowly. "I'll squeeze it in, but... I'm way behind with my regular work."

Dino ignored the reproachful undertone. "Thanks, Brian," he said and hurried back to his office.

Minutes later, Goodlette stuck his head in Dino's office. "Tonight, Dino. By 6 p.m. Not one minute later. Got it?"

"You can count on me, as always," Dino said.

***

A torrential rain pounded Dino's windshield on the drive home, but when he pulled into his gated community, the sun was out again, the small roads steaming like a sauna floor. He drove past the entrance to Brown Pelican Cove and was heading straight for Cat's house in Heron Bay, another subdivision.

He couldn't help remembering that four months earlier, when he and Cat had started dating, they had agreed that they wanted to keep their own houses and their independence. With Dino still hurting from a painful divorce, he was in no rush to move in together.

Cat stood on the front porch in a blue swimsuit, her hair wrapped up in a bun, a towel slung over her shoulder. "Just did a few laps in the community pool." Dino shot her an adoring look. She was definitely in much better shape than him.

He patted his stomach and vowed, once more, to lose a few pounds and exercise more regularly.

"How was your day?" he said.

"Okay. Busy, as always. But listen to this. I heard through the grapevine that we've had five more cases of opioid-like poisoning in the past few days. Two patients died of respiratory failure last night. Couldn't be rescued with Narcan, it was too late."

Dino frowned. "Oxy addicts? Or illegal drugs?"

"I'm not so sure. The patients—a sixty-three-year-old grandmother, a fifty-plus-year-old successful businessman, and a young mother of two—don't fit the stereotype of junkies."

"I respectfully disagree, Cat. Drug abuse occurs across all social classes, ages, and professions. No exceptions."

Cat shook her head. "Here's the really strange thing. All blood and urine tests were negative. In all patients. No traces of oxycodone or fentanyl or any other related drug, except, of course, Narcan, in their system. We don't really understand how that's possible. In fact, we briefly discussed the cases this morning during rounds. They don't know what exactly happened, or why. Same as your crash the other night."

Except I survived, Dino thought, his stomach suddenly cramping.

"I've got a crazy idea," Dino said, searching for Cat's reaction. "I think it could've been those tomatoes. Remember, I was the only one who ate them. You and Mia passed."

"Say again." Her incredulous expression said it all.

"Maybe I ingested a load of toxic pesticide residues. Some of those chemicals could have elicited similar symptoms as an opioid."

She looked at him for a long moment. "Yeah, right, tomatoes. Dino, get real. You are the specialist, I'm not—but I think you should drop this nonsense."

Cat was definitely the more rational and sober-headed person between them, and she was probably right again. But Dino couldn't help it—searching for answers was just his way.

The need to understand "why" was in his genes.

"Nonsense? Not so sure. I don't think my idea is so ludicrous. Just wait and see." It wouldn't be the first time his tenacity would pan out.

7

MIGUEL

Everything hurt. Breathing, lifting his head, talking. Especially talking.

Miguel Castro reached for the water bottle. His mouth felt dry as the Chihuahuan desert, his tongue shriveled like a dried prune.

The nurse had allowed the cops ten minutes max to question him. After a quarter of an hour, she'd kicked the two men out. Politely, but firmly.

The detective had pelted him with questions, relentlessly. The other cop, a Mexican-American woman, stepped in occasionally to clarify any misunderstanding. Miguel was glad they were pursuing a lead, but he doubted that his vague description of what happened that morning could contribute much to solving the crime.

He still hadn't the faintest idea why he'd been shot.

"Thanks, Mr. Castro," the detective said. "Let me know if you remember any details of what the attacker looked like." He placed a business card on the side table next to Miguel's bed. As if a sudden brainwave would unfold a close-up image of the guy's face.

He hadn't seen a damn thing.

Again, he tried to remember the episode the day before the attack.

Just before dusk, Miguel had driven his black Chevy pickup up to the loading dock of one of the packing centers of GR&S, looking for someone to help him load the produce into the bed

26

of his truck. As always.

The next day he would sell the tomatoes in Naples. Normally, GR&S did not do small retail sales, but Miguel's stall at the farmers market was an exception. The customers seemed to like the fresh vegetables and fruit, coming right from the fields to their tables.

He had stepped into the hall, wondering why nobody was around. Maybe because he was late. As always, the 25-pound boxes made of corrugated cardboard were stacked and ready for pickup. Each box had a picture of a ripe tomato on the side and featured a label that read, *TOMATOES. GR&S.*

Miguel opened a box halfway and peeked inside. There they were—large, firm, mouth-watering. He grabbed the boxes using the handgrips on the sides of the vented cartons and carried them to his truck.

A bit separated from the other boxes, but still at the site where his friends usually put out the goods for him, were two more cardboard boxes. The tomatoes in those boxes were slightly smaller, but he was sure they were intended for him too.

Miguel went around the truck and made a last check. Finished for the day, he removed his straw hat and wiped his dark face—a face etched with years of hard work, lined by sun and wind. Strands of thick, black hair stuck to his forehead. "*Listo para mañana,*" he mumbled to himself. Everything was ready for tomorrow.

He kept replaying the scene in his mind but couldn't think of anything that had been different from usual. Except, maybe, the two cardboard boxes on the side, labeled *Grand Captiva*.

A shy knock on the door jolted Miguel from his reverie.

A short, buff man with dark, wavy hair stuck his head in the door. Big smile, friendly eyes. No white coat, no scrubs, probably not a doctor.

"Mr. Castro?" the visitor said in a soft voice.

"*Sí?*" Miguel tried to lift his head.

The man carefully closed the door shut behind him and stepped up to the hospital bed. He reached out his hand, his smile broadening. "Hi, I'm Dino Stampa. How are you?"

Miguel stiffened, trying to sit up, but the pain in his chest told him to take it easy. Was this another cop? Or worse...

"Are you a reporter?"

Dino burst out laughing. "No, for chrissakes. How are you?"

"I'm better, thank you. Much better." The man looked friendly, *simpático*, but... what did he want?

"Sorry about what happened," Dino said, shifting from one foot to the other. "I just wanted to convey some get-well wishes. I had no idea what you might like, so I brought you some chocolates." He placed a box on the side table.

"*Oh, muchas grácias!*" How thoughtful. He would give the chocolates to his little girls.

"Quite a secure stronghold, your room." Dino jerked his head toward the door. "A guard is outside. Had to show my ID."

Miguel nodded. Another reminder that he was still in danger, that the cops probably hadn't caught the shooter yet.

"Not sure you recognize me," Dino said. "I'm a frequent customer of yours at your stall at the farmers market in Naples."

Miguel's frown morphed into a smile. "*Sí, lo recuerdo.* I remember now. Nice to see you."

"I'm sure you wonder why I'm here," Dino said. "My girlfriend, short, pretty blonde, blue eyes, and I recently bought some tomatoes from you. Grand Captivas, to be accurate."

Miguel's stomach suddenly hardened. That name, Grand Captiva, again. Everything he'd gone through that horrible morning of the shooting came back in a flash. His attacker had asked for Grand Captivas too.

He eyed the door, like a hunted animal searching for an escape route.

"What do you want, Mr. Stampa?" Miguel asked, his face stern.

"It's Dino. May I?" He eased himself down in the visitor chair. "Look, I can imagine how you feel, Miguel, but I need your help. A couple days ago, I ate some of those Grand Captivas, and I got sick, terribly sick. Had to be hospitalized. In fact, I almost kicked it—"

"Huh?"

"I almost died."

Miguel's heartbeat quickened. "So sorry. Why?"

"That's what I want to find out. I assume the tomatoes were organically grown?"

"That's right. Everything is organic and natural at GR&S—that's the big farm where I buy my produce in bulk to sell at the farmers market."

"Oh, I know. So what's so special about the Grand Captivas?"

Miguel forced himself into a more upright position. "I wish I knew. The guy who shot me asked me about them too. I swear I have no clue. Maybe they weren't meant to be sold." He shrugged. "I don't know why."

"That'd be no reason to shoot you." Dino stood up. "Maybe together we can find out what's behind all this. Listen—" he lowered himself to Miguel's level, talking softly now, "can you show me someday where they're grown?"

"Sure. Once I'm out of here."

"Of course." Dino gave him an appreciative nod. "You help me, I help you. We can make sure something similar never happens again. I hope they catch the son of a bitch who shot you." He put his hand on Miguel's arm. "I wish you a speedy recovery."

Miguel watched as Dino hurried out of the room, smiling, softly pulling the door shut.

He was still uncertain about what exactly Stampa wanted from him. Was he just another cop? The story he'd shared with him about the tomatoes that had made people sick was a bit confusing, sounded unreal.

But he had a hunch he had found a new friend.

8

DINO

Later that day, Brian was programming a test run on one of the computers as Dino entered the lab.

"Did you get a chance to finish—" Dino's voice was fraught with apprehension.

"Of course." Brian stepped up to a lab bench and reached for a pile of computer printouts. "I've got good news for you. It's negative."

It took a few moments for Dino to register the full meaning of the breaking news. "Negative?" *No way.* He had expected a high probability hit.

"Yup. Negative for the whole panel of pesticides that we normally check for," Brian said, his chin high. He stood tall, his legs splayed. "The tiny traces that we found for some of the compounds were just the usual background noise."

They both knew that the detection methods had gotten so sensitive that even minute amounts of contaminating chemicals could be identified, possibly stemming from other farms in the neighborhood and distributed through air and water. Meaningless, and too small to be of any significance to the consumer.

"How about malathion? Other organophosphates or carbamates?"

"Clean. Nothing."

"Did you repeat it?"

"Of course. Normal protocol, triplicate samples, and a repeat of the whole procedure. Why do you look so skeptical? Isn't that what you expected?"

"I don't know." Dino had drawn a blank. He tried to smother

his disappointment by taking a deep breath. "Thanks, Brian. I owe you one. A big one."

"You owe me several."

"I know, I know." Dino gave a wobbly smile. He knew his favorite technician well; Brian was indulgent, a bit shy, and insecure, but extremely reliable. Had he presumed on Brian's good nature too many times before?

Brian cleared his throat. "You said it was a personal project, had nothing to do with our regular work?" His indulgent tone was gone, his voice suddenly cagey, his ears turning red.

"Yeah, sort of. I know there is *something* on these fruits," Dino said.

"Fruits?"

I knew he would ask. "Yes. Tomatoes are fruits—"

"Oh, Dino, I thought I heard your voice." Jessica stood in the doorway, her favorite mug with the red hearts in her hand. "Don't forget the deadline for the government report. You know that I must do all the formatting before it goes out."

Dino hated it when Jess patronized him. He knew that she could afford to be snippy because she trusted that the boss would protect and defend her. There were even rumors that Goodlette and she were having a fling. Dino shuddered at the thought.

After she disappeared, Brian lowered his voice. "One more thing, Dino... what if the boss finds out that I did another unscheduled analysis for you, another private project? What if I lie to him and he finds out again?"

"Then don't lie," Dino said with a grim face. "Just tell him the truth."

Brian stared at him warily. "Goodlette talked to me yesterday. He was, how shall I put it, not really bubbling over with joy."

"He was probably beside himself," Dino said.

"You can say that again."

"What was the problem?"

"He wanted to know exactly what I'd been doing for the past days and weeks. As if he were my supervisor. He even checked the records on the autoanalyzer and looked at the raw data. Although I'm not sure he understood everything."

"He's a bean counter." Dino turned up his mouth. "He likes to ride herd on all our staff. Maybe I shouldn't tell you that—I don't want to undermine your allegiance to our company—but it's common knowledge. Goodlette should do his job, and that's running this place. He's the CEO, not a friggin' quality control officer."

Brian looked somewhat embarrassed. Being at the lower end of the corporate food chain, he apparently couldn't afford to join Dino in excoriating the boss. He gave a nervous cough. "The boss wanted to know why I was running that pesticide analysis when there were more urgent projects in the pipeline."

"What did you tell him?"

"That you gave me the order." Brian turned his palms up. "That's what it was, right?"

"A petty-minded pedant, that's what he is," Dino said, snorting. "It's none of his damn business in what order we finish our analyses as long as we finish them on time."

"Uh... maybe I should get back to work," Brian suggested. "I'm not sure I feel comfortable talking about this."

Dino turned and stepped away, his hot temper cooling down as fast as it had risen.

What now? What did the negative results mean? He was convinced that it had been the tomatoes that made him ill and caused his symptoms. They seemed to be clean. In fact, the data matched what their recent analysis for the government had revealed: *Southwest Florida's organic tomatoes were immaculate.* He had to accept it since he had nothing that refuted it.

Had it all been just a wild ass guess? A red herring?

The more he thought about it, the more the analytical results made sense to him. He had clearly overreacted. He needed to remain level-headed, keeping his feet firmly on the ground. Cat had told him repeatedly that his impulsiveness was his weak point, that he should make decisions based on his head rather than his gut instincts. And wasn't this what a scientist should do anyway? Stay realistic, and not let themselves get carried away by wild fantasies?

Dino shook his head in a how-could-I-be-so-witless manner. Sure, the most hazardous pesticides could be toxic if, say, the canisters were handled in an irresponsible way, or if the workers applying the pesticide didn't wear proper protection, but there's no way the small residues on a tomato would be acutely harmful. Impossible. The amounts were simply too minute. The real issue with pesticide residues on foods or in the water clearly were the long-term, chronic effects, if any.

With an unmistakable sigh of surrender, he strode into his office and tried to concentrate on the pending bread-and-butter stuff.

9

DINO

Later that evening, Dino and Mia were returning home from a bike ride across the neighborhood and parking their bikes in the garage, when Dino's phone buzzed. Unknown number.

"Dino? It's me, Miguel."

It took Dino a moment or two to link the flustered voice to the fruit vendor. He had left his number with him at the hospital. "Miguel! What a surprise. How are you?"

"Thanks, getting better every day. Listen, I'm sorry to bother you, but I need your help. My wife..."

The squeaking garage door drowned the rest of the sentence. Dino sent Mia inside and slouched against his car. "Say again?"

"Maria, my wife, and one of my kids got sick. They had trouble breathing. And they threw up." Dino could hear the anxiety in the man's voice.

"What happened? Where are they now?"

"They are fine now. A neighbor took them to a walk-in clinic. The doc had said it could be from food, something... *tóxico*."

Dino wiped away the appalling thought of Dino's family falling victim to an intangible poison. Who would be next? "Did they..." he hesitated, outguessing the answer before he even asked the full question.

"They ate some of the unsold tomatoes I'd taken home from the farmers market. Luckily, they didn't eat much of it, but do you think that's why they got sick?"

Dino used his sleeve to dab at the rivulets of sweat running down his face. "Miguel, tell them not to touch those tomatoes anymore. By no means." His voice was firm, with a commanding tone. "Do you understand?"

"*Sí, comprendo.*"

No way this could be a coincidence. Dino's scientific curiosity was only one of the motivational forces that drove him to find out what was behind it—now it had become a personal thing.

"There's something else," Miguel said. "My wife kept the cardboard box that contained the tomatoes. She's smart." Dino heard the proud undertone. "She took a picture of the label and sent it to me. Want to see it?"

A moment later Dino heard the *ping* of a new text message. He stared at the pic with the printed label on the cardboard box.

GRAND CAPTIVA—CH-304 / R2

His stomach churned. "What's that number after the name?"

"The location where they grow them, at GR&S."

He blew up his cheeks and gave Miguel an imaginary high-five. "Thanks a bunch, my friend. We'll be in touch. Hope your family will fully recover and you'll be out of the hospital soon."

Dino clenched his jaw and gazed into the distance. He knew it.

And he would get to the bottom of it.

Back inside the house, Dino found Cat ensconced in her favorite armchair, flipping through TV channels. She threw him an appraising glance and instantly muted the TV. "What's up?" He briefed her on the phone call.

"It's magnanimous that you want to help Miguel find out who attacked him, and why, but isn't this a wild-goose chase?" Cat asked. "Wouldn't you rather leave it to the officials?"

Dino grunted. He walked over to the fridge and grabbed a beer. "You want one?" he shouted from the kitchen. Before she could answer, he dropped into an armchair next to her and twisted off the cap.

"I have a gut feeling I'm on to something big. Maybe I'll be debunking a myth even. The myth of pesticide-free organic farming," he said with a grim smile.

"Geez, your imagination is running wild. Get real, Dino. This sounds like a conspiracy theory."

"How about me getting poisoned after eating organic tomatoes? How about the other mysterious cases at LCH you told me about? And now Miguel's family."

Cat remained quiet, fiddling with her ring.

"And how about our friend Miguel being shot? All figments of my imagination?"

Cat slanted a look at him. "Listen to reason. There's no proof these two things are related to each other. Not a single piece of evidence."

"I'm not crazy. Too many strange things have happened." He inhaled sharply. "I think I will definitely pay a visit to Tomato World."

"Say again?"

Dino winked at her. "Yup. GR&S. Site visit."

Cat gave him a wan smile. "You've gotta be kidding."

"Tomorrow," Dino said. He caught a glimpse of annoyance in Cat's expression, but his mind was made up. He would check the organic farm out the next morning. And should he sure enough find something illegal, he would bring it to light.

10

DINO

Dino had done his homework overnight. *Green, Red & Sustainable's* main business sector was vegetable and fruit farming and distribution, with emphasis on organic production and green farming. The farm complex sprawled over a large area off Sementina Road.

As he was pulling up into the visitor parking lot at the main office building, he had to admit to himself that he was impressed with the place. It was easy to see why Sementina Springs was called "America's Tomato Capital." Large farms, wide fields, greenhouses, interspersed with warehouses and packing and shipping facilities dominated the area. The GR&S spread was huge.

He killed the engine and took a deep breath. His mouth felt suddenly dry.

Dino opened the heavy wooden door and stepped into the reception area. A sweet scent lingered in the air, reminiscent of fresh apples and tropical wood. The interior was simple, functional, clean, and had a touch of something charmingly wholesome.

After he introduced himself at the reception, he glanced around as he waited to talk to someone with the company. Baskets of fresh, ripe, red cherry tomatoes were scattered about, inviting visitors. Like after dinner mints at a Chinese restaurant. The tomatoes were beautiful, innocent looking, but somehow his stomach heaved when he looked at them. *I'll pass.*

He tried to catch a glimpse of what was beyond the glass doors at the back of the lobby, but all he could see was a dark corridor. He hoped whoever emerged was as gullible as the receptionist had been; Dino had turned on all the charm he could muster but wasn't sure if everyone would buy his story.

The man who stepped through the door looked to Dino more like an airplane pilot than the manager of an organic farming plant. Asian complexion, clean-shaven, muscular build, short-sleeved white shirt, black pants.

The man bowed almost imperceptibly and spoke quietly. "Somporn Wattanapanit."

Dino extended his hand. "Dirk Spino. Nice to meet you, Mr. Watta..."

"Just call me Sompy, that's easier. Thai name."

Sompy's handshake felt limp and clammy. Dino furtively wiped his hand on the back of his pants.

"So, how can I help you today? I hear you're interested in our company."

"Well..." Dino hesitated for a second. This guy might not be so easy to con. "You know, I'd love to learn more about organic tomato farming and—"

Sompy grinned. "That's a pretty broad subject. Are you a journalist?"

"Oh, heaven forbid, no," Dino said, with a repelling gesture.

"Any bad experiences with journalists? You act like they are the devil in disguise. No, seriously, what do you do, if I may ask?"

Dino had prepared for this. "I'm writing a book on nutrition—a holistic lifestyle, in general, organic farming, in particular."

"That's fantastic." Sompy was perceptibly delighted. "Make sure to include a picture of our wonderful tomatoes." He puckered his lips. "There's a lot to discuss, and quite a few things I could tell you." He motioned for Dino to sit down in one of the more comfortable armchairs near the window.

Friendly guy, Dino thought. "You have time? I mean, barging in on you like this..."

"Don't worry. We always welcome visitors who are interested in organic tomato farming. What exactly would you like to know?" Sompy's expression was serious, quizzical, yet cautious.

A lot. For example, why did the Grand Captivas almost kill him? Or why was the vendor who sold them to him shot?

"I do know a lot about the nutritional value of tomatoes and their health effects—even beyond lycopene—" Dino winked as if signaling, *aren't we both insiders and on the same page?* "I'd like to learn more about the breeding and cultivation of tomatoes, and also... about pesticides."

Sompy shot him a skeptical glance. "We don't use pesticides." He sounded alarmed, if not horrified, by the mere mention of the word.

"I know. No synthetic pesticides. But how about *natural* pesticides? Those that still match the criteria for being allowed to use the term *organic*?"

"None." Sompy closed his eyes and raised an appeasing hand. "Tell me, you're not from the FDA or the USDA, are you?" The question hung in the air, half in jest, half serious.

"Me, an undercover agent? Yeah, right." Dino flashed a disarming smile. "If I were a spy, I would show up here with a fake mustache and apply for a job as a field worker. I wouldn't ask the key questions upfront."

Sompy's face relaxed somewhat, but Dino wondered if he was overplaying his hand.

"Organic produce is still in vogue, right?"

"Very much so. For decades now, the market has been soaring, and so has organically managed farmland." Sompy furtively checked his watch. "A book—that's really cool." Then he paused for a short while, his expression unreadable.

"Look, I don't have a lot of time now, got to run to a meeting. But if you make an appointment, we could show you a couple of our greenhouses and outdoor fields, if you wish."

"I'd be delighted," Dino said. *Now or never.* "Just a couple of quick questions. Do you happen to know a certain Miguel Castro? He works here at GR&S, I think." He always liked to use the element of surprise.

A shadow crossed Sompy's face, and he momentarily looked flummoxed. It was hard to tell whether it was because he felt abashed or simply because of the brusque change of subject.

"Of course, everybody's heard about Castro. Why do you ask?"

"Read something in the paper." Dino made sure his expression showed genuine concern.

Sompy's face clouded. "Terrible story. Castro doesn't work directly for us, but he is a subcontractor of sorts. Sells tomatoes and other produce at local farmers markets. Shot the other morning, right in front of his house. Poor fellow."

"Robbery?"

"No. Police still don't know. The shooter's still at large." If Sompy knew more than the TV reporters, he didn't show it.

Dino set up for match point. "I heard he sold Grand Captivas..."

Sompy's gaze told Dino he had served an ace. Uneasiness radiated off the man, but he didn't comment. He stood.

Dino thanked him and proceeded to the reception desk to make an appointment. "As soon as possible," he said. "I'm flexible."

Back in his car, he fist-pumped. He had one foot in the door.

11

KUZMINSKI

The phone buzzed. Again.

Alone in his office, Karol Kuzminski, the founder and CEO of Green, Red & Sustainable, Inc., was checking some reports from the head of accounting. Reclined in his leather chair, he picked up the phone. "Yeah."

"Chuck, how are you?"

Kuzminski smiled as he recognized the familiar voice—euphonious, but heavily accented.

"Hey, Sompy. What's up?" Somporn Wattanapanit was manager of GR&S's new Traditional Herbs and Healthy Food branch.

Kuzminski waited. He was not a friend of small talk. Get to the point, keep it short. And Sompy was known for long windups.

"Business is not so good at this time. Slow, much too slow."

"What else is new? That's not the reason you're calling, right?"

"No, indeed not." Sompy's voice grew louder. "Well, there is something else. I need your advice."

Problems, problems. Kuzminski sighed. "I'm listening." Chuck glanced at his watch. He had scheduled a lunch meeting at his golf club in half an hour.

"Someone was snooping around this morning. A strange guy showed up, uninvited, asking a lot of questions."

"A guy?" Kuzminski jingled his car keys. "Who was he? What did he want?"

"He signed in as Dirk Spino. He wants firsthand information for a book he plans to write."

"A book? About our company?"

"Well—about organic farming. Tomatoes."

"I see." Kuzminski scratched his chin. In contrast to Sompy, he didn't conjecture a deceptive intent behind every first-time visitor. He didn't get it. "So, why are you worried? I mean... why are you telling me this?"

"Just a gut feeling... He seemed a bit too keen on the subject. He could have been an undercover cop, you know, or someone from the EPA or USDA."

"So what?" Kuzminski let out a guffaw. "We're not hiding anything, right?"

"He inquired about Castro."

"It was in the news, everybody knows about it. Look, it's nothing, Sompy. Don't panic. Look, I gotta go. Anything else?"

"Yes. He quizzed me about the Grand Captivas."

Kuzminski tapped a pen against a notepad on the desk. "If he returns to gather more information, let me know. We will grill him on his professed interest in tomatoes."

Kuzminski hung up and stared at the ceiling, absorbed in his thoughts.

"Careful now," he mumbled to himself. "This whole thing might blow up."

They had to prevent this by all means.

The stakes were simply too high.

12

MIGUEL

Miguel had just received the good news—he'd be released from the hospital in a few days. The doctors had told him that he made a good recovery, quicker than anticipated, because his underlying physical condition was excellent. Strong body, the doctor had said. Miguel still smiled to himself when he thought about it.

Just as he was about to pick up his cell phone to call Maria, there was a faint knock on the door and a man entered the room.

"How are you doing today, Mr. Castro?" he said, wheeling in a trolley. "Any pain?"

Miguel didn't know why, but he took an instant dislike to the guy in scrubs. Not that he was less friendly than the other nurses, but there was just something about him...

"Doing great, thanks. The doc told me I could go home soon. Can't wait to be with my family again."

"Wonderful news. I'm happy for you." Warm words but cold eyes. Eyes that looked vaguely familiar to him. Maybe reminded Miguel of someone, but he couldn't pin them down.

"You new here?"

"No, just moved over from another ward. By the way, I'm John."

"I'm Miguel. *Encantado!*" Maybe John wasn't so grouchy as he'd first appeared to be. Maybe just tired.

John closed the door, let his eyes sweep the room, then walked up to the bed.

"You taking my vitals, *again*?" Miguel asked. Another nurse had been with him just an hour ago. He was no longer

43

in critical condition, so—

"I'm taking what?"

"My vitals."

John didn't reply. He either didn't hear well or he was slow on the uptake.

Miguel kept his eyes glued to the nurse who, with his left hand, grabbed a hypodermic syringe from the cart.

"I'm gonna give you a painkiller," John said. He pulled off the cap, held the needle up, and squeezed the piston until a fountain of yellowish fluid squirted high up in the air.

A painkiller? Miguel didn't need another painkiller. He could bear the pain, but if the doctors insisted... He was just about to ask the nurse why he didn't use the Y-shaped piece of the IV drip, like all the other nurses did when they gave him an injection, when he realized what was going on. He jerked, pulling his arm tight to his body.

He figured out who that haggard face, those sunken eyes, belonged to.

The nurse grabbed Miguel's arm with a firm grip and bared his teeth like an aggressive dog.

"*No!*" Miguel swung his free arm around and launched a blow, knocking the syringe out of the man's hand. "¡*Sé quién eres!*" He had no doubt who this guy was now—the *tipo* who had shot him in his driveway.

The man who called himself John emitted a guttural groan and shot forward, punching Miguel in the face, then smashing his fist down on Miguel's chest.

A lightning pain exploded in Miguel's body, and he felt as if someone had poured acid into a wound. His vision blurred, and his surroundings danced in front of his eyes.

He held his arm over his head in a protective gesture as the white pillow came down on his face. He felt the pressure, fighting for air, gasping...

13

CAT

Overworked, sleep-deprived, and dealing with the emotional burden of a higher number of patients dying in the hospital than under normal circumstances, Cat was having a hard time coping with her emotional stress.

She was on the early shift at LCH.

She didn't understand what was happening. Nobody understood. What was most puzzling was that these emergencies did not occur randomly but were clustered together, triggered by *something*—some common denominator. But what? It could happen again, anytime.

She thought of Dino, how he was frantically trying to solve this mystery that seemed unsolvable for a whole team of experts. How could Mr. Amateur Sleuth believe all this was related to tomatoes? She shook her head. Dino could be so hardheaded. And yet—Miguel, the tomato vendor, had been fiercely attacked in his own driveway by a man looking for Grand Captivas. Tomatoes.

Miguel. Poor guy. She'd heard from Dino that he was here at LCH.

Cat checked her watch—coffee break.

Abandoning herself to an impulse, she hurried toward the elevators.

"What's the patient's name again?" the receptionist asked with bored efficiency, staring at the monitor.

"Castro, Miguel Castro."

"Which department? You know?"

"In-patient. Probably General Surgery, but I'm not sure."

"Are you family?"

"No. I work here. Immediate Care Center," Cat said, pointing to her name tag.

The receptionist reached for a clipboard. "Got it. This is an exceptional case, I'm afraid. You need to fill out this form, and I need to see your ID." She picked up the phone, turning away slightly as she spoke.

Cat glanced down at the form. Room 407. That was all she needed. This was going to be a surprise visit. Poor guy, he'd always been so friendly—and now an innocent shooting victim. Cat felt somehow connected to him, and she knew Dino had established some sort of a friendship with the man.

She would quickly cheer him up with get-well wishes.

The security officer was on duty in the corridor. She asked for Cat's ID, gave her the once-over, and patted her down. Cat wondered why—she was hospital staff, after all.

"Special precautions, I guess," Cat said.

"Yes. Special patient too." The officer put on a forced smile. "You're good."

Cat knocked shyly, opened the door, and closed it behind her without a sound. A tsunami cloud of isopropanol disinfectant hit her. She still hadn't gotten used to it, and it still gave her an occasional headache. She turned up her nose. Some nurses just seemed to overdo it.

She peeked at the bed, but all she could see was the low end and some messed up blankets. The rest was curtained off.

She walked around the bed. "Miguel?" she said softly, not wanting to scare him. Was he asleep? The body under the sheet didn't move. Cat couldn't see Miguel's face because his head was buried in a mountain of bulgy white pillows. Another fat pillow was on the floor. She picked it up and laid it gently back on the bed.

"Mr. Castro?... Miguel?"

No reaction.

Cat cleared her throat. She had hoped Miguel would have recuperated from his injuries and be amenable to a conversation. She stepped closer.

The pillow was wet and spattered with blood.

Cat recoiled, stared at the blue, ghastly face of the man. His lifeless face still radiated pure terror, but what made her heart hammer against her ribs was that the man lying in Miguel Castro's hospital bed was not Miguel.

Cat felt for his pulse—nothing. His eyes were glazed over. It took her only an instant to activate *Code Blue* and *Code Silver*. Then she stepped quickly out into the corridor and walked in the opposite direction. Far enough away not to be noticed in the excitement, but close enough to still see his room. Nurses from the ward rushed in immediately and a doctor arrived moments later. The security officer bolted into the room two minutes after that.

Cat watched in stunned silence.

I'm not letting myself get involved in this, she thought, shivering. But she knew, of course, that it was too late for that.

***

"So, you were the one who found the man and set off the alarm?" the big man who had introduced himself as head of security asked in a peevish tone. It was obvious that situations like this weren't daily fare.

Cat nodded, still out of breath. She still couldn't fully grasp what had happened.

"What were you doing up on this floor?" He pointed a finger at her name badge. "You're from another department, in another wing of LCH?"

Her gaze shot upward. This guy apparently had no idea of the daily routine of a busy nurse. "This was personal. A short visit to see how he was doing and cheer him up." She glanced at Miguel, who was slumped back against the chair, his blue hospital gown loose and coming off a shoulder, his dark eyes flitting back and forth. She was looking for a blanket but couldn't see one within reach. "I know the patient."

The windowless, small staff room was cold and smelled of a mixture of hand lotion and coffee. Palpable tension hovered over the four people seated around a plain, square table.

"The police are on their way, but I have to ask you a few questions before they arrive," the security guy said. He turned to another nurse with olive skin and jet-black hair who apparently acted as a translator. "Ask him what happened."

The translator flipped her head to the other side. A torrent of words gushed out of Miguel's mouth, accompanied by wild movements of his arms and hands.

Cat waited. Her command of the Spanish language was vestigial, most of what she'd learned forgotten. She was glad they'd called for a translator who could catch the subtleties of both languages—the important, if tiny, nuances in a conversation.

The nurse raised a hand, interrupting Miguel's flood of words. "He says the man who attacked him in his hospital room was the same man who shot him at his home. He says he clearly recognized the guy—not at first, but then without any doubt."

Cat watched Miguel barraging the translator with the rest of his story.

"Mr. Castro says the fake nurse stepped up to him and tried to drug him with some fluid in a syringe, then smother him with a pillow."

Miguel accentuated the translator's exposé with a vivid pantomime. If it weren't dead serious stuff, the scene looked almost like taken from a standup comedy.

"I got it," the security guy said. "He must have panicked. Acted in self-defense." He waited again for the translator to summarize the rest of Miguel's incoherent outburst.

It takes inordinate guts to lie in a hospital bed, recuperating from shot injuries, and then fight back a man who shows up to kill you, Cat mused. *Then sneak out of the room and surrender.*

"Great." The security guy turned his head to Miguel. "Very helpful, and thanks for cooperating. What you need now is a lawyer, a good one." He gave a grim smile, and Cat wasn't sure whether she could detect a hint of naked schadenfreude. She wondered whether the head of security shouldn't rather be concerned about having to explain how it was possible for someone from outside, even in deceptive scrubs, to bypass the guard at the door.

A hospital employee stuck her head in the door. "The detectives are here."

The security guy jumped to his feet. "You'd better make yourself available for interviews," he said.

Before leaving the room, Cat stepped up to Miguel, putting her hand on his bare forearm and giving him a gentle squeeze. She leaned closer. "¿Por *qué lo hiciste?*" she said in a low voice. "Why did you do it?"

"Because it was payback time," Miguel said, loud and in perfect English.

14

DINO

It was past 9 a.m. when Dino stepped into the lobby of Rainbow BioLabs. He held his dripping wet umbrella away from his body. "Quite a deluge," he said, smiling at Jessica. He noticed that she didn't return his smile but instead pointed with her thumb toward Goodlette's door.

"Yup, dark clouds over there too," she said in a meaningful tone. "The boss wants to talk to you ASAP."

Dino stepped into the lion's den.

Goodlette was perched in his executive chair, his sour face and the deep furrow north of the base of his nose boding ill. He didn't offer Dino a seat. Obviously, he wanted to cut to the chase.

Okay, Dino thought, let's talk about the fucking government project report. I'm ready.

"Couple things," Goodlette said. "There's so much bullshit on your plate, I don't even know where to start." He gave an angry snort. "First, the government project. Your report is overdue, Dino. I—"

"It's done." Dino tried to sound casual. "I put it on Jess's desk last night, about seven o'clock. The draft, that is."

Goodlette ignored Dino's explanation. "I gave you a deadline, quite some time ago. I reminded you, gently at first, then more firmly. Then, I gave you an ultimatum. But what did Dr. Stampa do? He decided to take a day off, then schedule a couple of dental appointments." Goodlette raised his voice. "Then take sick leave, then sneak out early and show up in the afternoon—but where's the report?"

"I had a medical emergency, Jason. Quite a serious one, in

case you've forgotten. I was in the ER, then admitted to the ward."

Goodlette remained unimpressed. "Look, this is serious stuff. Sorry to tell you, but you were a much more reliable person in the past. To be honest, I'm not happy with your job performance." He wheeled the chair close to the desk and leaned forward. His massive upper body rested on his elbows. "When you were married, you were a much more stable and self-balanced person. And more reliable, too."

"Keep my private life out of this," Dino snapped.

There was a loaded pause.

"You don't deliver. Period. You don't deliver." Whenever Goodlette was agitated, he tended to repeat phrases.

Dino felt the blood rush into his ears as he sat down. This could take longer than anticipated. He leaned forward, staring into his boss's eyes. "Look, I admit, I was busy, and sick, which, by the way, was totally out of my control. But the draft of the report is ready. The ball is now in Jess's court. All she needs to do is polish it. That's basically it. All you'll have to do is read it and sign. Big deal."

Goodlette chewed on his lower lip. "There are a couple of other unpleasant things, unfortunately." He hesitated.

Geez, what else is coming? Jason must have a whole laundry list. Dino leaned back again, glanced at his watch, exhibiting deadly boredom coupled with an increasing unwillingness to dally away any more time.

"Here's the worst part. Don't even know where to begin." Goodlette sighed. "Here—read this." He reached for a newspaper clip and flung it under Dino's nose. "Read it, and then explain."

Dino glanced at the text, then at Goodlette, and then at the salient fat headline of what seemed to be a recent article in *Gator News Today*.

"NEW PHANTOM OPIOID VICTIMS HOSPITALIZED, MORE DEATHS," by Susan Farewell.

Dino went down a few lines. Goodlette had highlighted a subtitle with a yellow marker.

"Southwest Florida Laboratory Confirms Elusive Nature of the Drug But Says it Could Be Pesticides."

"Southwest Florida Laboratory?" Dino mumbled.

"That's us," Goodlette sputtered.

Dino gazed at the headlines in disbelief. Susan Farewell, a reporter for *Gator News Today*, who frequently contributed to the *Health & Food* section of the newspaper, had done it again. It looked like she'd sensationalized another story. After they'd talked earlier, he'd had an undefined gut feeling, a sense of unease, but he couldn't put his finger on the problem. Now—the bombshell.

Susan had contacted him after he got out of the hospital. She had informed him that she planned to write a column on the recent aggregation of the opioid epidemic in Southwest Florida, and that she'd like to meet up with him to get some expert advice and clarification.

They had met for lunch at the Tropical Breeze Café in south Fort Myers. He had educated her on the chemistry of opioids and provided details on some technical aspects of opioid analyses in patients. She appeared to be on fire and said that this was hot stuff.

And now this—red-hot stuff.

Dino had asked her whether he would get a chance to vet the draft before it went to press. She had warded off his concerns. "Of course, Dino. Who do you think we are?"

Of course, she'd never sent him a draft and here he was reading, for the first time, a gonzo-journalism text that was sensational more than anything.

"That's outrageous," Dino said and got up from his chair. "Distorting the facts." He slapped his hand against the newspaper clip. "True, we talked about the recent cases, but I never said that the phantom opioid might be another chemical that would simply emulate the effects of a classical opioid drug.

And yet, here she goes suggesting that it could be a pesticide, maybe even one that is used in organic farming. And she's citing our company. That's outrageous."

Goodlette narrowed his eyes to slits. "So you admit it, you talked to her. You probably told her to go ahead and pop the story and feel free to mention Rainbow BioLabs."

Dino paced up and down the office, brandishing the paper in the air. "You're barking up the wrong tree, Jason. Just for the record, I never mentioned our company and I never spoke disparagingly of organic production. In fact, I explicitly urged Susan Farewell to be careful. Had I known..." He didn't finish his sentence.

Dino sat down again. "We could be sued for false allegations."

"I think you are finally getting the point," Goodlette said. His neck and face were turning purple. He undid the collar button of his shirt and loosened his necktie.

"Well, I can see why you're upset." Dino tossed the paper back on the table. "This journalist comes up with a half-baked story and produces fake news. It's just unprofessional. But look, after all, it's her job to bloodhound scandals, fraud, and misconduct."

"For heaven's sake, get real." Goodlette was spitting fire. "Get real. I don't give a damn whether the reporter distorts the science or accuses the plant protection manufacturers. What bothers me—I mean, really, really pisses me off—is the fact that they mention our company. We are the ones who apparently discovered a fishy story or even unveiled a fraud. Who authorized you to talk to that journalist and comment on pesticide analyses done here at Rainbow? That's confidential information until a client discloses it to the public." Goodlette painted an imaginary arc in the air with his hand as if to underscore the blatant advertising of his company.

Dino was speechless. Right now, he could care less whether this reflected badly on Rainbow BioLabs. What bothered him was another question. Who did Susan Farewell get this information from? Did she simply fudge her own story, or did she have other sources?

"Here's the *real* problem, Dino. The core of the fucking problem." Goodlette jabbed a finger at Dino's face. "I know that you ran one or several unscheduled analyses for a series of pesticides on your own. Who the hell authorized you to do those tests, here in our lab? Who approved it, and who's gonna pay for it?"

"Me," Dino said.

"I can't believe this. I can't believe it. You siphoned off company resources for this rogue undertaking. You wasted your time, your tech's time, used analytical tools, blocked our UHPLC and mass spec facility—for something that you never discussed with anyone here, something that's basically your private affair. But—hey—our company's name is now in the news, and on everybody's lips tomorrow, and I can already see some creepy lawyers showing up at our door. This is not just deception, this is plain old fraud."

"Let me explain," Dino said, raising his palms. "It was just a small, quick test. I would have discussed it with you, but, you know, the government project report had highest priority—"

"Don't give me that BS," Goodlette boomed. He paused and leaned back. "You are suspended for the rest of this month. Afterwards we'll see," he said quietly.

"Come on, Jason," Dino protested. "Let's discuss it."

"You heard me. You are suspended for the rest of the month. And stay away from the lab—I don't want to see you around. Do I make myself clear? Jessica is preparing the paperwork."

"You cannot fire me just like that," Dino objected with a constrained laugh. "No second paycheck then, this month?"

"You are temporarily fired. Suspended, it's called. You have all the time in the world for your dental appointments, ER visits, and inspections of organic farms." Goodlette got up.

"That's it for now, Dino."

What a jerk, Dino thought. *He'll probably change his mind in an hour or so.* For sure, Goodlette would revoke his hasty decision.

"I'm sure you'll like the government project report," he added. "It's a real page turner. Can't put it down. You'll gobble it up." He walked across the threshold and closed the door behind him without looking back.

Outside his boss's office, he immediately regretted his outburst. His sarcasm only made things worse.

15

DINO

The next day, Dino spotted the unmarked white sedan parked on the street in front of his driveway before the doorbell even rang.

Two men in white shirts and blue ties, who looked like sales reps filled with purpose, stood on the porch. On a Saturday morning?

The older of them flashed his badge. "Detective Brad Roberson, Bureau of Criminal Investigation, Lee County Sheriff's Office," he said.

Dino hadn't expected the police to turn up on his doorstep. "Yes?"

"You're Dino Stampa?" Roberson asked, jutting his chin forward.

Dino nodded, curious to know what all this was about.

Roberson pointed to his younger colleague. "This is Detective Kenyon. I'd appreciate it if you could answer a couple questions for us, sir. It won't take long."

"Of course, come on in."

"Just a routine thing," Roberson said as if reading Dino's thoughts. "You know Mr. Castro, right? He mentioned your name. We're investigating the double assault on him and the death of the alleged perp."

"Miguel? Yeah, met him a few times. Poor guy. Could've been killed."

Roberson didn't follow up. He scanned the living room and the open kitchen. "Nice house. Been here a long time?"

"Two years." After the divorce, he and his ex-wife had sold their property, and Dino plunged into debt and purchased this small bungalow in the Brown Pelican Cove subdivision. He completely refurnished his new home, beach-style, and got rid of his old, more traditional stuff. Symbol of a new start.

"Nice view," Roberson said, jabbing a thumb toward the lake and preserve. Kenyon studied a framed picture on the side table. "Your family?"

"My girlfriend and her daughter."

Was Roberson ever going to get to the point? Dino decided not to wait on him. "Did you find out why Miguel Castro was shot and then almost killed in the hospital?"

Roberson jutted his heavy chin forward, sniffling. "The investigation's still ongoing. We can't comment on *why*, except that we're making progress." He let his hands slide into the pockets of his navy pants. "But we know *who* did it. It's been released to the press, by the way. The putative attacker, now dead, has been identified. A drug trafficker from a Miami neighborhood, well known to the police. Apparently hired as a hitman this time. Our people had secured his truck in the hospital's parking lot and seized a handgun in the car. Forensics will soon be investigating whether it is the same weapon as the one used in the shooting." He stopped and watched Dino, grim-faced.

Dino swallowed. What the hell did they want from him? They hadn't mentioned Cat with a single word so far. After all, she'd been the one who had found the thug. "Can I offer you anything... water... coffee?"

Both men raised their hands. "Thanks, I'm fine," they said in unison.

"What do you know about a tomato variety called *Grand Captiva*?" Roberson asked, out of the blue, stressing the name.

The question came unexpectedly. Dino felt a twinge of panic. Miguel must have told them. "Nothing. Why?"

From the blank look Roberson shot him it was impossible for Dino to guess whether the detective believed him or not. Probably he didn't. He exchanged a look with Kenyon.

"Because we believe those tomatoes might be somehow related to the aggravated assault and the attempted murder."

Dino was bursting with curiosity, but that was not the reason his heart pounded. He wasn't dreaming up. There must be something about the mysterious Grand Captivas. Looked like the theory he'd posed wasn't totally off-the-wall.

"You familiar with a company named Green, Red & Sustainable? GR&S?" Roberson asked.

"Why? I mean... Yes. I've heard about it. Tomato farm in Sementina Springs. Huge. Organic tomatoes." What lead were the cops following? Did they follow him around? What an abrupt swerve... Dino crossed his arms on his chest. He didn't want to confide to the police his secret activities at GR&S. Not yet. Not until he had something substantial, something incriminating on them.

"Ever been there?" Kenyon asked.

"Nope," Dino said. He started to chew on his lower lip. Had the cops been there, asked around? He had signed-in under a false name. They probably didn't know about his recent visit *incognito*.

Roberson inhaled sharply. "Do you know Dr. Andrew Timberlake?"

Holy cow, Dino thought. *These detectives are all over the map.* They were relentless in grilling him and certainly excursive. Where were they going now?

"Andy Timberlake, the cancer researcher? Sure, job-related, if we're talking about the same person. I don't know him well, but I know he's successful, well respected in his field. Why?"

"Timberlake has tight connections with the Sementina Springs company. He's collaborating with a few scientists at GR&S. On a tomato project."

"*Tomatoes?*" Dino gave a short, spiky laugh. "Really? Andy Timberlake is a pretty big shot in immunology and cancer research, but I didn't know he's into vegetable farming."

"They're collaborating on a drug development project."

The detective leaned forward for emphasis, his eyes piercing. "About anti-cancer drugs. We wonder whether you, as a scientist, could answer a few questions for us lay folks, to clarify."

"Frankly, I think it'd be easier if you talked directly with Timberlake. Cancer research isn't exactly my area of competence—"

"I'm afraid that's no longer possible," Roberson said. "Dr. Timberlake is dead. He died of a drug OD. Opioid. In his home."

Dino's head spun. "What?" He choked on the word.

"Somebody injected him with a massive dose of fentanyl. We don't know yet who did it," Roberson said, his face lined with concern, "but it wasn't an accident. It was a homicide. We're still investigating."

Dino felt his hackles rise. Another assault on someone who had connections with GR&S. This couldn't be a coincidence.

"From what we've learned," Roberson said, "Timberlake and his research team were developing new treatments for prostate cancer."

Dino nodded, wondering where this new avenue was leading.

Roberson briefly glanced at his notebook. "With *PMPs*, short for plant-made pharmaceuticals. Any idea how this could be related to tomato farming?"

"Plant-made pharmaceuticals?" Dino registered the disapproving tone in his own voice. "*Good* natural products in plants, as opposed to *bad* synthetic pharmaceutical drugs?" He air-quoted the contrasting words, his voice becoming louder. "To be honest, I'm not necessarily a friend of dried leaves and plant extracts and such mumbo jumbo. For several reasons. Number one—too unsafe. Number two—they don't work." He flashed on the image of Cat, the "all-natural" health freak, and their endless discussions.

Dino registered that the two detectives were watching him intensely. He took a deep breath and stopped short in what he realized had been another of his rather dogmatic outbursts.

He should learn to control his temper better. Cat had told him several times that he should be more open-minded in discussions, less opinionated.

"Tomatoes and prostate cancer? Sorry, Detectives, I can't help you there. I've no clue."

Without another comment, Roberson got up and Kenyon followed suit. He stretched out his hand. "Thanks for your time, Dr. Stampa. Most helpful."

"My pleasure." Dino wondered what on earth he had said that could even remotely have been helpful to them.

They knew more than they'd told him, he was sure of that. But what he'd learned confirmed his suspicion.

Something strange was going on at the tomato farm.

16

DINO

On Monday morning at 8:25, the text message from Jessica was brief, but concise. Could he please drop by the office at his earliest convenience for a meeting with Mr. Goodlette?

Dino frowned. The boss? Would that be good news or bad news? Probably Goodlette had changed his mind, and Dino would be reinstated. Rainbow was short of experienced staff, and they needed him.

He briefly informed Cat that he was back at work, and headed out.

Forty-five minutes later, he pulled into the last empty parking spot at Rainbow.

Jessica looked up from her computer screen, deadpan. "Dino, I'm so sorry about what happened the other day." She lowered her voice. "Jason can sometimes be a bit, well..."

"No problem, Jess, I took it in stride. Can't wait to get back to work." Dino winked at her. "Look—I brought you something for your coffee." He handed her a paper bag with a couple of cinnamon and sugar-sprinkled donuts, her favorites. "Is the boss...?" he asked hesitantly, pointing with his thumb toward Goodlette's office.

"He's on the phone." Jessica's face clouded. "Thanks for the donuts, Dino, but you really shouldn't—"

Dino nodded and went straight to the lab, where Brian stood in front of the buzzing printer, watching the pages of an obviously voluminous document piling up.

"Any exciting new data?"

Brian jumped. "Boy, you startled me. I didn't expect you, frankly. Why are you creeping up on me like that?"

"Morning, Brian. Sorry for frightening the hell out of you. Just wanted to give you—"

"Oh, please, not another heads-up, Dino. I'm swamped."

"No worries, man. Just wanted to thank you again." He paused for a moment. "You know, my life's a bit upside-down right now." He patted Brian on his shoulder, taking the opportunity to glance at the pages spewing out of the printer, dense with chromatograms and mass spectrometry analyses and chemical structures.

"So, you'll be back in two weeks?"

"Probably sooner," Dino said with a confiding smile. "Maybe tomorrow, or even today."

Brian shot him a befuddled glance. "Okay."

"I'll explain later," Dino said. He walked sideways toward the door, looking back over his shoulder. "Thanks a bunch for your help, Brian. But listen—no word about those tomatoes if he asks again, okay? Tomorrow, when I'm back—"

"You won't be back, my friend," a deep voice thundered.

Dino spun around into the red face of Jason Goodlette.

"You're fired."

The words hung in the silence like a reverberating shot.

Dino's heart gave a lurch. "What do you mean, fired..."

"Fired, as in axed. Discharged from employment. With immediate effect."

"Jason, you can't just..."

"Yes, I can. Enough is enough." He sliced the air with his hand as if it were a Samurai sword. "Enough is enough."

Dino clenched his teeth, this time succeeding in swallowing down a bunch of insults before they left his lips.

***

Coming to grips with his new situation after that humiliating sacking was one thing, admitting the smackdown to Cat was another. Dino resigned himself to the ordeal, knowing she would let him have it.

"What do you say to this, Cat?" Dino slid a piece of paper across the table. "I still can't believe he'd follow through with it."

"Can I go for a bicycle ride with you?" Mia interrupted. "You promeeesed..."

"Maybe a bit later. I need to discuss something with your mom."

Cat grabbed the letter that Dino had brought home from work. It took her only a moment to go through it. "You got a pink slip?" Her expression had taken on a livid touch. "Seriously? You're a complete ass, Dino. You lost your job because of your silly actions—crossing the line several times." She threw her hands in the air in a snit. "You're such a stubborn idiot. Irresponsible, too."

Dino looked at her in utter astonishment. Her cheeks were beet red. Strands of her blonde hair hung loose from the ponytail. He hadn't expected such a blowup. "Okay, maybe I went too far."

"You think? I told you, but you wouldn't listen to me."

"Thanks for the moral support. I haven't heard the *I told you so* pearl of wisdom since my mother died."

He could tell from the glowering look she gave him that his poor-little-me attitude galled her.

"Granted," Dino continued, "I might have stretched it. But that's no reason to fire me, just like that. Jason could've talked to me first."

"Isn't that what he did? Last week? And probably before?"

Dino brushed his hand through his wavy hair. "Look, maybe I behaved like a jerk, but—"

"Glad you can finally admit it."

"But Goodlette's reaction is inappropriate, and totally out of proportion. His retribution is excessive."

Mia, meanwhile, sensing that trouble was brewing, looked timidly at her mother and slowly withdrew to her room.

Cat hammered her hand flat on the kitchen countertop. "You're such a blockhead. The mistake is never yours. You always blame others. Whereas you, you're always Mr. Perfect." She was panting with rage. "Shit."

Dino was stung by her words but didn't say anything.

"What are you going to do?" Cat asked after she simmered down a bit.

He shrugged. "Look for a new job."

Easier said. He had no idea where to start.

17

DINO

When he woke the next morning, Dino felt the full impact of his new situation. He'd botched it. He'd lost what he thought was a secure job because he had cast Rainbow BioLabs in a negative light. He had used his best technician for a personal investigation, spent company resources and time, and been away from the office without properly informing anyone. He had missed deadlines, repeatedly. And yet—was all this a persuasive reason for him to be dismissed without notice?

He got out of bed and trudged into the kitchen to make coffee, accidentally knocking over a dirty glass. *Shit!*

He glanced at the pile of letters he'd ripped open earlier. He needed to pay the bills. Jobs tailor-made for him were few and far between—and he was almost forty. There was that tightness in his chest again.

Had it been worth it? His hunt for the elusive chemical that had made him stop breathing and killed several other people had been unsuccessful. His efforts so far to identify a harmful pesticide on those tomatoes had been in vain. He was still where he'd always been—at square one. Was it true what Cat had said, that he was chasing a shadow?

He stared at himself in the hallway mirror. Disheveled, ashen-faced with dark half-moons under his eyes, and a two-day stubble. His tongue had a furry sensation; probably he'd drunk a bit too much wine last night. The dispute he'd had with Cat had eventually turned ugly, and he'd gone home.

He could do better than feel sorry for himself.

***

65

Around ten, he left home and stopped at a nearby gourmet market off Tamiami Trail, where he bought a large coffee and a prosciutto ciabatta. He sat on a bar stool, suddenly remembering what the detective had told him. He pondered whether he should call Sompy at GR&S and ask him about their alleged collaboration with Timberlake. On second thought, however, he abandoned the idea. If Sompy knew anything fishy, he wouldn't tell Dino upfront. And if he didn't know, it probably wouldn't be a good idea for Dino to red-flag a well-kept secret and fan the embers.

As he stepped outside, he noticed that the parking lot in front of the gourmet market was still relatively empty, except for a few delivery trucks, a shiny Cadillac, and a polished Acura. Two black vultures, hopping a few yards away, turned their featherless gray necks, eyeing him defiantly.

Waiting for roadkill.

A second before he consciously apprehended what had happened, his gut signaled that something was wrong. It felt like a punch to the solar plexus. The front window of his car was smashed. A small round piece of the glass in the center was splintered, and from there, numerous cracks radiated out like the spokes of a spider web.

"What the—" Dino stammered. He looked left and right, but saw no one. He stepped closer to assess the damage. It was only then that he detected the folded paper slip that was stuck under one of the windshield wipers.

"MYOB. NEXT TIME IT COULD BE YOU."

Mind your own business.... In a subconscious move, Dino held up his hand to protect his head from an imaginary baseball bat.

***

The police officer wasn't helpful. "Maybe the damage was caused by a flying object, a stone maybe."

Dino was dazzled by this logic. As if flying stones were as common in this part of the world as winging crows or sailing seagulls. He held up the handwritten note.

"Someone is threatening me."

The trooper scratched his head. "If it's a person, though, it'll be hard to catch him, unless someone observed the whole scene."

Dino took a snapshot of the damaged windshield. The thought alone of some thug smashing that window made him shudder. Who could it be? Someone from the tomato farm who disliked him—because they thought he'd vilified the clean, organic managing of crops? He couldn't imagine who could be so menacing. Maybe the goons who attacked Miguel? But why would they put him, Dino, in the crosshairs? And how did they know where he was?

Someone was watching him, 24/7.

Dino felt the sweat trickle down his forehead as he looked to his left, his right, and behind him.

PART TWO

Pomme d'Amour

18

DINO

One elbow propped up on the kitchen counter, his pen flitting across a blank sheet of paper, Dino began to jot down a mind map. Trying to piece everything together.

Opioid abuse had skyrocketed in Southwest Florida, and the number of people with OD symptoms that had been admitted to the regional hospitals in recent days and weeks had soared. They all exhibited symptoms consistent with opioid toxicity, but for many of them the labs had found no opioids in their bodies, which was surprising.

The effects hadn't been an illusion, they were real. They just defied analysis.

Dino was convinced, but couldn't prove it, that *something* on those "organic" tomatoes he'd eaten must have been the cause of his recent health emergency. He'd suspected an illegally applied pesticide, but, again, couldn't find any.

He circled the word *pesticide* and added a big question mark. This was the only weak link in his whole story. Plus, he didn't know whether any of the other patients had consumed the same type of tomatoes. But that would be easy enough to find out. He boxed the word *Grand Captiva* and scribbled two exclamation marks next to it.

Dino was closing in on the characters in the plot. Timberlake, the cancer researcher, collaborated with GR&S and had been killed from an opioid overdose. Or did he know something that had cost him his life? Miguel Castro, who innocently sold Grand Captiva tomatoes, had been assaulted and nearly killed. Dino had visited the tomato farm and been warned.

Someone must be terrified that the truth will be exposed.

71

The truth about what? He tossed the pen on the counter. *All roads led to GR&S.*

Before he'd pay them a second visit to clear up the guarded secret, however, Dino had arranged to meet up with Miguel for a happy hour drink. The lucky guy had been released from the hospital the previous day.

***

When Dino arrived at the taqueria, he spotted Miguel sitting on a bar stool, elbows propped on the counter, a sweating can of Tecate in one hand, a bowl of chili lime peanuts in front of him.

Miguel looked up as Dino slid onto the stool next to him and wiped his mouth with the back of his hand. He broke into a broad smile. "*¡Hola amigo! ¿Cómo estás?*" He gave Dino a bear hug.

Dino remembered not a moment too soon that Miguel was recovering from injuries and refrained from slapping him too hard on the back. "So they finally released you?"

"Yeah, it was about time. The hospital food is so boring. Oh, *cerveza?*" Miguel asked.

"Thanks. Corona, please," Dino told the bartender.

"Couldn't wait to get back to my family." Miguel looked great, strong. Hard to believe that he'd just survived two near-death attacks.

"How's the family doing? Fully recovered from that alleged food poisoning?"

"*Muy bien.*" His smile said it all. He reached for a handful of chili nuts, gesturing for Dino to help himself.

"What have you done now? You were supposed to be in a hospital bed, recuperating. Instead, you made short shrift of that goon."

Miguel shot him a quizzical look, then nodded with a grim face, probably having guessed the meaning of Dino's words.

He took a deep breath.

"Dino, the police said that I need a lawyer. Can you help me find one, please?"

"Sure. I know someone. A friend of mine. I'm sure he can help." He could see Miguel frowning and knew what must have crossed his mind. "He won't charge much. Let me talk to him."

Miguel's furrowed face lit up, his right palm pressed to the heart.

The two men high-fived, without saying a word.

"When will you go back to work?" Dino asked.

"The doc said a week from now. I'm not allowed to lift anything heavy yet."

Dino nodded and fidgeted on his stool. "Aren't you a bit scared? Afraid someone might... I mean, honestly, after what happened to you?"

"No." Miguel's chin went up, his chest out. "Why? Are *you* afraid?"

Instead of an answer, Dino rotated the ice-cold bottle in his hand.

I'm shit-scared.

Miguel looked left and right, then turned to face Dino. "Listen, did you find out anything about the—" he lowered his voice to an arcane whisper, his lips accentuating the words, "Grand Captivas?"

Dino took a long swig off his beer, waiting for the waitress to move out of earshot.

"No, I'm still stuck. Didn't find a damn thing on those tomatoes. They seem to be clean. Looking so harmless."

"What did you expect to find? Frankly, I didn't see anything on them," Miguel said.

Dino stifled a laugh. "Dunno. Chemicals. Something toxic. Something you wouldn't see with your naked eye. But something that almost put me in the ground."

Miguel's eyes grew big as tortillas. He sat in silent thought for a few moments, then inhaled sharply. "You said you didn't find anything bad on those tomatoes?"

"That's right. I've run out of ideas."

Miguel's smile sent creases up his cheeks. He reached across the bar and picked a single pistachio from a bowl that the waitress had placed in front of Dino. He cracked open the shell and held the green nut under Dino's nose.

"What if the bad stuff is not on the outside? What if it's *inside?*"

The word hung in the air for a few seconds before Dino's mouth fell open. So obvious, he hadn't thought of it.

He fist bumped Miguel on the shoulder in solidarity. Only when Miguel winced did Dino realize that Miguel's machismo belied the lingering effects of the ruthless attacks he had suffered.

Dino had just received a dazzling idea from Miguel. Not based on rocket science, but simply on streetwise shrewdness, and plain old common sense.

"We'll be in touch, my friend," Dino said as they parted an hour later. "I'll keep you posted." *About GR&S and the Grand Captivas*, he thought, but didn't say it.

"*Pues claro.* And..." Miguel stalled as if he wanted to add something. "Please, don't forget to ask about the lawyer," he finally said.

19

DINO

Dino's jaw muscles bulged. This time, he was determined not to come back empty-handed. He was convinced the key was in those Grand Captivas, and he needed to get to the bottom of it.

He slowly pulled up to the main building at GR&S. As he killed the engine, he took a deep breath. Time for action.

Only mid-morning, but it felt muggy and hot already. Out here in the back country, he heard not a sound. The familiar tinge of wood smoke lingered in the air, probably from a small wildfire.

He had called ahead this time and been given an appointment with a Ms. Martinez.

The receptionist gave him a blank stare when he walked into the lobby. Apparently, she didn't remember him and his flim-flam spiel from before.

"Dirk Spino to see Ms. Martinez," Dino said, removing his sunglasses and giving her one of his charming smiles. She motioned for Dino to take a seat and picked up the phone.

"Samanta? Dirk Spino is here to see you. Yes... Five minutes? Perfect."

She smiled. "While you wait, please help yourself to today's cultivar sample."

Dino glanced at the basket on the elegant pedestal, this time filled to the rim with chocolate-brown mini-tomatoes. Evidently the *dernier cri* in the tomato fashion world.

"Thanks. They'd be great with coffee," he said, jerking his head toward the shiny brown little spheres, "but I should cut down on sweets."

Moments later, a young woman garbed in a long green lab coat breezed into the lobby, appearing from nowhere, holding a stack of papers, staring directly at him.

Dino jumped to his feet, his gaze fixed on her.

"Oh, would you mind signing in as a visitor?" The receptionist handed him a clipboard, but he didn't take it. "Sir?"

It took a few seconds for Dino to tear his eyes away from the woman in the green lab coat and her inviting, radiant smile, but eventually he scribbled his name out of force of habit: STAMPA. First name: DINO. Company: *Blank*. The dense fog that had shrouded his person had magically dissipated. His disguise was gone in an instant.

***

Samanta Martinez was an extremely attractive woman in her mid-thirties, her dark hair cut short, large almond-shaped eyes, olive skin, and a disarming smile that exhibited flawless white teeth.

"Ms. Martinez?"

She nodded.

"Sorry to unexpectedly drop in on you like this and—"

"That's okay. I like unexpected things. I'm Samanta."

"Dino. Pleasure to meet you."

"So you're a journalist writing an article about pesticides?"

"Dead right, except I'm not a journalist, and it's a book about organic farming and pursuing a healthy lifestyle."

"Oh," Samanta said. He wasn't sure whether her tone reflected a slight disappointment or whether it was a sign of admiration. "What are you expecting to see here?"

The unexpected? "Everything. For example, how you're able to control the pests and vermin that are after your crops without using any pesticides and how you develop new tomato varieties."

"I can certainly show you that, but it'll be easier if we go to another building." They stepped outside and hopped into one of three repurposed golf carts parked in a neat row.

"Are you an agricultural engineer?" Dino asked.

"No, I'm a plant geneticist."

Plant geneticist. "Wow! Trying to lift the secrets of the tomato plant's DNA?"

"Among other things. By the way, the tomato genome has been sequenced. Its genetic code has been cracked."

"No kidding. So what you're doing is... genetically modifying tomatoes? Cutting out some DNA and inserting other pieces? Making super-tomatoes?"

Samanta threw her head back and laughed. "It's not so easy."

"Didn't they generate the *Flavr Savr* tomato brand, some time ago, by genetic engineering?" Dino asked. He had read about it and wanted to show off.

"Oh, you're familiar with the *Flavr Savr?* I'm impressed." Samanta smiled. "That was a long time ago. Turned out to be a total flop. That company in California thought those engineered tomatoes would have a longer shelf life."

"But everything was FDA-approved and ready to go—they got a green light for human consumption, right?"

"Absolutely. But they stopped producing them after a few years."

They drove up to a second, larger building and walked across a graveled area to the entrance. "You seem to know a lot about genetic engineering," Samanta said. "Do you have a scientific background yourself?"

"Yeah, I'm a toxicologist. University of Florida at Gainesville."

"Oh, you're teaching at a university?"

"No, I..." *just got fired from a senior position in a contract lab in Fort Myers*, he wanted to say, but didn't. "I do contract work."

Samanta jerked to a halt and peered at Dino. "I just knew it. You can't hide it; it seeps through the pores of your skin. You're talking like a scientist, not like a journalist or a popular book author. You wouldn't make a good actor."

"How about an undercover agent?"

Samanta threw back her head and let out a guffaw. She closed her eyes, and her whole body was shaking. Three seconds later she was back to normal. The abrupt change of expression, without any subtle transition, was fascinating. Dino had never seen someone laughing like this, let alone a beautiful woman.

"So, this building is your research facility?"

"No, the big research building with all the labs is further down the access road—" Samanta threw her head to the side, pointing westwards. "I'm afraid I can't show you around there. Restricted corporate premises. Confidential. I'm sure you understand."

"Of course I do," Dino said. He had a fleeting fantasy of a dark warehouse full of canisters with highly toxic chemicals, novel nerve agents to kill bugs, and corrosive fluids that would annihilate weeds in an instant. Hunched men in yellow chemical splash suits...

"This is just an experimental station. With a greenhouse in the back." She led the way around a few more corners. She removed the long green lab coat she had been wearing and threw it on a chair in an anteroom.

Dino couldn't help noticing Samanta's curvaceous figure that was enhanced by her tight white T-shirt and a pair of white jeans. He had to make an effort to avert his gaze before it became too obvious.

"You asked me what we do to increase the plants' resistance to pests or environmental stress, since we strictly avoid the use of pesticides?"

"Yeah. You genetically modify the tomatoes, I guess?"

"You mean here at GR&S? No. We don't meddle with the DNA. For consumer products, that is. We do use some limited genetic engineering for research purposes, though."

"Fascinating. What kind of research?"

"Applied biomedical research. That's all I can say, unfortunately. I'm sure you appreciate the confidential nature of this work."

"Oh, of course." Dino wondered what *applied biomedical research* could mean.

"To come back to pest control—what we do is apply biological pest control. *Natural* insecticides. Besides, of course, using insect traps, physical barriers, and so on. But no synthetic pesticides. That's a no-no."

"But what I don't get," Dino said, a perplexed look on his face, "is that some of the natural pesticides, isolated from plants, can be quite toxic too."

"I know. But their use is permitted. Approved for organic farming because they're *natural*."

Was there a touch of irony in Samanta's voice?

They chatted some more about tomato breeding and new varieties and their health effects. He even caught a glimpse of the experimental greenhouse.

"Anything else you'd like to know?" Samanta asked, checking her watch.

"Yes." Dino cleared his throat and looked her straight in the eye. "Tell me what the Grand Captiva strain is."

A hint of a frown flickered across Samanta's face. "It's a *cultivar*, not a strain—we're talking about plants here, not lab mice. The Grand Captiva is just one of the many varieties we have."

Dino rubbed the back of his neck. "Anything special about it?"

"Not really. They look appealing to the customers and have a lot of the good stuff. Vitamins, antioxidants. How come you know—"

"Are they available on the market?" Dino was quick, deflecting her scrutinizing question.

"Oh, no. Still in the experimental stages."

"So you don't sell them yet, right?"

"Of course not, as I just said."

If she was becoming suspicious, she didn't show it. Maybe she was just curious.

Dino sniffed a chance. "Would it be possible to get me a few of those?"

"Sorry, I can't. I'm sure you understand." Samanta paused for a few moments. "Any particular reason why you are so interested in those tomatoes? There are so many others available on the market."

Dino met her gaze without flinching. "It's the name—Captiva. Silly but... we just love that island." He shoved his hands in his pockets.

"*We?*"

"My significant other and I."

"Oh."

The pause was too long, awkward.

"That was interesting." Dino's voice was overwrought. "Thank you so much for your time. Maybe I should be heading back now."

"My pleasure. Let's take the shortcut through the greenhouse," Samanta suggested. "It's faster."

She led the way through patches of tomato seedlings and endless beds of different varieties, all neatly labeled with small identification plates stuck into the soil.

"All these—" Dino moved his outstretched arm in a 180-degree bow, "—are organically grown?"

"Sure." Samanta stopped short, picked up a few small lumps of soil and crumbled them between her fingers. She took a sniff and, obviously satisfied, brushed the earth off her hands.

"I need to wash my hands," Dino said.

"Sure, men's room's over there to the left. I'll wait outside. Take your time. I have to make a phone call."

Dino dawdled toward the rear of the greenhouse, making sure Samanta was out of sight.

What he had spotted a minute earlier was of much more interest to him right now than finding a place to empty his bladder. In a small area, roped off from the other patches, were some small, green, healthy-looking tomato seedlings. What had caught his attention, though, were two large, unmistakable signs; the first read, *KEEP AWAY—DO NOT TOUCH*, and another was labeled, *GR. CAPTIVA—CH-304*.

He glanced furtively up and down the aisles of the greenhouse. At the opposite end of the building, three men were bent over a row of seedlings, seemingly absorbed in their gardening. Dino strolled slowly toward the patch of interest, making sure he turned his back on the three workers to hide what he was doing. He crouched down as if to admire the small plants. Time for a gutsy move. He yanked a handful of seedlings from the ground with a fast hitch, brushed the earth from the tender plants, and stuffed them into a pocket of his baggy khakis. He slowly stood up and casually walked to the bathroom. Nobody seemed to have noticed.

As he exited the greenhouse, Samanta was pocketing her cell phone.

"Sorry it took me so long," Dino said, wondering whether she had noticed his gait. He didn't much care, though, what Samanta might speculate about a sore tush or a struggle with extra-tightly fitting underwear, as long as the precious small plants stuffed in the pockets of his pants suffered only minimal injury.

***

Eric Clapton was blasting away on his car stereo as Dino pummeled the steering wheel, his head bobbing to the music. Mission accomplished. Not only had he found a knowledgeable and trustworthy contact person—did he mention charming—but he now possessed some baby Captivas, admittedly pilfered from the greenhouse, but if they survived, he could grow dozens of tomatoes and study them inside out.

He peeked at the seedlings that he had carefully wrapped

in a wet paper towel from the men's room and placed on the passenger seat. They looked miserable, but he was positive they would recover from the rough transport.

On his way home, he stopped at Lowe's Garden Center and purchased a small pot with Heirloom Beefsteak tomato seedlings to use as a comparator.

"How long will it take until I can harvest these tomatoes?" he asked one of the assistants at the garden center.

"Dunno, for sure, sir," the guy said, "but with seedlings this size... a couple months, maybe. Remember, they need a lot of water, but let them dry out first. They don't like damp feet."

"Is there any way I can speed up the growth process?"

The man laughed. "Can't wait to eat them, right?"

Dino's stomach clenched, but he didn't say anything.

"Lots of sunlight—shouldn't be a problem around here. But, no, otherwise, there isn't much you can do. Maybe feed them. Tomatoes are heavy feeders, but you have to wait until they get bigger or you'll burn the tender plants. Just gotta be patient."

Patience, again. Not exactly his prime virtue. Dino was on edge, time was against him. He hoped there wouldn't be any more casualties from phantom opioid OD, that the streak of bad luck could be stopped.

20

SAMANTA

Kuzminski picked up the phone on the first ring, which astonished her. "Sam?"

"Hi, Chuck," Samanta said. "Just a heads-up. There's more to the Castro affair. A visitor I met today here on the premises asked me if I could help him get some of the tomatoes that Castro sold. What do you think?"

"What's his name?"

"A certain Dino Stampa, aka Dirk Spino."

"Same guy who showed up the other day? The one who talked to Sompy?"

"Not sure."

"What's he like?"

"Good-looking fellow, forty-ish, rather short, burly, muscular build, dark wavy hair combed back. Likeable."

"Could be him." Kuzminski paused. "Suspicious-looking? You think he could—"

"Nah, don't think so. He's a scientist. Rather naïve, angular. I think he's harmless. Cute, but harmless."

"Harmless? So why are you calling me?"

"Because he mentioned the Grand Captivas."

"No shit?" Kuzminski sounded a bit fazed. "What did you tell him?"

"I feigned ignorance."

"Keep an eye on him, Sam. Could be one of those damn journalists. They're like bloodhounds. If he shows up again, try to get him off your back. If there is a problem, let me know."

"Sure, will do. I suspect he hasn't a clue what he's blundered into."

Samanta finished the call and leaned back in her chair. Dino Stampa—an interesting man. Why had he used a different name the first time? Dirk Spino—seriously? A scientist... who pretended to write a book about organic farming and healthy nutrition? She didn't buy that. What the hell did he want from her? He had certainly indulged his subterfuge. He'd asked for the Grand Captivas...

Was he looking for something other than tomatoes?

Also, it seemed he had taken a genuine interest in her when they met. Was he attracted to her... just suspicious?

She lifted her shoulders in a shrug of uncertainty.

21

SNOWHILL

Dr. Robert Snowhill sat in the front row of the small auditorium in the west wing of Lee County Hospital. He had been invited to join the weekly round where some of the latest cases of uncommon or unexplained incidents were being discussed. The medical staff usually discussed uncommon adverse drug effects, unexpected reactions to certain procedures, or complications of rare diseases.

Among this week's cases—*phantom opioid poisonings.*

Some of the attending doctors had elaborated on the symptoms and treatments the patients received. Most of these most recent patients had been released the following day, but, unfortunately, three more of them had died of respiratory failure, despite efforts to rescue them. The patients had received airway ventilation and been given naloxone, the most widely used antidote for opioid poisoning, but it had had little effect. Everybody agreed that the clinical picture strongly resembled acute opioid poisoning, but the real nature of the disease eluded them.

The resident who chaired the meeting asked Snowhill to comment on the puzzling situation. "I've had the privilege to review the analytical report that was done by a contract lab in Fort Myers," Snowhill said slowly as if to organize his thoughts and present them in a logical manner. "Serial blood samples were obtained from each patient, taken shortly after admittance during the day, then around 8 p.m., and finally around 5 a.m. the next morning. Analysis of the plasma did not reveal any detectable levels of the major opioids, including morphine, methadone, or fentanyl. This had to be expected as none of the patients had been treated with an opioid analgesic here in the hospital."

Dr. Chang, a clinical pharmacologist, brandished his outstretched hand. "Sorry for interrupting."

Snowhill paused and glanced at his colleague over the rim of his reading glasses.

"Could the reason for the absence of opioids in the blood simply be that they had already been eliminated from the body? I mean, morphine has a rather short half-life..."

"Good point, thanks," Snowhill said. "However, it would have been detected in the early samples. And other drugs, like methadone, for example, have a much longer half-life, up to forty hours."

"How about recreational drugs?" Dr. Clifford, a well-respected internist, threw in.

"I was just going to address that," Snowhill replied. He didn't like being interrupted before he had even finished his comments. "Of course, the lab checked for heroin and oxycodone, hydrocodone—all negative. The list of available opioids is much longer, but for obvious reasons they could only test for the most commonly used, or abused, drugs."

"So how do you explain the paradoxical clinical picture of these patients?" a final-year resident asked. "Typical symptoms of opioid overdose—pinpoint pupils, nausea, partial unresponsiveness, shallow breathing... then coma, respiratory depression—yet total absence of any opioids in the body?"

"Well," Snowhill said slowly, searching for a plausible answer. "*Either* we're dealing here with a rarely used opioid drug of abuse, which is highly unlikely to be found in all patients at the same time..."

Heads went up, alert, eyebrows raised.

"Or, we have a flaw in the analytical procedure. Again, highly unlikely."

"Who did the analysis?" asked Dr. Johnson, Chief of Immunology.

Snowhill glanced at the report. "Rainbow BioLabs, a contract lab in Fort Myers, not too far from LCH. It was a rush order, given the pressing circumstances. We've used this lab before, several times, and they seem quite trustworthy."

"*Quite trustworthy?* The analysis must be one hundred percent reliable. We're talking about a life-and-death situation," Dr. Johnson admonished.

Thanks. I didn't know that. Snowhill hated being patronized by some of his colleagues. "The contract lab *is* reliable. The reason the analysis was outsourced and not done here at LCH, I was told," he pointed to Dr. Chang, "is that our own analytical facility is understaffed. Right, Ed?"

Dr. Chang gave a nervous laugh. "Understaffed is an understatement. We are hopelessly shorthanded in the clinical-analytical lab. I have repeatedly raised this issue and talked to hospital management, but no new personnel have been approved yet."

"Maybe this would be a good time to raise the issue again in light of the current case in point," Johnson suggested.

The chair of the meeting pledged to file a high-priority request directed to the attention of the personnel management. Then he announced that due to time constraints, they needed to move on to the next case.

Half an hour later, Dr. Snowhill was striding toward his office, lost in thought and oblivious to a group of nurses who greeted him in the corridor. Phantom opioids? He didn't believe it for a minute.

22

CAT

Cat bit her lip, trying to tamp down a twinge of uneasiness. Things hadn't been going well with Dino recently. Since he lost his job, he had withdrawn from her. Hopefully, a passing phase. He had been an idiot, granted, and she had let him have it, but that was no reason for him to be in a sulk for days. Normally, he would storm into a temper, but afterwards things would be argued out quickly and domestic harmony was restored.

The other day, she had been over at his house.

"Wow. Didn't know you liked gardening," she had said as she and Mia stepped out onto his lanai. She gazed at the collection of pots, garden soil, and plant fertilizer.

"I didn't know either," Dino said. "But I've decided to start growing my own veggies."

She turned his way, flustered. "What are you growing—carrots? Or your own strawberries?"

"I love strawberries," Mia reminded everyone, just in case they had forgotten.

"Nope. Tomatoes."

Cat darted a concerned look at him. Dino had been acting strangely of late. Staying away in the evenings more frequently than before, avoiding discussions both about their work and personal decisions, brooding over some murky projects that he didn't want to share with her—to name a few things that had struck her. And now his recently developed obsession with tomatoes. Probably this unusual behavior was related to his being laid off. Maybe the stress and uncertainty of finding a new job.

She shrugged. It was his own fault, after all. She decided to broach the subject with him, when the time was ripe.

Or were these the first signs of their relationship cooling off? At the beginning, when they started dating, it was she who had held back her feelings. She was still healing from a recent divorce and another unhappy, albeit short, affair. When she started to get to know Dino better, she had gradually let go and invested deeper feelings in their blossoming relationship, hoping for a lasting commitment that would go beyond the first few weeks or months of that intense romantic fire. Now it was Dino who seemed to be withdrawing. Did he feel that she put Mia first and him second? Probably not—he appeared mature, and displayed affection for Mia, who adored him.

She knew deep inside that if she needed him, he would be there. He was reliable, and he cared. Nevertheless, she had expected a bit more of a sense of responsibility from him. He came and went as he pleased. And he acted crazy sometimes, flouting the rules, especially in recent days and weeks.

Maybe it was just a temporary thing that would pass. But right now, her mind was a roiling mess of conflicting emotions.

"Let's go home." She took her daughter by the hand. "Say bye to Dino."

"Already? We haven't even eaten," Mia said.

"We'll grab a bite at our house," Cat said. She wanted Dino to realize that she was miffed. She had felt neglected, if not rejected, in recent days. Yes, that's what it was. She'd always gone out of her way to reconcile her work with her private life, her daughter, and her partner. Dino didn't seem to appreciate her efforts.

She searched Dino's face for any reaction to their leaving. He brushed the soil from his gardening gloves, rose from his crouched position, and stood up looking somewhat helpless, a blank look on his face.

***

Several days later, late in the afternoon, Cat was standing on her front porch, wearing her oversized designer sunglasses and a white visor cap. Dressed in shorts and a pink belly tee-shirt, she was ready for a jog, eager to unwind from a stressful day. As she did her stretching exercises against the wall, she spotted Dino pulling up into her driveway.

She hadn't expected him so early, but she had called him earlier and invited him over.

"You look great," Dino said. He handed her a bag of groceries.

"I have some news for you, Dino—you want a job?"

The newsflash must have taken him totally by surprise. Dino creased his face into a frown that could not conceal the waggishness in his eyes. "A job? No, thanks. I'm perfectly happy with my current life. Sleeping in, joining the old retired geezers at the coffee shop at 10 a.m., taking a swim in the afternoon. A job is tedious, plus it takes away too much of my free time. The bucks could come in handy, though." He threw up his hands. "What a question. Of course I want a job."

She knew that he had sent out cold job applications as well as responded to advertised positions at several companies located not only in the greater Fort Myers-Naples area, but also outside Southwest Florida, even out of state. So far, he had gotten either no reply or been met with a standard refusal. It was obvious that those polite brush-offs had clouded his mood and started to erode his self-confidence.

They stepped inside and Cat closed the door shut.

"Listen—they might be looking for an analytical chemist or a toxicologist pretty soon." She jabbed her index finger at his chest. "That's you."

"Who's *they*?"

"LCH. I heard rumors today that they urgently need someone to support the clinical chemistry lab. It appears that they want to ramp up the capacity and increase the efficacy of the diagnostic lab."

"No kidding." Dino's expression turned dead serious within a millisecond. "How do you know about this?"

"Oh, through the grapevine."

"Is the position advertised? I haven't seen anything—"

"No, not yet," Cat said. "Needs to be approved first. But from what I hear, that will only take a few days."

She told him the rest of what she knew. Not only did it sound like a dream job, but it also seemed tailor-made for him. And LCH was close to where they lived—she would have been sad to see him move away from the area.

As she watched him, Cat registered the change in his expression—a man who had been severely shaken by his recent job loss and who had turned stir-crazy suddenly looked like the living embodiment of a smiley badge.

Dino pumped his fist. "I'll call human resources first thing tomorrow morning, and then I'll send them my résumé."

You haven't got the job yet, Cat thought, but didn't say it.

"How about reference letters?"

Dino looked flummoxed for a moment. "What do you mean?"

"Goodlette," Cat said. "He was your last boss. Who fired you. They will certainly check with him. And they will probably ask that *would-you-hire-him-again* question. I hope he'll play fair." She was familiar with the encoded language of reference letters. Most likely his former boss would either slander him or ruin his chances with nice, lukewarm praise—either one of which would kill Dino's chances of getting the job.

"Oh, please. Forget Jason."

Cat could read Dino so well. Contrary to his feigned assurance, he was dead worried about Goodlette.

23

DINO

The job interview had been a breeze.

"You're the perfect candidate for this position," the Human Resources director had said. "We need someone with your kind of experience."

"Experience?" he said, winking at her. "Nothing else than the ability to immediately recognize when you make a mistake... that you've made it before."

She glanced at the papers on her desk without any apparent response to Dino's quip. Was he doing it again? Being a smart ass at inappropriate times.

"Something else—I don't think I'm breaching any confidentiality rules by telling you this." She removed her stylish red glasses and held them in one hand. "We have received some *very* strongly worded reference letters on you—I mean, you rarely see this."

Dino felt a knot growing in the pit of his stomach. Strongly worded. Shit! He knew it. That bastard Goodlette.

"Don't look so embarrassed," she said, grinning. "By strongly, I mean strongly supporting you, praising you as a world-class scientist, speaking of you in the highest terms." She got up and came around the desk to exchange a cursory handshake. "We'd be honored to have you aboard."

Dino signed the contract that evening.

Time for a change and a new beginning. This was Dino's second day at the new job.

He smiled when he thought of how everything had gone

off without a hitch.

He readjusted the name tag pinned to the lapel of his new immaculately white lab coat. *Dino Stampa, PhD, Head of Analytical Services.* He puffed himself up—if only Goodlette could see him. Dino still couldn't understand why his former boss had apparently given him such a favorable reference. What did he have to gain by endorsing him, Dino, as a new Lee County Hospital department head? Unless the personnel officer's remarks were to be taken ironically. Anyway, that was irrelevant now—he'd gotten the job.

The first several days went quickly—the grand tour, introductions, paperwork. Dino felt a flood of exhilaration as he realized what a significant improvement this new position was compared to his job at Rainbow.

He was determined to step up to the plate, to face the added responsibility.

He picked up his phone, then shoved it back into his pocket. Part of being a responsible professional was not calling his girlfriend at work unless he really needed to. They had agreed to be silent about their personal romantic relationship, at least in the beginning. It was better to keep their professional life separate from their private.

He gathered his new team and announced that he'd like to have a short briefing session each day at 9 a.m. Two-way communication was crucial, he said. They should drop the formal *Dr. Stampa.* He was Dino. They were all in the same boat. One team with one vision, striving for efficiency and top quality.

Even though Dino was determined to concentrate on his new job, he hadn't blanked out the phantom opioid poisonings, much less the possible link to the Grand Captiva tomatoes and GR&S. Maybe he would learn more about the mystery soon—he was right in the thick of the action.

***

Patience had never been one of Dino's strong suits. He had to use all his cogency and power of persuasion to cajole the administrative specialist at LCH into giving him the names of the mysterious phantom opioid victims admitted to Lee County Hospital with opioid overdose symptoms between May 10 and 13.

Dino had to act the big shot, repeatedly shoving his new name tag in the officer's face, until she relented. She glanced at the list before handing it over to him, visibly stumbling over one particular name. She looked up at Dino, blank-faced, as if he were a ghost.

Dino smiled at her. "Stampa. Yup, that's me. I was one of them. But I survived. Thank you, appreciate it."

Later, in his office, with the door closed, it took considerably more time than anticipated to reach some of the people on the victim list by phone. He had decided to start with the survivors, as he didn't want to bother the families of those patients who hadn't made it. Two of the patients who recovered lived in Naples, one in Bonita Springs. It was possible that all of them had shopped at the same farmers market off the Tamiami Trail and purchased tomatoes from the same vendor—Miguel Castro. Dino needed to be hot on the trail.

He called John Taylor, an insurance agent, first. Mr. Taylor was tied up with meetings the entire day and wouldn't be available.

He hit it lucky with the next two survivors.

***

Ms. Jane Oldenheimer lived in a gated community in Bonita Springs. She greeted Dino with a friendly smile but seemed a bit wary. He flashed his hospital badge and spoke briefly with her over the noise of kids clamoring in the background. She remembered having eaten some tomatoes from the farmers market the day she had that terrible reaction.

"I know it's probably too late," Dino said, "but do you happen to have any of those tomatoes left?"

She looked perplexed. "I'm afraid I don't. That was quite a while ago. After I came back from the hospital, I threw the rest of them away. They had all turned bad. Why do you ask?" Ms. Oldenheimer asked, a quizzical look on her face.

Dino made a flimsy excuse about food safety monitoring, thanked her, and drove away.

Dino asked the same question of Ms. Paula Lambertini, an elderly lady from upstate New York who lived in a luxury retirement community in North Naples. After inspecting his LCH badge, she invited him in to sit down in the living room. She showed him framed pictures of her grandkids and offered him ice tea, which he politely declined.

Familiar with the farmers market off the Tamiami Trail, Ms. Lambertini knew Miguel and his tomatoes well. "Yes, I bought quite a few tomatoes from him just a couple of days before I got sick. He has the best tomatoes in Southwest Florida. I always buy my veggies from him. Why do you ask? Does it have anything to do with my medical emergency that day?"

"Maybe." A possible hit. But no evidence yet. "You don't happen to have any of those tomatoes left, do you?" Dino ventured.

"Oh, no, they would have been rotten by now."

"Of course." This was to be expected.

"You think it could've been food poisoning? They wouldn't tell me at the hospital what it might have been."

Because they had no clue, Dino thought. "A type of food poisoning, yes, maybe, but in a different sense. Well…" He waved it off with a hand, implying that things were too complicated to explain.

"I usually prepare my own spaghetti sauce," Ms. Lambertini said. "You know, it's in my blood—my Italian ancestry." She smiled proudly. "You think it's safer to throw everything away then?"

Dino sat bolt upright. "You mean, you still have some of it

left? The tomato sauce?" What were the odds?

"Sure. I usually make portions and freeze them. You think it'll be okay to eat it, or should I..."

It didn't take a lot of effort to convince Ms. Lambertini to cede a portion of her frozen genuine Italian *sugo al pomodoro* to him. Dino told her to keep the rest separate from the other frozen foods and not to touch it.

"It's not worth it," she said, and gave him the remaining two frozen plastic jars.

Dino promised to let her know if he found out the tomatoes had made her sick.

Ten minutes later, he was back in his car, heading back to his lab.

Maybe a lead—finally.

***

Dino had always thought of himself as a practical man, but Cat had dubbed him a theorist. Sometimes he would come up with the weirdest ideas and offbeat hypotheses. Unlike Cat— when presented with a riddle, she'd choose the most plausible and obvious explanation for an unexpected result first and look for the quirkier reasons later. She was a fiery advocate of the Occam's razor principle—the more assumptions one had to make, the more unlikely was the explanation.

His mind drifted off to Cat—what would she say now? *If it walks like a duck...* If the symptoms he and others had developed after eating those tomatoes closely resembled those of an opioid overdose, they were probably caused by an opioid. Why look for other, less probable explanations like pesticides?

Truthfully though, a tomato contaminated with an opioid wasn't a mundane thing either.

Dino walked up to Laurie, one of his new technicians. She was the most senior one among his new team, radiating authority, orchestrating the daily assignments like an experienced emergency dispatcher. Tall and slim, her white lab coat loose-fitting, her hands donned in blue nitrile gloves. Dino had never seen someone handle a bunch of test tubes and pipettes simultaneously, deft with her long fingers, like a con acrobat.

"I have a request, Laurie," he said in a low voice. "Since you're doing a couple runs for opioids this morning, is it possible to include a few extra samples for me?"

"Sure, why not?" Laurie said. "More in-patients? Or from the ER?"

"No, actually not. It's something different. Not patients. Not humans."

Laurie gave him a puzzled, almost disgusted look, as if he were asking her to analyze alien blood.

"I'd prefer for this to stay between you and me," he added. "Actually, it's *tomatoes*."

Laurie laughed sheepishly.

Dino went to one of the freezers and removed a small transparent plastic box labeled STAMPA—DO NOT OPEN.

"Take half of the sample for the analysis and put the rest back in the freezer. Homogenize and dilute it, take an aliquot, lyse it, and precipitate the proteins. Then treat it exactly as you'd treat a blood sample."

Laurie wrinkled up her nose. "Looks to me like frozen ketchup or something. What is it?"

"No worries," Dino said with a grin. "It's plain old Italian tomato sauce."

"You gotta be kidding," Laurie said, seemingly lost. "Are you pulling my leg?"

"No, I'm dead serious. It's important, believe me. And, please, don't store the analytical data in the hospital database. Put it on a thumb drive, or give me a printout, and delete the data from the computer." Dino leaned toward her in a trustful manner. "Thanks... I appreciate your discretion."

At the door, he looked over his shoulder. Laurie was rooted

to the same spot where he left her, gawking at him in disbelief, scratching her head.

Dino smiled and buried himself in his office. It seemed he had a personal and discreet assistant again, someone reliable, quick, and accurate—like Brian, his previous assistant at Rainbow. Most importantly, she kept quiet.

He wondered whether he should talk to Cat.

Instead, he dialed GR&S's number and asked for Samanta Martinez.

24

DINO

"Dino, you? What a surprise." She sounded genuinely pleased to hear his voice.

"Samanta, hello. This a good time to talk or...?" He stared into the distance, reclined in his chair, both heels propped on the corner of his melamine-coated desk, feet crossed.

"No problem." He heard the low muttering of background talk. "Let me just shut the door. One sec..."

She wants privacy, Dino thought. He rehearsed his strategy once more.

"Okay, I'm back." She sounded cheerful. "What's up?"

"Business. Purely professional interest. Wanted to thank you again for hosting my visit the other day. But, needless to say, I'm also delighted to hear your voice again."

"Likewise. How's your book coming along?"

"My book?"

"Your book project. What's the title?"

"Oh, the book." *The Tainted Tomatoes?* "Don't know yet."

"Make sure you send us a copy when it's published."

"Sure, will do."

There was an awkward pause.

Dino was ready for the run-up, focusing on the target. "I wonder whether you could tell me what you know about Dr. Timberlake."

No immediate response, but he heard her breathing.

"Timberlake? You mean the scientist who was recently murdered in his house? Yeah, I saw it on the news. But why are you asking *me*? Why should I—"

"Because I know he collaborated with GR&S."

"That's true. But—why are you interested in that?"

Dino inhaled sharply. He had expected this question. "Because I want to learn more about PMPs. Plant-made pharmaceuticals."

Another pause. Dino could virtually hear her turning things over in her mind. He pictured her assuming a rigid posture, licking her glossy lips.

"I didn't know him personally," Samanta said. "He worked primarily with Dr. Harrod."

"Who's he?"

"Clayton Harrod. He's one of the plant scientists in our research department."

So are you, Dino thought. She *must* have known Timberlake. Piecemeal tactics. It was evident—she only admitted so much at a time. Only what he already knew or could prove, hiding everything else.

"What did your colleague and Timberlake collaborate on? I mean, tomato research and cancer research are not exactly..." Dino said with a constrained laugh, searching for the right word.

He thought he heard a touch of indecision in her voice before she continued. "Look, Dino, truth is, we tried to keep it on the down low. We have enough problems with the press, and we didn't want to needlessly stir things up."

"Because of the Castro story?" Another punch. Dino removed his feet from the desk and sat upright.

"Yeah, among other things. The gossip factory has been working overtime already. But tell me, why is all this so important to you anyway?"

"Because I want to know what's behind the tomatoes that Miguel Castro was selling at the farmers market." How much of his intention should he reveal? A tightrope walk. "Some folks who bought them got sick. Seriously ill, that is. This has to stop before more people end up in the hospital."

"What do you think is behind those tomatoes?"

"I don't know but they're dangerous. They could kill some-one." *Like me, or Miguel's family.* "I want a chemical analysis."

"Of what exactly?"

"Of those tomatoes."

"Yeah, that came across." She sounded as if she'd regained her balance.

Dino cleared his throat. "For xenobiotics, chemicals that shouldn't belong there."

There was a short, tense pause. Then he heard a faint, almost inaudible wheezing. He remembered what it was. He could picture Samanta throwing back her head, closing her eyes to slits, her whole body shaking with soundless laugh-ter. As if someone had switched her to sound-off-vibrate-on mode.

He didn't quite grasp what was so funny about what he'd just said.

A few moments later she was her normal, solemn self again. "Why didn't you tell me before? We could have chatted about it earlier."

"Really? Would you have?"

"Sure. I can tell you more about what we're doing here. About how we improve the genetic makeup of plants, cross-breed and select novel tomato cultivars, and other stuff. And, please... call me Sam."

Was this a side step or a true sign that she was willing to cooperate?

"All right, Sam." Dino hesitated. "Maybe we could have a drink somewhere?"

"Sure, why not? But not today. Some other time, okay?"

His heartbeat quickened as they disconnected the call.

25

DINO

Laurie popped her head into Dino's office. She looked tired, if not dispirited.

"I'm done with the regular runs. All the data is updated and accessible in the LCH database."

"Great, thanks." Dino gestured for her to come in. "You didn't get a chance to..." He left the sentence open for Laurie to guess what he meant.

"Yes, I'm done with it." She held the printout in one hand. "But I got strange results."

"Strange? What do you mean?"

"It's all negative. Nothing. Not even traces." She had a hangdog look on her face.

"Let me see." He reached for the papers. "How about the positive controls? The standards?"

"Everything's okay. The method works fine. It's the sample. There's nothing in it."

"Don't despair, Laurie. It is what it is."

"But didn't you tell me there was something in that tomato sauce?"

"I didn't tell you that you *had* to find something at all costs. In fact, I had no clue. But now we know."

Laurie looked somewhat relieved. "Anything else you want me to do?"

"Nope. Thanks for the excellent work. Why don't you call it a day?"

Dino slumped back against his chair. He was back at square one.

The negative results meant that the tomatoes from Paula

Lambertini that came from Miguel Castro's veggie stall at the farmers market did not contain opioids—which made sense. How would they have ended up there in the first place?

No pesticides, no opioids... Yet a dramatic effect. On him and other people. A lethal effect. By something invisible. Would anybody believe his story?

Dino buried his head in his hands. *I'm not crazy. Am I?*

Was the *something invisible* still there, the deadly effect still lying there in ambush?

His head shot up.

There was only one way to find out.

***

Dino walked up to the counter of the spacious LCH pharmacy. He flashed his ID card, pointed to the name badge pinned to his white lab coat, and introduced himself as Dr. Dino Stampa, head of Analytical Services.

"I need two flasks of Narcan nasal spray, please."

"Are you an MD, or do you have a prescription?" the pharmacist asked.

"I don't have a prescription, but it's for our analytical lab. As a standby rescue medication, if you wish, not for personal use. My team works all the time with different kinds of opioids, and I would like to have a fast-acting opioid antagonist at hand, just in case someone inadvertently gets a dose. We need something to counteract the dangerous effects quickly, if needed."

"I understand," the pharmacist said, "but I need an official paper or a valid license. Sorry."

Dino realized he had hit a stone wall and left empty-handed.

Ten minutes later, he got lucky with the head nurse on one of the wards in the Oncology Center. She gave him two flasks of the naloxone nasal spray for exclusive use in the

Analytical Lab. She wrote the details down on a worksheet, and he signed for it. He would leave one of them in his lab and take the other one home.

He still had some of Ms. Lambertini's Grand Captiva tomato sauce frozen in the lab. A risky endeavor, but he'd be one step ahead... or dead.

***

Initially, Dino had considered running the test in his own house. However, in view of the small but real risk that it could backfire, he had decided to run the experiment at his workplace, at the hospital.

The following day he asked Laurie to stay a bit later than usual. Normally, the technical personnel left around five, hardly ever later than six, so he and Laurie would be the only ones in the lab, except the two techs assigned to the night shift. He promised to treat her to a nice lunch in return. Laurie agreed to the overtime, provided it didn't turn into a regular thing. She declined lunch.

He had instructed Laurie to remain in the lab, where she could do some paperwork or read, while he was in his office behind closed doors doing an experiment. Everything should be over by eight or so. If he called her, she should come into his office immediately; otherwise, she should stay clear of him.

"Why don't you perform that experiment during the day?" Laurie had asked.

"Nah, too much distraction during the day. I need full concentration and privacy."

Laurie had looked at him with skepticism. He was pretty sure that she didn't consider him a threat. Maybe a bit whacky, but harmless.

With the voice-recording app ready, he placed his cell phone on his desk, a pair of pointed forceps that he had borrowed from the lab next to it. Finally, he mounted a digital blood pressure monitor on his left wrist.

Dino took a deep breath.

He checked his watch. Once more he glanced at the door and then started recording.

"Tuesday, June 15, 6:15 p.m. Baseline data." He inflated the blood pressure cuff and waited for the beep. "145/85." A bit on the high side, but that was to be expected; he was obviously a bit edgy.

He turned on the selfie mode on his phone, inactivated the flashlight, and brought the camera as close to his right eye as possible, making sure there wasn't a bright light source next to him. He brought his eye into focus and shot a picture.

Snack time.

He carefully opened the plastic box containing the tomato sauce that he had defrosted and warmed up in the break room's microwave a while ago and reached for the spoon he had snitched from the cafeteria. No pasta today, just plain tomato sauce.

"6:25 p.m. Time zero," he said loud and clear, then shoved a couple of spoonfuls of the red sauce into his mouth.

The sauce tasted... well, he wasn't sure how to describe it. Not bad. Strong, concentrated, sweet-spicy—a savory tomato taste. A hint of oregano and a strong touch of basil. He cocked his head to the side and slowly turned the sauce around in his mouth as if tasting wine. Good actually. Not like the insipid, preservative-laden stuff from a can, but the full, sweet, aromatic taste of ripe tomatoes that only the local farmers could offer.

He fed himself more, swallowed, and waited.

Half an hour later, Dino smiled to himself. He felt great. He wondered how long it would take for any effect to kick in, if there was any. He spooned up the delicious sauce. As he did, he felt tired, but this could be the earlier tension draining from his body.

A slight wave of nausea seized him, but he shook it off.

Everything seemed to tally. *Wonderful.* He would provide the proof. He would win.

He took his blood pressure again. "104 over 70," he said in a clear voice. "7:34 p.m." A clear drop from the previous baseline value. *Who cares?*

He shot a second pic of his right eye. The pupil seemed like a pinhead.

Fifteen minutes later, he realized his breathing had become shallow. He'd planned initially to do an analgesia test on himself, but decided to forgo it. The sharp forceps were right in front of him, but he was in no mood to pinch himself and see whether he could feel the pain or not. He could care less about it right now.

He put his elbows on the desk and rested his head on his arms. Just for a few minutes.

A soft, sweet breeze flooded over him. It felt like a warm, salty wave from the Gulf of Mexico. A curtain of tropical flowers engulfed him. So sweet, so peaceful.

He was gliding, falling, as if suspended by a parachute, through a sea of red clouds. These clouds fell to pieces into small, round pieces that swirled around him. He wanted to reach for what looked like cotton balls, except that their white, fluffy texture gradually turned into red balls. Cherry tomatoes....

Then everything went black.

26

LAURIE

At 8:40 p.m., Laurie knocked on Dr. Stampa's door. She hadn't heard a sound for over an hour. He had insisted she leave him alone unless he called her, but he had also said that the experiment would be finished by eight or so. She was hungry and tired and wondered why she had agreed to assist him at all in this dubious game.

There was no answer, so she decided to sneak a peek. She opened the door slowly and peered in.

"Oh my gosh," Laurie stammered, her jaw dropping.

Her boss lay on the floor, arms stretched out, his mouth wide open, his expression lifeless.

Instantly she knelt and took his head in her hands. He didn't seem to be breathing. His symptoms seemed vaguely familiar to her—weak pulse, clammy, cold skin, eyes half closed. A million thoughts raced through her mind.

What had he been doing? "An experiment," he had called it. How silly of her to agree to stay without knowing what this was all about. Had he suffered a heart attack? She was not a nurse, just a lab technician. She had never had formal first-aid training, but she knew that every minute counted.

Laurie turned Dino over on his back and started applying rhythmic pressure to his chest. She had heard that a cardiac massage would help maintain blood circulation and that this could save someone's life after a heart attack. He remained unconscious, but still there was a pulse. Probably not cardiac arrest.

She was breathing heavily as she whipped out her phone and called the hospital's emergency number. Thank goodness it happened right here with doctors and nurses just a few levels above.

As she waited for the rescue crew, she glanced around the office, noticing a blood pressure device lying on the floor. What the hell had he been doing? On Dr. Stampa's desk sat an open plastic box with the remains of an ugly-looking red mass, a spoon sticking out of the leftovers. It reminded her of something that she'd recently seen, but she couldn't quite put her finger on it.

Her eyes wandered around and spotted an unopened vial of Narcan nasal spray. Then she knew. She had used an identical plastic box for the opioid analysis she had done for Stampa. *Tomato sauce.* Did Stampa really have the guts to ingest that stuff?

The emergency team arrived in record time; as she watched them, the young resident had to make a quick decision.

"Prep an IV," he said calmly but decisively to a nurse. Laurie gawked at him as he pulled up Dino's eyelids. "Miosis, pinpoint pupils. Respiratory depression."

"He works with opioids," Laurie said. "But I don't know whether..." She didn't finish her sentence.

The doctor stood up and shot her a glance. "Thank you." He talked on his phone while the others heaved Dino onto a gurney.

Laurie didn't get everything the doctor said, but she clearly understood some of it.

"Prepare for tracheal intubation and naloxone. Looks like we have an opioid OD."

Laurie watched in dismay as the team rushed the unconscious Dr. Stampa to the elevator. It was only after she was alone that the tension was released, like a deflating balloon. Her mouth was dry, tears welling up behind her eyelids. It looked like her new boss was in safe hands for now, but he had behaved in a bizarre way. Whatever that "experiment" was, it was an irresponsible thing to do.

She stared at the internal phone number the doctor had scribbled on a piece of paper. She would page him soon to follow up on his health situation.

What the hell was going on?

27

DINO

"You had a close call," the young resident told Dino. "Luckily, you were in the right place. Had you been somewhere other than the hospital, I'm not sure you would have made it." Dino could see the concern on his face.

"Thanks, guys. Was it really that bad?"

"You bet. We had to ventilate your airways and give you an IV infusion of naloxone. Naloxone competes with and displaces the opioid drugs from the receptors—"

"Yeah, I know what naloxone does," Dino interrupted.

"You seem to be familiar with the terminology—are you an MD?"

This seemed like a *déjà-vu* moment. Dino shook his head. "No, I'm an analytical toxicologist. I work here at LCH."

"I see." The resident flashed him a faint, derisive smile. "A laboratory person. Not much clinical experience with real patients, right?"

A joke or a cheeky comment? Dino wasn't sure which, but the man had saved his life.

The young doctor took a seat next to Dino's bed. "Tell me, what on earth did you do?"

Dino had anticipated these kinds of questions. *Devoured some tomato sauce.* These guys had no idea. All he wanted was to get out of here. Explaining his suspicions was useless, and describing his self-experiment would severely impeach his credibility as an expert. In his imagination, he already heard the whisperings in the corridors—the newly hired head of Analytical Services, a total nut.

He had to come up with a subterfuge, now. "I was in pain,

severe pain. And since I had some fentanyl in my lab, I took some. Silly me. I guess the dose was too high." The lie dangled in the air.

"Where did you get the fentanyl? You know it's a prescription drug—"

"Of course, I know, but we have it in our lab. We have to run opioid analyses all the time, so we use it as a standard."

"How much did you take?"

"Half a milligram, I think."

"You *think*?" The resident stared at him in disbelief. "Well, it sure knocked you out. You know that fentanyl is a hundred times more potent than morphine?" He shook his head. "Dabbling in self-medication. You should leave it up to us. Self-medicating can be dangerous."

Dino knew the doctor was right, except Dino had eaten tomato sauce, not fentanyl. "Anyway, doc, thanks again for quickening the dead." Dino sat upright. "I feel fine now. I assume I can leave?"

"We'd better wait until all the stuff is out of your system. In a few hours, I think, we can let you go. We're preparing the paperwork." The resident got up, reached out his hand, then quickly withdrew it. "Oh, one more thing—you mentioned you had severe pain—what kind of pain?"

"Back pain." Dino touched the small of his back. "Sometimes it's unbearable." Another lie.

"You'd better have it checked soon."

This time, the resident shook hands and left.

Dino quickly got out of his bed and reached for the slippers. He lurched for a moment and realized he still felt a bit dizzy. Strong stuff—whatever it was. The second time the effects had kicked in faster than the first time when he had eaten the fresh tomatoes, probably because he had ingested much more of it from the concentrated sauce. The previous chemical analysis hadn't revealed anything, but the results of his risky self-experiment were crystal-clear. He could demonstrate the effect, but he couldn't determine the cause. He reached for the water bottle and took a long gulp.

Although Dino felt a prickle of remorse about what he had done and how he had lied to the resident, he had gathered compelling evidence.

No doubt, the Grand Captivas were a potential poison, a deadly poison.

But nobody would believe him.

***

Later that evening, Dino told Cat everything that had happened. Without embellishing the story, without justifying himself, just in a matter-of-fact way.

Cat shot him a quizzical look. "That's what you did? Seriously? I can't believe it. You're a complete fool." She shook her head. "I just can't believe it."

Dino assumed an unfazed expression. He knew all too well that she was right, but he didn't want to admit it. It was true. He had acted irresponsibly and unwisely. So much for his promise to himself and Cat to become a responsible, trustworthy adult male.

"You know what? You could have killed yourself. Easily." She shook her head again in utter disbelief. "You'd think once would be enough. But, no, you wanted to bring this to a boil. Deliberately poisoning yourself a second time. Wonderful." She blew the air sharply out her nose. "And you call yourself a toxicologist? A specialist?"

"The first time wasn't deliberate," Dino said. "I had no clue then." This was the best he could come up with to justify his reckless behavior. He thrust his hands deep into the pockets of his jeans.

"Why didn't you tell me? And why did you swallow that stuff while you were alone?"

"I wasn't alone. Laurie, my new assistant, was with me. I mean, outside. She was waiting outside the room," Dino snapped. He didn't like Cat heaping accusations on him.

"Ah, here we go. You let your sweet little assistant in on your secret intentions, but you keep your partner completely in the dark. I bet she's cute as hell."

Dino took a deep breath. He'd never become inured to Cat's jealous taunts.

"Stop it, Cat. Let's not start again with these ridiculous allegations." He realized that, within seconds, the topic of their conversation had shifted away from the phantom opioids in the tomatoes to her delusional perception of omnipresent female rivals. He had never given her any reason to be jealous of another woman. Every time she started this, he realized he defended himself, although he hadn't done anything wrong. He decided not to pander to her whims this time.

A pregnant silence filled the room. Dino could virtually feel the friction from their discussion.

After what seemed a long time, Cat looked down at the glass-covered coffee table, avoiding Dino's gaze. "I'm tired," she said. "I'd rather be alone tonight. Perhaps it's better if you leave now."

"All right," Dino snorted. "Fine." He snatched up his keys from the side table in the entrance area and stepped outside on the front porch, resisting the urge to slam the door.

28

SAMANTA

The somber conference room felt stuffy and smelled of musty carpet. *What am I doing here?* Samanta thought. She wasn't a big fan of the boring bimonthly GR&S Research Staff meetings, but it was a good opportunity to catch up.

Somporn Wattanapanit entered the meeting room. He moved like a cat—soundless, soft-footed, discreet, but always on high alert.

"Since you're here, Sompy," Kuzminski said, "you might as well give us an update on our new campaign."

"The *Red L&T* project?"

Kuzminski leaned back in his chair in anticipation. "You got it."

Sompy connected his flash drive to the laptop and started the projector.

Samanta watched as the man moved around quickly. He was stocky, but deft and agile, dressed in an immaculate white dress shirt without a tie, black pants, and shiny black leather shoes. As he walked past her, she couldn't help noticing the discreet and pleasant lemony fragrance, with a hint of something tropical, that he exuded. Coconut, maybe. Sompy always looked like he'd just come out of a long shower. Fresh, clean, balmy—but not that perfumy, sweet-scented overpowering stuff that some men seemed to bathe in. And then his fancy hairdo—his thick black hair slick and shiny, sticking out in spikes.

He explained how they had made considerable progress in pushing the marketing of the nutritional value of tomatoes, advertising them as a healthy alternative to less wholesome snacks. The company's goal was to promote tomatoes as medicinal food.

"*Medicinal food?*" an old stager from agrochemistry interrupted. "How are you going to justify that term?"

"Thanks, that's a good point. Nutraceuticals—medicinal foods—have the potential to be safely used therapeutically. In the clinic."

"Pardon me? Tomatoes? In the clinic? Because they contain some vitamin C and some lycopene?"

Sompy smiled knowingly. "Want to see the latest? We have developed super-tomatoes. You won't believe this." His green laser pointer nervously wandered across the projected graph. "See, the lycopene levels are sky-high, about ten-fold higher than normal. And look at this—" he pointed at another graph "—alpha-tomatine is almost a hundred times higher than the values you would find in normal tomatoes. Massive amounts of these antioxidants."

"How on earth did you do this?" the agrochemistry expert asked, seemingly impressed.

"Two strategies. First, organic soil and treatment, of course, and second, more importantly, careful selection and cross-breeding of those varieties that have high lycopene and alpha-tomatine content," he said, with a proud undertone.

"So that's why you call them *Red L&T*—for lycopene and tomatine," a woman from Marketing said.

"You got it," Kuzminski said, as if he were the project leader who had coined this term.

"Okay, they're antioxidants, we know that. But why *clinical use?*" Samanta asked.

"Because a combination of high levels of lycopene and alpha-tomatine has the potential to dramatically reduce the incidence of new cases of prostate cancer and to greatly decrease the mortality of those with existing cancer." It sounded like a statement Sompy had memorized beforehand.

Its meaning took a few moments to soak in.

"Are you saying that eating a lot of tomatoes, let's say the Red L&Ts, will protect and ultimately cure prostate cancer patients?" Samanta asked, leaning forward. "Seriously?"

Before Sompy could reply, Kuzminski jumped in. "Time will tell."

"According to whom?" someone asked.

Kuzminski cleared his throat. "According to someone who knows—or knew, I should say— more about this than all of us in this room." His eyes wandered around the table. "The late Dr. Timberlake at ImmuneTherix."

"The cancer specialist?"

"That's him, big shot," Kuzminski said. He took a deep breath. "So sad he's no longer among us."

Samanta stole a glance at Harrod, their resident super brain geneticist, then locked eyes with Kuzminski. He held her gaze and slowly, almost imperceptibly, shook his head.

***

"Fantastic. You folks really have a green thumb," Kuzminski said during a short coffee break.

"I'd call it a *red* thumb, Chuck," someone from Green Chemistry said.

"*Super Toms* indeed," Kuzminski said. "Our lawyer tells me we're close to filing the patent."

"You should perhaps change the name of the new cultivar, Red L&T, to something more appealing, for marketing reasons," the Marketing lady said. "But don't call it *Prostate Savr*, that would be too much of a turn-off."

Kuzminski clapped his hands. "Back to work, folks."

For the next half hour, Clayton Harrod filled them in on his latest results with genetically altered tomatoes. Harrod was a tall, skinny man with a pale, gaunt face, who looked older than his thirty-nine years. He had large, sleepy eyes set deep in their sockets. He moved with slow, deliberate steps, emanating a sense of insecurity that sometimes verged on plain disorientation. Everyone knew, however, that he was an extremely sharp, highly intelligent and creative molecular geneticist, who usually made decisions blazingly fast and worked with the utmost speed and accuracy.

He's an introvert at best; if not borderline autistic, Samanta thought. Harrod ignored people, looking straight through them as if they weren't there.

His presentation was pithy but studded with too much scientific minutiae and too many abbreviations like CRISPR. Although Harrod reiterated that, nowadays, everybody should be familiar with the game-changing technology called CRISPR, Kuzminski seemed lost, judging from the questions he threw in every few moments. He leaned back in his chair, clasping his hands behind his head.

Harrod appeared annoyed by the constant interruptions that interfered with the flow of his presentation.

"I have a question," said Kuzminski. "You said you can insert a piece of foreign DNA into the genome of the tomato plant, right?" He air-quoted the word *foreign*.

Harrod nodded.

"So—this tomato plant starts making a certain foreign product that it wouldn't make normally, from the recently inserted blueprint, which is not a tomato gene, but a foreign gene?"

Harrod seemed to wriggle for an answer. "Yes... it's not that simple, but... yes."

Kuzminski waved any objections away with his hand. "Let's keep it simple. Just for me. So—if you inserted a gene coding for lycopene, and another one for alpha-tomatine, and a few others coding for other antioxidants—couldn't you generate a real blockbuster tomato, full of all that good stuff?"

Harrod rolled his eyes. A murmur went through the row of the other participants.

Samanta glanced at her watch. These sluggish meetings

had a good side to them. They were a fascinating lesson in applied psychology—studying the participants in-depth, watching their reactions, analyzing their questions, deciphering their non-verbal behavior, and, importantly, how they related to each other.

Kuzminski would claim another ten minutes just for having explained to him what a gene product was.

"I'm not sure I'm following you," Harrod said. "There isn't a single gene for lycopene, nor for tomatine."

"Why not?"

"Because they are not proteins. Lycopene is a carotene, and tomatine is an alkaloid coupled to a sugar." Harrod seemed to struggle with explaining something complicated in simple terms. "To biosynthesize these chemicals—to make them—a plant needs to go through a complex, multi-step pathway, involving many enzymes and precursors and—"

Harrod took a deep breath and let it out slowly, frustrated that his explanations seemed over Kuzminski's head.

"So... what you're saying is that you can only take a stolen gene and implant it into the host tomato if the gene product you want is a protein?"

"Basically, yes."

"So—you cannot simply insert a gene for, say, any pharmaceutical drug and then the plant would start making that drug?"

"Only if the drug is a protein," Harrod said, "and the vast majority of drugs aren't proteins."

Some of the attendees started fidgeting in their chairs.

Samanta, for the umpteenth time, checked her watch. A private lesson in basic biochemistry. She had things to do, but unless she had a solid reason, she couldn't possibly leave—she might miss something important.

29

DINO

On Sunday morning, coffee mug in hand, Dino stepped out onto the lanai and checked the status of his tomato seedlings. Both the Grand Captivas and the normal twins were growing fast.

He could see small yellow flowers on quite a few of the plants from a distance already. The first fruit would develop soon. Getting the ripe tomatoes would be crucial to finding out what was so special about them.

Carefully, almost tenderly, Dino touched one of the small plants. The delicate stems were already several feet above the ground and covered with tiny hairs. He looked at the pinnate leaves with their serrated margins. Beautiful. Actually, he had never looked at a tomato plant that closely. He, who had never had the slightest idea about, let alone interest in, gardening and could care less about growing plants, had now become an expert. He had turned into the ultimate tomato pundit.

"Keep growing," Dino mumbled.

***

Sunday night. A sweet, heavy scent of frangipani hung in the humid air.

It was getting late, and Dino was tired. He had just reviewed a proposal he had written on the need for a new and expensive UPLC-MS/MS for his lab, an ultra-high-resolution tandem mass spectrometry apparatus, when he thought he heard a noise in the front of the house. Like someone knocking at the door. At this hour? He glanced at his watch—it was past midnight.

He shut down his computer, grabbed a beer from the fridge, popped the top, opened the front door, and stepped out onto the driveway.

The oppressive heat hit him like a wave. Coming from the comfortably cool rooms inside the house, the contrast was stark, and he closed the door to keep out the hot air and humidity. The neighborhood was quiet, except for the monotonous croaking of frogs and the shrill nagging sound of the cicadas in the trees of the preserve across the lawn. The houses were dark, his neighbors early sleepers.

A large, dark object moved slowly down the street, some fifty yards from his driveway. As it approached and then stopped, he recognized that it must be a car whose driver had forgotten to turn on the headlights. Or a couple making out, not having the heart to say goodbye to each other.

As he took the last swig from the can and turned to go inside, out of the corner of his eye, he saw a shadow emerge from behind the large palm tree next to the driveway. Reflexively, he spun around, totally taken aback.

The impact caught him off guard. He fell hard on the concrete driveway. His beer can flew into the air and plonked down on the ground. Befuddled, Dino gasped for air. The next moment he felt a heavy knee on his chest. The punches to his face were brutal, the kicks in his side and loin savage. There was no way he could cry for help as he panted for breath. A sharp pain kicked in, and then things went blurry. More blows—and then... nothingness.

30

DINO

"Oh my gosh—what happened?" Laurie burst out, clapping her hands over her head, sounding half amused, half frightened at the sight of him. "Were you run over by a truck?"

"Close." Dino felt miserable. His head was bruised. His left eye a swollen, dark shiner, likely to develop into a gradually changing rainbow pattern in the days to come. His whole body ached and he walked with a limp. Luckily, nothing was broken except two ribs, and his lungs were unharmed. Coughing, sneezing, even laughing felt like a stab with a butcher's knife. Things could have been much worse, the attending doctor at the ER had told him.

It seemed as though he was tumbling from one emergency to the next. Part of it was brought on by his own fault, but not this latest incident.

The aftermath of last night's painful assault still hovered over him. He couldn't shake the strong feeling that he was in danger. Who was threatening him and why? He didn't know.

First, his smashed car window and now a vicious nighttime attack. Clearly it was a warning; the intimidation was escalating.

After he'd regained consciousness—he must have been out for just a few minutes—he had reported the ambush to the police. They said they would do their best to catch the attackers—which probably meant nothing was going to happen.

He had also checked with the security guards at the main entrance of his gated community. They were strict about who gained access to the huge community, but hundreds of cars drove in and out of the four gates during a single day. The guards said they were going to look into it but hadn't found anything unusual or suspicious so far, which seemed strange in view of all the modern surveillance networks in place.

Dino touched his head, as if to make sure it still hurt.

"Let me tell you what happened, Laurie. You won't believe it. Over the weekend, I tried to skateboard for the first time. Old guys like me shouldn't be allowed to even try to get on a board. I lasted about two seconds before I kissed the pavement. Silly me. God punishes idiots instantly." He grinned awkwardly. Another lame lie. He hoped nobody could see that he had been scared to death, and still was.

"So sorry," Laurie said, trying to look sympathetic while trying not to laugh. "Wish you a speedy recovery." She shot her boss a skeptical look. "Just wanted to let you know that it's finally working." She gave him the thumbs-up sign.

"What? What is working?"

"The tandem mass spec analysis of the protein mixture you gave me the other day. No need to enzymatically chop up the proteins first. I can run the analysis with the intact proteins."

Dino sat upright as if on cue. "That was the test run with a known protein, right?"

"Correct," Laurie said, lifting her heels and rising slightly to emphasize the importance of her successful analysis.

"Great. That's wonderful news." He cleared his throat, stalling. "Soon I'll give you something new. An *unknown* protein. Try the *SEQUENCE* software program, and if you can't identify it there, let's determine the sequence and ID of the peptide ourselves."

Laurie's eyes widened. "I've never done that before."

"I'll help you. No worries," he added quickly.

"Okay." She shoved her hands into the pockets of her immaculate white lab coat. "It's just that..."

"What?"

"I'm so far behind with the regular work. The hormone

report is overdue, and the immunoassays—"

"Don't worry. I'll assign someone else to the routine work. I want you to concentrate on the protein analysis—highest priority." Top priority for him, not necessarily for the hospital.

"If you say so," Laurie said. "Where's the sample?"

"I don't have it yet. I'll give it to you in a few days." He placed his index finger across his lips. "Not a word to anyone about this, okay?"

"About what?"

"About the protein analysis."

Laurie nodded, then cocked her head, as if to say, "Why are you acting so mysterious?" She shrugged and resumed her work.

Dino went back to his office and settled in his creaking chair. The pile of reports and documents he should vet and sign was growing bigger by the hour.

His new job was interesting, but his mind was somewhere else.

31

DINO

"What in the world..." Samanta said. "You look terrible."

"I warned you on the phone." Dino had heard the *what-happened-to-you* question a million times in recent days. "What happened is..." he said preemptively, "last Sunday I did a reverse double somersault from the diving board when I realized in mid-air that there was no water in the pool." He touched his sore eye; it still hurt like hell.

"Must be awful. How badly damaged is the pool?"

"Thank you for your empathy."

They had agreed to meet for a Happy Hour drink at a bar off Sementina Road.

"Did you call me to discuss tomato breeding or because you wanted to see me?" The irony wasn't lost in Samanta's voice.

"To be honest, both," Dino said as he sat down.

Samanta glanced furtively at his hands. "Are you married?"

"No, divorced. You?"

"Same here. I'm single now and enjoying the freedom to do what I want. And you—are you living with someone, Dino?"

"I *have* someone, yes, but we have separate houses."

"Is it serious?"

"Sort of."

"So, you're not available?"

Boy, does she get right to it. "No, I'm afraid I'm not." He wondered where this was going.

Luckily, their drinks arrived. They clinked glasses.

She looked gorgeous and obviously enjoyed teasing him, but Dino didn't feel comfortable continuing on this topic.

"Tell me a bit about your research," he said, trying to change the subject.

Samanta stared at him for a few seconds, then gave him a knowing smile.

"I can tell things aren't going well for you, Dino, in your relationship... am I right?" she persisted.

For a moment he pondered whether Samanta had misinterpreted his motive when he called her and suggested getting together after work. On the other hand, the better they knew each other, the more likely he could squeeze some insider information out of her. He needed to be extra careful though, and not overstep the bounds.

"Things could be better, yes," he said, "but I guess it's temporary. Ups and downs are normal in a romantic relationship." He mimicked a rollercoaster with his hand. "I'm sure you know that too."

She threw back her head and exhibited that inaudible laugh again, mouth open, eyes narrowed to slits. Although a bit off-the-wall, her demeanor held a certain fascination. Her body shook for a few seconds, then everything returned to normal. "When a man tells me that things are going up and down, that usually means their relationship is below the freezing point."

I hardly know this woman, Dino thought, *and here we are, talking about personal—intimate—stuff, almost like in a counseling session.*

His mind wandered. Cat had not been her normal self lately. He hadn't heard her play the piano or seen her painting. She had gradually, almost imperceptibly, changed from her jolly, good-natured self into an over-critical person who blamed him when things didn't go as planned. She said she didn't understand why, out of the blue, he was withdrawn and would no longer spend time with her and Mia. Not true. His perception was that it was Cat, not he, who was becoming aloof. Maybe one of these days they needed an honest, upfront talk to resolve the issue before it became more serious.

But he knew who his heart belonged to, and he had not

the slightest intention to change that.

Determined to get her back on the subject of tomatoes, Dino turned his focus from Cat back to Samanta. "You said the other day that you joined GR&S about six months ago. Where did you work before?"

"University of Miami. Masters in Biological Sciences."

"Wow, that's wonderful. Coral Gables, I guess. Never been there, but it must be a nice place," Dino said. "What's your specialty?"

"Plant genetics." She leaned forward and winked at him. "Helps me better understand the sex life of tomatoes. How about you?"

"What about me? Do I understand the sex life of tomatoes? I'm afraid not. Have a hard time understanding my own."

"What I meant was, where did you work before you joined LCH?"

"Oh." Dino tried a dismissive look. "Rainbow BioLabs, a small company in downtown Fort Myers. They do routine analyses for the government, but also for medical centers. Boring. I decided I needed something new, the winds of change blowing... you know. So I tendered my resignation—"

"I'm sure they didn't like your decision to leave."

"Yeah, probably not, but, you know, they understood." One of Dino's eyelids started to twitch uncontrollably. If she was aware of it, there was no indication of disbelief on her part. Dino fidgeted in his chair.

"Who was the boss of your former company?"

"Rainbow BioLabs? Goodlette. Jason Goodlette. Good guy. You heard of him?"

Samanta looked straight through him. "No. Doesn't ring a bell. You're still in touch with him?"

"No, I'm not. We weren't friends, if that's what you mean. We never socialized. Why do you ask?"

She shrugged and then quickly lifted her head and signaled their waitress. "I'm hungry. How about you?"

They ordered food and another round of drinks.

"So, who did you say was collaborating with Timberlake?" he asked.

Samanta's smile froze. "Clayton Harrod. Told you before, I think. Not sure whether you've met him?"

"Harrod? Don't think so. What exactly is he working on?"

Samanta put down her glass. She stopped playing with her earrings and leaned forward. "It's an open secret. I'm not blurting out anything." She briefly gazed at the table next to them, then lowered her voice.

"Super tomatoes. To kill cancer cells."

The time passed without Dino realizing how late it was. The place had been filling up, and the noise level increased.

"Did you know that the French sometimes call the tomato *pomme d'amour*? Apple of love? What a seductive attribute for a fruit." Samanta laughed, gently touching Dino's arm. Her hand lingered just a bit too long.

Here she goes again. She's attractive, but she knows it, and she thinks she's irresistible. He preferred to stay on firm ground and talk about science. On the other hand, he had to admit that being with Samanta gave him a rush.

Dino chugged his beer. He felt her thigh brush his leg under the table. It could have occurred by accident, but she held the delicate touch. After what seemed a long pause, Dino pulled away, confused, but it had been enough to give him a frisson of excitement.

Dino suddenly decided he needed some distance, to get away from this—now. He wanted more time to make sense of everything. Samanta, though, wasn't giving him any quarter. She was in a playful mood, to say the least, and not inclined to discuss work any further.

He was clearly taken with her, but he did not want to succumb to her overtures. He didn't consider himself prim, but they had only just been getting to know each other. At this point in his life, he didn't want to be drawn into greater intimacy. And, most importantly, he was committed to someone else.

While Samanta continued to talk, his mind veered off. What had he learned that he hadn't known before?

Dino leaned back and turned his head to look around the cozy, dimly lit room. He absent-mindedly scanned the crowd at the bar—chatting, laughing, drinking, flirting—and then he froze. Samanta's words came from far away, and he didn't hear what she said.

He stared at a face that was both sad and determined—eyes he knew only too well—that were now both beautiful and cold. Cat's eyes.

The few seconds Cat held his gaze felt like an eternity.

Then she turned and was gone.

32

DINO

Dino leaned against the front door jamb, his shoulders sagging, conscience-stricken. "Would you stop for a second, Cat? I can explain everything."

Cat was standing in the hallway, her cheeks flushed, her blonde mane unkempt, her eyes red and swollen. "That's what men always say... *I can explain.* Stupid frigging nonsense!"

"It's not what you think, Cat. Why don't you give me a chance to tell you what it's all about?"

Cat sniffed but remained silent. At last. He stepped inside and closed the door.

After the awkward incident at the bar, Dino had abruptly terminated his date that had gone south. He'd said his jealous girlfriend had chased them down and that he needed to leave, picked up the tab, and said he'd call her soon. Samanta had just put on an arcane smile. She didn't really understand why he felt uncomfortable being around her, she said, and added that she'd been under the impression he enjoyed her company.

"You can call me at work if you want to discuss business," she said. "But after work, when I go out on a date, I want to have some fun. What's wrong with that?"

Furious with himself that he had screwed up, he mumbled something that sounded like an apology. She could have been a perfect source of insider information. Maybe there would be another opportunity, but he wasn't sure. Right now, it looked like he had blown his chance.

He had driven immediately to Cat's house, where he had found her, arms crossed in front of her chest, shouting insults. Obviously pissed off, she had bombarded him with accusations that went far beyond that evening's event. She rained down on him a violent outburst of built-up blames and reproaches that had been accumulating over the past weeks.

"It was a business meeting," Dino continued, immediately realizing how ridiculous that must sound.

"Yeah, right," Cat snapped. "In a dim bar with a slut that just couldn't stop trying to get off with you." She shoved a flick of hair out of her eyes, her expression sullen.

"Why don't you listen to me, darling...?"

"Oh, don't you *darling* me," she snarled.

Dino made a renewed attempt to shuffle out of this situation. "She's not a slut. Samanta Martinez is her name. She's a scientist, works at GR&S. I met her the other day, up there in Sementina Springs, and we agreed to finish our discussion outside the company. That's all."

"Why couldn't you finish your discussion right there, during your visit to the tomato factory? I guess you knew it would be easier to grope that skank in a bar than in a business environment." Cat was shouting. She stopped long enough to blow her nose loudly.

"Listen, Cat, don't yell at me. Where is Mia, by the way? Is she upstairs, asleep? I don't want her to—"

"And you leave Mia alone, do you hear me?" Cat hissed.

This is getting out of hand. Dino scratched his head and vented a deep sigh.

"Look—there's something going on at GR&S. Something fishy. I think I'm on the scent of a really big story. A fraudulent story of unforeseen dimensions. I—"

"You never told me about this. You never tell me anything anymore."

Dino ignored her remark. "I'm on the verge of unraveling a potentially dangerous, far-reaching plot, believe me. I hope I can bust the whole damn thing soon. I just need some more time and a bit more understanding and appreciation from you. A trifle of tolerance—"

"Tolerance? Aargh!" She threw her hands up in the air. "I can't believe you're saying this."

Dino stepped closer to where Cat was slumped on the couch. "Okay, I can tell you the entire story now, if you wish. But I must ask you to keep absolutely mum. Otherwise, we could be in danger, both of us." He let himself fall onto the sofa, splaying his legs apart.

Cat sat up, trying to get control of herself. "Sorry, not now. I'm dead beat. I'm going to bed. And you, please leave. Just go."

Dino shook his head. He pounded his flat hand against the coffee table and rose from the sofa. "Okay, if you don't want to hear the truth, that's fine. I'm leaving."

Cat got up too. "One more thing," she said in a soft voice. She braced herself. "I need a break, Dino. From us. From you. I need time to reflect." Her face suddenly bore a stony, determined expression. "I don't want you to call or show up at my house. No texting, no emails. I need a time-out. Do you understand?"

Dino stayed rooted, mouth gaping wide. No, he didn't understand. After a few seconds, he slouched and walked toward the door.

"Just one more thing," he said, turning around. "Why were you spying on me? Why did you follow me to that bar?"

Cat said nothing.

Dino shrugged and walked out, slamming the door behind him.

33

DINO

Before the next encounter with Samanta, Dino wanted to get a better idea of what the researchers at GR&S were working on. Sitting in his office with the door closed, he spent a couple of hours hunched in front of his computer, not to become an expert, but at least so he could be on the same page when he talked to her again.

The first disturbing fact he learned was that "plant-made pharmaceuticals" were not what he thought they were. He'd been dead wrong when he delivered a lecture to Detective Roberson about the myth of using plants and herbs as an alternative treatment for cancer. He'd gotten all worked up over the topic—for nothing.

What he just learned about PMPs was quite a different story.

"I got it," Dino mumbled to himself as he shut down the computer. "If one can insert a piece of foreign DNA—a 'blueprint'—into the genome of a mouse cell or a bacterium, why can't one insert it into a plant cell as well?"

And the machinery, the biological factory that could translate that inserted blueprint into a foreign protein that normally would not be generated, could be... a tomato, for example. Genetically engineered to crank out a given pharmaceutical drug. *Plant-made pharmaceuticals.*

Dino sucked in a quick breath. Mind-boggling. Why didn't he think of that before?

Sounds like science fiction? Not feasible, not doable? Dead wrong. The technique had been widely used, he read, allowing scientists to go forward at ultra-high speed.

Dino's mind snapped into sharp focus. He had tracked down the first major clue to the mystery. Timberlake and Harrod had been up to artificially making a therapeutic drug—in tomatoes.

But there was one aspect of his theory he didn't understand. If there was nothing secret, nothing new about this technology, why did Timberlake have to die? And why had Miguel been attacked?

He strode up to the window, watched a group of doctors in white coats rushing past, a nurse pushing a patient in a wheelchair, an old man in a robe holding on to an IV pole, seemingly lost, an ambulance whooshing by in the distance...

A flash of insight hit him out of the blue.

Was it possible that they—somebody, whoever—tried to turn tomatoes into making things other than therapeutic drugs? Other proteins? Something that people inadvertently ingested? Something that had almost killed him and others...

There was only one person he could think of at this moment who could shed light on that, who would perhaps blurt out a secret. Risky, but worth a try.

Dino fished for his phone and thumbed through the *contacts* list.

The receptionist put the call through, and Harrod answered on the first ring.

***

Dino was sifting through his mind for all the questions he needed answers to—tomatoes... foreign DNA... foreign proteins—when his thoughts were interrupted by a subtle, almost inaudible swish behind him. Startled, he spun around.

"Sorry," the man in the checkered shirt behind him said. He had a long, earnest face and looked tired, if not exhausted.

"Boy, you made me jump," Dino said and stood up. *Harrod.* He must've been hiding under the lounge table—Dino hadn't heard anyone walk up or seen anyone coming in.

"Mr. Harrod? I'm Dino," he said, stretching out his hand. "Nice to finally meet you in person. Thank you for making time for me in your busy day."

"Clayton," Harrod said, staring right through Dino, as if he were made of glass.

Dino registered that Harrod was the first person who hadn't commented on his bruised face. He didn't even seem to notice.

Dino had pictured him differently. He'd expected to see a nutty scientist in a spotty white lab coat, perhaps overdue for a haircut, eager to talk shop. But the real Harrod was different. He was casually dressed in shorts and a short-sleeve shirt and wore sandals. He fixed his dark, almost black, piercing eyes on Dino like a snake that never blinks.

An uneasiness radiated off Harrod, who certainly wasn't a blatherer. He had barely said a word so far.

Dino tried to reassure him. "I just have a few questions; it won't take long."

"This way." Harrod gestured for Dino to move on down the corridor that led toward the back of the building.

"Why don't you go ahead?" Dino suggested. "You know the way."

Dino had hoped Harrod would take him to his office, but the two of them were seated at a long, oversized table opposite each other, in a small meeting room, crushed by the silence and emptiness of the room. *Awkward.* Harrod had left the door ajar. Dino hunched his shoulders and rubbed his hands. The room felt ice-cold.

If Harrod was bothered by the blasting A/C, he didn't show it. He kept staring at Dino. "Yes?"

"I heard you were collaborating with Dr. Timberlake, and I—"

"You heard it from whom?" The question came quickly, knifing through Dino's preamble.

"Samanta Martinez. She told me about your plans to develop plant-made pharm—"

"No way she told you about our research plans. We keep everything confidential."

So it *was* true.

"I just wonder..." Dino scratched his head. His eyes narrowed to slits. "Since it's possible to turn tomatoes into a biological factory that produces therapeutic drugs, wouldn't it also be possible to program tomatoes for producing... other chemicals as well?"

"I don't know what you're talking about. I was under the impression you wanted to discuss breeding tomatoes, generating new cultivars to increase their nutritional value."

Dino leaned in aggressively across the table as if to challenge the other man, but the two were still at a ridiculous distance. "Look, Clayton, let's just stop playing games. It's time to lay our cards on the table. You can't fool me. I know everything."

The effect was uncanny. Harrod's pale, sunken cheeks flushed red. He swayed his upper body sideways, fixing his gaze on Dino, like a king cobra zeroing in on him, ready to strike. Dino almost expected to see his split tongue dart in and out.

"I'm not willing to discuss any corporate secrets. If you don't stop, I'll call security."

Dino forced a smile, extending a palm in a *can't-we-just-talk* gesture.

"You're producing chemicals, in those tomatoes, right? C'mon, Clayton. I know it. Just tell me what it is and how you do it." Dino spoke quietly, but his breathing became faster, his chest heaving. This was risky. Maybe outright dangerous. But there was no way back.

"Chemicals? In tomatoes? That's ridiculous." Clayton's voice was high-pitched, strained. "What kind of chemicals are you talking about?"

"Drugs, for example. Drugs of abuse."

The silence sang in Dino's ears like the buzzing after the boom of a powerful gun.

"*Drugs? What drugs?*" a sharp voice cut in from behind them.

Dino spun around.

Samanta Martinez stood in the doorway.

34

DINO

"You?" Dino stammered.

Harrod jumped up from his chair and, without a word, slithered out of the room.

"Didn't expect you to be here either," Samanta said. "What's going on?"

"Oh, I just had a nice little discussion with Harrod."

"I can see that. About drugs?"

"Pharmaceutical drugs."

She was wearing that green gown again. The only things not covered were her white tennis sneakers. She flashed Dino her perfect smile.

Samanta stepped up to him, ignoring his hand, and holding him by his shoulders, pecked him on the cheek. "Gosh, it's cold in here. Want to chat somewhere else, where it's more... cozy? My buggy is parked in the back." She ushered Dino through the door bearing the sign, ACCESS FOR PERSONNEL ONLY.

"Real nice to see you, Sam," Dino said. "You just saved me."

"From Clayton's chattering and bubbling personality?"

Dino squelched an urge to touch Samanta's arm. He had to perform a balancing act—to appear friendly, but not physically attracted to her. He needed to keep his distance and not give her any reason to accuse him of sexual harassment, especially in the workplace. He liked her, but his goal was to get her to pass information to him without realizing she was giving away well-kept corporate secrets. A tightrope act.

Samanta stopped and inched closer. She cocked her head and looked at him. "Don't be so formal, Dino. Just relax."

"My apologies again for the recent incidence the other evening."

"Stop it. We talked about it. Now let's just forget it."

"My lady friend was upset. I mean really upset. I had a hard time convincing her that it was a misunderstanding."

"A misunderstanding?" Samanta said, mockingly. Then she touched his arm. "She jilted you. Right, Dino?"

Dino didn't know for a moment whether she was quipping or whether she felt sympathy for him. "She is..." he started, and then stopped, realizing that he was on the verge of defending Cat. He felt a sudden twinge of uneasiness. He wanted to keep Cat out of this.

"I came to ask you a few things, professional things," he said, a clear sign that he intended to change the subject.

"Professional things... Oh, sure."

Dino squeezed into the seat of the golf cart. As they slowly drove over to Samanta's office, Dino carefully pushed her right hand off his left thigh.

***

Samanta removed her green gown and flung it casually on another chair. She wore tight white jeans and a black T-shirt. Simple, but elegant. No jewelry, hardly any makeup.

"You work directly with Harrod?"

"Clayton?" She gave a weak smile. "You've asked me that before. No, I don't work with him. Never have. I mean, we're colleagues, but... Why?"

"He told me that he collaborates with you and that he has something cooking. *Pretty hot stuff*, as he put it."

"Clayton told you that? He's quite withdrawn normally, to say the least. What did he tell you?"

"Oh, he mentioned that he uses tomatoes to make certain proteins. Proteins that the plant normally wouldn't make. Pharmaceutical drugs. PMPs."

She flinched, and Dino thought he caught her swallow.

"He told you that, really? I don't know. We talk sometimes, but mostly we exchange methods, and new technologies."

"Exchange methods? Bloody Mary recipes?"

Samanta placed her empty soda can on the table. "Want another one?" Her question came a bit too fast.

Dino prepared for another go. "Something doesn't tally. Let's assume Harrod—or you or anybody—has finally come up with a therapeutic tomato that generates a ton of those artificial anti-cancer drugs. You pick the fruit, wash it, probably admire it, and then, what happens?" He glanced at her.

Samanta sat on her chair, reclined, fingers of both hands joined together to form a tent, her head tilted, question marks in her eyes, waiting.

"Then you eat it," he said. "Correct?"

"The patient eats it, not me."

"Here we go. The patient—not you—eats it, digests the tomato, and, guess what?"

She opened her mouth like she was going to say something, but then waited for Dino to finish.

"Being a protein, the therapeutic drug, made-in-tomato-land, is digested too. Denatured, chopped up in your gut into smaller peptides and individual amino acids. The protein is gone long before it is absorbed and circulated in the bloodstream, let alone reach its target, the cancer cells. So, nice try, but it won't work. It simply won't work."

"Are you done with your biochemistry lecture, Dino?" Samanta started to tap her outstretched fingers. "Coupla things. Number one, it would be easy to isolate the proteins from the tomatoes and purify them. That's peanuts for a chemist."

"And number two?"

Samanta smiled. "Then they could be *injected* into the bloodstream. As opposed to being eaten." She tapped her head. "We're not stupid."

We, she had just said, *We're not stupid.* Was she in bed with

Harrod? And Timberlake? He needed to sort things out. Clear his mind. Later. He didn't want to waste this opportune moment.

"Sam, before we get totally lost in tomato genetics, let me ask you—could we get together for dinner sometime? What do you think?"

Samanta turned around quickly, blinking with one eye. "Sure." She looked as if she had expected his question.

He smiled and stood up. Maybe a couple of drinks and some wine would ease the flow of information that he so badly wanted to obtain. "How about Saturday? You like seafood?"

She agreed.

"I know a wonderful place in North Naples on the beach. Wonderful sunsets."

"Sounds enticing."

She gave him a ride back to the main lobby to check out.

On his way back to work he reached a sober conclusion. Everything dovetailed nicely with what he already knew, but there was a catch. Actually, more than one.

He and the other phantom opioid victims *had eaten* the tomatoes. An obvious truth. Any protein would have been digested.

But—more importantly, a simple truth: *opioid drugs are not proteins.*

Dino was back to square one.

What the hell was going on? He was all amped up about saving more people from getting poisoned—who knew how many highly dangerous tomatoes were still floating around in the area, waiting to be sold in local markets, lying on kitchen tables, sitting on lunch plates? He had the moral obligation and the professional knowledge to stop this, even though nobody believed him. Not even Cat, who normally was a rational thinker. When he'd broached the subject, she reacted twitchy, dismissing his concerns as irrational fears. And not to mention the police. They thought he was an eccentric scientist with the most abstruse theories.

The only person who truly believed him was Miguel. The poor fruit vendor who didn't know a bloody thing about plant-made pharmaceuticals but who had experienced firsthand what it meant to mess with the wrong people.

Dino pummeled the steering wheel. Shit.

But what if... What if they all were right? What if all this was just a hallucinatory fantasy of his? Was it worth the risk of sneaking away from work with lame excuses? And even more importantly, was it worth dancing on the edge, slithering into a potentially explosive, remorse-laden, and meaningless relationship with Samanta, making Cat even more jealous and unhappy?

Dino didn't know the answer, but the doubts niggled at the back of his mind.

35

DINO

The silence was eerie, the house empty. He felt tiny needles in his heart.

Dino pressed his fist to his lips. What had he done that was so terrible? Why didn't she want to at least talk about it? Cat was taking umbrage at his behavior, but he had never before met her truculent side. He put his elbows on the desk and buried his head in his arms.

He remembered, in searing detail, when, a few days before, he'd run into her at the hospital.

"Do you want to talk sometime?" he had ventured.

"About what?"

What a question. "About us."

"No, Dino, I'm not ready for that yet. I told you, I need a time-out."

"Okay, okay, I understand." Dino sighed. "I'll be here whenever you're ready. You can call me anytime. I miss you—"

She walked around him and hurried swiftly down the corridor.

He had tried to reach Cat at least ten times. She hadn't tried to call back, not even once. He didn't understand her motive for remaining silent. A time-out he could accept, but she had totally cut all connections.

Late the previous night, Dino had driven over to Cat's house in Heron Bay. Her car was not in the driveway. The wooden garage door did not have a window, so he couldn't see whether her car was in the garage. He rang the bell and knocked on the front door, but nobody answered. She had insisted he return the spare key to her house; now he felt like a complete stranger. He walked around the house and peeked into the screened lanai, but the rear door was locked.

Dino walked across the street to her neighbor's house. Kevin greeted him rather reservedly and threw him an appraising glance, then called his wife, Kim. Probably Cat had told them about their current difficulties. No, he said, Kim had not seen Cat or Mia for a couple days, and no, she had no clue where they were. They were in the midst of summer break, after all. They could have gone away on a short vacation or be visiting relatives or friends out of town.

Without having learned anything useful, Dino drove back to his house with a stony face. He took a deep breath. Cat could at least maintain some basic level of low-key communication. He felt a painful tightness in his throat.

On top of that, there was Samanta. Dino's mind reeled back to her. He knew that he needed her, not necessarily as a friend, although he liked her company, and definitely not to start a clandestine romance. He needed her as an accomplice. She knew more than she had told him, he was certain of that. And she had excellent connections.

To find the truth, he needed to confide his secret findings and assumptions to her.

36

DINO

The next day, when Dino got home from work, he tried to compose himself, but it was difficult. He walked onto the lanai with a cold beer in his hand, jangling his keys in his pocket, pacing up and down.

"Enjoyin' the breeze?" From ten yards away, Bill, his neighbor, waved at him, rolling the grill cart into position on the freshly mowed lawn. "How ya doin'?"

"Just wonderful."

"What the hell is wrong with your eye? You run into a door?"

Dino instinctively touched his eye, which he knew had shifted from violet to a greenish-brown color, and winced. "Oh, nothing serious."

Bill stepped away from the grill. "Haven't seen your lady for a while."

Dino said nothing.

"You remodeling the house, or just having some repairs done?"

"Remodeling my house?" Dino raised his eyebrows as he stepped forward toward the screen that separated his lanai from Bill's. "What makes you think I'm remodeling my house?"

"Oh, it's none of my business, but I just saw two guys going in and out of your house this afternoon. Looked like contractors, so I thought—"

"Contractors? Going in and out of my house? What? When was that?"

"Today, around three or so." Bill laughed. "I was home—enjoying my day off—and just thought you had them do a paint job or something. You weren't expecting them?"

"No, I wasn't expecting anybody. Hey—" he stepped through the screen door out onto the lawn, walking up to Bill. "Who were they? What did they look like? A paint job, you say?"

"Take it easy, man," Bill said. "Yeah, they came in a light-colored minivan, with a bright logo. *Painting something*, can't remember. Two guys in white T-shirts and white pants. They looked like... well, painters."

Dino's face had turned red. "You said they went into my house?"

"That's right. I didn't think anything of it. You'd better call them to check it out."

"Thanks, Bill," Dino shouted. "Always good to have observant neighbors."

He dashed inside.

It took him about twenty minutes to go from room to room. Nothing. Everything looked normal, exactly the same as when he had left the house. Nothing seemed to be changed or removed. The main door had been locked when he came home. The garage was closed, and so were the windows. Nothing was missing, not even from his den, where he kept some money, credit cards, and electronics. There was not the slightest trace that anyone had been in the house.

He called the guard at the security booth and asked him to go through the list of contractors who had checked in at the community entrance that morning. Dino was told that there were four different gates and that he should come by with an ID. No information over the phone.

Maybe Bill had just misinterpreted the situation. Or the contractors realized they were at the wrong address and left.

He shrugged. Time to water his tomato plants. He stepped to the sun-exposed corner of the lanai where he had parked the pots. A second later, Dino knew why someone had forced entry into his house and what they had taken.

Three pots of tomato plants were gone. Only a few crumbles of gardening soil remained on the tiled floor of the lanai.

The thieves had left the other three pots untouched. Dino gazed at the wire-legged plant markers stuck in the soil. The small, zinc-coated nameplates read HEIRLOOM CONTROLS, *Garden Center*. It looked like whoever had been in his house had filched the three pots of Grand Captivas and left the normal tomatoes he was growing as a negative comparator.

Except the intruders didn't know—couldn't have known—that Dino had swapped the nameplates after he planted the tomatoes. It had been Miguel's idea. He was out of the hospital, and they'd met for a beer. "Change the labels," he'd said, "best way to hide your precious *especímenes*." Miguel had burst into laughter, his whole body shaking.

Dino was upset about the burglary in plain daylight, but he had stiffed the thieves. They had unwittingly stolen the normal tomatoes.

He still had the Grand Captivas.

37

HARROD

As Clayton Harrod was about to call it a day, the door to his lab opened halfway, and a technician peered in from the hallway.

"Clayton? We just got a new batch—where do you want me to put it?"

"A new batch of what?" He hated inaccurate statements or incomplete sentences.

"Grand Captivas."

"The new ones? The real ones, this time?"

"Yup. From *R2*."

Harrod nodded. All greenhouses labeled *R* were designed for research, not for commercial production.

"Okay, great. Put them in the minus-eighty, please."

After the technician left, Harrod stepped over to the -80°C freezer, donned the heavy cold-protective gloves, and opened the top drawer. Just to make sure the samples were correctly labeled. He couldn't afford to have another disaster. The previous mistaken identity, when Castro had grabbed the wrong tomatoes on his last pickup, had been severe enough. The whole thing could easily have blown up. He couldn't imagine the consequences. The mere thought of it gave him chills. That Castro guy had screwed up, but they couldn't go back now. The cops had been here before, here at GR&S, and he was sure they would show up again.

Harrod knew that he was deep in the mire.

He opened the plastic container the technician had brought in. Inside were three medium-sized, red, fully mature tomatoes. He would analyze them tomorrow.

Harrod closed the top drawer and focused his attention on the bottom drawer, just to make sure the other important specimens were still there. He stared at a white container neatly labeled in clear writing with the date and the description of the contents: *Grand Captiva – C.H.* His initials. And the red masking tape around the container: *DO NOT TOUCH.*

He carefully shut the door of the freezer and made sure the alarm was on.

***

KUZMINSKI

Chuck Kuzminski looked up from the report he was reading in response to a quiet knock on his office door. Peering over the rim of his glasses, he barked, "Come in."

The door opened slowly, and Harrod's thin face appeared, almost as if in slow motion.

"Clayton," Kuzminski said, removing his reading glasses. "Come on in—don't be shy. What's up?"

Harrod moved soundlessly toward Chuck's executive desk and lowered himself into the visitor chair. "I have good news, Chuck."

"Great." Kuzminski wheeled his chair back, crossed his legs, and after a few awkward moments uncrossed them. "Well?" *If only Clayton weren't such a sleepyhead*, he thought. "You want some coffee?" Maybe that would animate him a bit.

Harrod ignored the offer. "I think we got it, finally." He paused.

Kuzminski gave him an encouraging nod, opening his eyes wide to show eager anticipation. He wished Clayton would be less monosyllabic. Clayton Harrod was one of the best scientists in the company's research department, but he was not exactly a brilliant communicator.

Harrod's eyes flashed. "The blueprint works fine," he said, pausing again.

"You're talking about the PMP project?"

"Yes."

"Just tell me the full story, please." Kuzminki's tone was still polite but growing impatient.

"I just told you, Chuck." The words came gushing out. "The blueprint works. We now have five different proteins, antibodies linked to a potent toxic component. They bind with extremely high selectivity to their respective targets on the malignant cancer cells, including CD22, CD11c, CD103, and—"

"Whoa, whoa, hold on a sec," Kuzminski said, holding up his hand, interrupting the sudden unexpected flow of highly specialized biomedical information. "It's great to hear that you've been successful with developing these antibodies, but, look—I'm just the CEO. I happen to know a little bit about economics and tomato farming, but I'm neither a biochemist nor a cancer specialist, so—" He stopped short when he became aware of Harrod's long face, and then quickly continued. "Try again, in simple terms." It was not Kuzminski's intention to be condescending to Harrod. Yet he noticed the other man stiffen a bit and thought he detected a flare in his eyes.

Harrod drew a deep breath. "Okay. We think we have cleared another hurdle. We're still a fair way off, but definitely another step closer, inching our way to achieving a major breakthrough. We've found a new way of treating certain cancers. By doing the most natural thing in the world." He paused—only this time he did it deliberately, to increase the suspense.

"Which is?" Kuzminski had already guessed the answer.

"Which is—" Harrod dragged out his words, "by eating tomatoes." He burst out cackling hysterically.

"Well—kudos to you. We need to find someone to follow in the late Dr. Timberlake's footsteps and collaborate."

Harrod stared at him without blinking.

"Keep me posted on the progress, please," Kuzminski said.

"As a businessman, I like to understand where the research money goes." He put on his reading glasses; a clear sign that the conversation was finished and he would like to get back to work.

Harrod remained glued to his seat.

Kuzminski cleared his throat. "Great news, Clayton, but if you don't mind, I have work to do." He shook his head ever so slightly as he watched Harrod rise and slowly walk toward the door.

What a strange guy—brilliant, indispensable for our research department, but definitely from another planet...

38

DINO

"Somebody broke into my house yesterday."

They were seated at a small cozy table on the terrace of the *Dorado Bay* restaurant, just a short distance from the sandy beach. The night was warm, but not muggy. The sparkling water reflected the moonlight, and the Gulf was still and peaceful. The perfect evening for a romantic *alfresco* dinner.

"Really? Sorry to hear that," Samanta said. "Must be an awful feeling. Did they take anything of value?"

"I don't keep any money in the house. Computer, home audio system, and my new ultra-HD TV are still there."

"Did they leave a big mess?"

"No, not at all. Everything looked exactly the way I left it in the morning."

"So, how do you know someone was in your house?"

"Good question," Dino said, his mind racing. He rubbed his jaw. "They stole a plant from the lanai," he added casually, watching her.

He thought he saw Samanta cringe, but it may have been his imagination.

"They didn't take anything else?" Samanta had a doubtful look on her face.

"No. That's why I didn't even report it to the police. You think I should have?"

Samanta shrugged. "I don't know. I'd change the locks if I were you, just to be on the safe side." Her shiny earrings and the matching turquoise bracelet enhanced her dark, beautiful eyes.

He wondered to what extent he could trust Samanta. Was she friend or foe?

They clinked glasses.

The red snapper was delicious.

Dino gazed at his companion as she slowly took a bite of fish and relished the ginger and orange sauce. Samanta's full lips had a silky sheen of dark red, her black tank top flattering her ample curves. She had slipped out of her role of serious, demure scientist and adopted that of highly attractive, seductive woman.

"This afternoon, the cops showed up at our research facilities," she said. "A certain Detective Robinson, I think—"

"Roberson."

"You know him? He was all over the place, talked with everyone who happened to be at work on a Saturday."

"He talked to you too?"

"Yup. Told him I didn't know Timberlake personally and never met Castro—"

I knew it. If the police didn't think there was a connection between Miguel's vicious attacks, Timberlake's death, and the mysterious tomatoes, they wouldn't have gone out to GR&S.

"What did they tell you?"

"They didn't tell me anything. You know the cops. They grill you. They want to explore all possible links, pursue every lead, search for every piece of evidence, but they leave you in the dark."

Dino put down his fork and leaned forward. "Sam, who do you think killed Timberlake?"

"If I knew I would tell the police."

"I didn't ask whether you *knew*. I asked who you *think* did it."

"It's irrelevant what I think. But since you insist—I think it was a crime committed at the personal relationship level."

"How do you know?"

Sam threw her head back. "Dino, don't contradict your-self. You asked me what I *think*, not what I know." She tapped her glass. "Most violent crimes are related to interhuman rela-tionships, by the way. Jealousy, dammed-up anger, frustration, humiliation, rejected love, abuse, you name it."

"Maybe. But, as we also know, some are based on mundane motives such as money, or drugs, or—"

"*Drugs?*" Samanta's answer came fast.

She looked at her empty wine glass and held it up in the air. Dino refilled both glasses.

"Have you ever taken drugs, Dino?" She cocked her head and put on a mischievous smile.

He looked at her fleetingly and then stared into the dis-tance. The memory of his late brother flitted into his mind, triggering a wave of equal pain and upwelling anger. Tony, who had to pay with his life for abusing drugs. "No. I would never touch the dangerous stuff, like coke or meth. Never ever."

"How about opioids?"

"Inadvertently, I guess, when I had surgery a few years ago. They're great as painkillers, but they have unpleasant adverse effects. But—taking opioids as recreational drugs? For chrissakes. Never." He held out his palms as if to stop some-thing. "How about you?"

"Do I look like a junkie, Dino? Nope, not for me. If there's anything, then *this* is my drug—" she pointed to the wine bottle in the ice bucket. "In moderation, of course." Then she leaned forward and fixed him with a patently teasing and tantalizing gaze. "And, occasionally, someone as sexy as you, Dino."

His head was spinning for a few moments. He was hardly ever stumped for an answer, but he didn't know what to say. The best way to get out of this awkward situation would be to revert to something non-personal.

Dino signaled to the waitress and asked Samanta whether

she still had some room left for dessert. She ordered a *mousse au chocolat*, while Dino passed on the sweets.

He watched her revel in her mousse for a while, realizing that he found himself unaccountably drawn to her.

"Oh, another thing that I wanted to ask you," she said. "Why are you so interested in the Grand Captivas?"

Dino almost choked on his espresso.

"You've asked me before. Because I believe they are genetically modified." Dino tried to sound casual.

"You didn't answer my question. Of course, they are genetically altered, like all the other new cultivars. By NBTs... Sorry, *New Breeding Techniques*. Insider slang," she added quickly. "I'm sure what you mean is whether they contain *foreign, non-tomato DNA*." She shook her head. "Let me assure you that that would be way too dangerous. Those plants are kept apart, under tight security, in the research buildings and labs. Not outside. Harrod's in charge, he has control over those."

"Why dangerous?" Dino asked. "Too risky because they could be stolen, and the technology given away?"

Samanta again shook her head and put down the spoon. "No, forget it, the technology has been out for quite a while. Dangerous for the environment, for people. Imagine what could happen if the foreign genes, the artificially introduced new DNA, escaped and mixed with normal plants that are used by everybody? This is an obvious safety concern. If these transgenic plants escaped into the wild—and this could occur through a number of... *accidents*—" She placed the word in air quotes.

"Escape? Plants? How—on their little feet?"

"How? Simple. If, for example, pollen from transgenic tomatoes somehow or other fertilizes normal food crops. Or by contaminated farm equipment. We must take precautions. We take this very seriously." She leaned forward. "The secret is *containment*. Containing the foreign gene."

"Easier said than done, probably," Dino said. "How do you actually do it?"

"The most important thing is isolation of the transgenic plants. No way we could grow them outdoors, for example. That's one reason why we keep all these plants in greenhouses."

Dino thought with horror about his little tomato plants on his lanai that had just started to propagate.

Samanta put her hand on Dino's arm and looked straight at him, smiling. "This has been quite serious talk, Dino. Talking tomatoes—on a Saturday night date—how sexy—" She acquired a devilish look. "Why don't we loosen up a tad? Let's have some fun."

"Yeah, we could take a few steps on the beach," Dino said, patting his stomach.

"Let's see what else we could do. The night is still young."

Dino felt Samanta's leg gently brush against his thigh. He looked up at her. She winked at him and then let her tongue glide slowly along her shiny upper lip.

He felt a powerful rush of excitement, but an internal voice told him to be careful. How far would he allow himself to go to get what he wanted? He knew where to draw the line.

The waitress appeared from nowhere. "Another one for you, ma'am?"

Samanta looked at her empty glass. "Sure."

"How 'bout you, sir?"

Dino held up his palm. "I'm good."

What he needed more than anything was a clear head.

39

DINO

"Quite a selection of keys," Dino said, glancing at the key ring with a dozen or so keys of all sizes and types. "Like a janitor. How do you know which one is for what?"

"I know them all," Samanta said, giggling, "except when I've had a bit too much to drink." She fumbled around with one but was unsuccessful. The condo door didn't budge.

She has had one too many, Dino thought. "Let me help you," he said, reaching for the key ring. "Maybe you're confounding your house key with the one to the high-security greenhouse."

"No way," Samanta mumbled. "Those I keep in the office. No tomatoes on Saturday nights." She giggled again and tried to kiss Dino.

"One sec," he said, keeping her at bay with his left arm, "let me try to get us inside first."

Samanta had long ago lost her cool, controlled, all-scientist face and replaced it with a salacious, sexually aggressive demeanor. Instead of Dino's suggested after-dinner saunter on the moonlit beach, she had coaxed him to have one for the road. He barely touched his glass and mostly drank water. As it became clear that she was unable to drive home, he had suggested she leave her car in the restaurant's parking lot and he'd take her home in his car. She could always get her vehicle the next day.

Once across the threshold, she slapped the keys on a side table in the hallway and pulled Dino close to her, slamming the door shut with her foot. "Don't act so prudish." She let out a sultry breath. "Why don't you loosen up a bit?"

Dino felt her yanking at his belt and fumbling with the buttons on his jeans. He grabbed her arms. "I need a drink first. Want one?"

She mumbled something incomprehensible and reeled toward the living room, where she collapsed on the sofa. "There's a bottle of champagne in the fridge," she said. "The glasses are... somewhere."

As he opened the bottle, he glanced around the kitchen—well-organized and clean. Modern equipment. The stainless-steel appliances looked shiny and like new. He wondered whether she cooked at all. She had insinuated that she lived alone. He noticed a small round table in the center of the breakfast nook. A blue designer bag and a couple of unopened letters lay on it.

Dino found two tall flutes and poured some champagne. He didn't hear a sound coming from the living room, which was strange as Samanta had been boisterous until just a few minutes ago.

"Look—" he started as he steered for the living room and turned the corner, but choked on the word. Samanta was voluptuously sprawled out on the sofa. One arm was trailing from the side, hand touching the floor, next to her blouse. Her bra was open and had slipped out of place. Her eyes were closed, and she exhaled a faint snoring sound.

She was obviously blind drunk, and sound asleep.

Dino stopped dead in his tracks. He couldn't take his eyes off her. While devouring her with his eyes, he had an increasingly unsettling feeling. His mouth felt suddenly dry, and he felt a jolt of excitement. But he also knew that this would be the last moment when his rational cortex would still be able to control the situation. One step further and he would be in another state of mind, where his reptile brain and primal instincts would take over. A sudden flood of exhilaration and desire washed over him. At the same time he felt a pang of remorse and guilt. Lust versus a strong sense of wrongdoing, slugging it out. He couldn't help picturing Cat, sitting somewhere, alone, unhappy...

He took a deep breath and averted his eyes. Get a grip, for heaven's sake.

Dino stepped back into the kitchen and put down the two glasses, spilling some of the contents. He realized that his hands were slightly shaking. He went straight to Samanta's blue shoulder bag and pulled on the loop. While he rummaged through lipsticks, packages of tissues, a small red booklet, mints, a wallet filled to bursting with member cards and coupons, he detected a small red plastic ball that looked like a toy, but which, on closer inspection revealed its real nature—a miniature plastic tomato. He reached for it and pulled out a metal ring with four keys. Undoubtedly, these must be the keys to the lab and office. Dino let them glide quickly into his pocket and closed the shoulder bag.

If he were lucky, Samanta had sunk into a deep, semi-comatose sleep and wouldn't wake up for quite some time. He could sneak out, drive to Sementina Springs, and—

"Sweetie, where are you?" a raspy voice sounded from the living room. Oops, it looked as though the snooze was over.

"Coming," he shouted, desperately looking for a way to maneuver out of this situation. In the absence of a better alternative, he whipped out his cell phone and started a loud mock conversation.

"It's that bad? Really? No, I'm busy right now. No way. I can't." He walked slowly into the living room. Samanta sat upright, smirking, her hair disheveled, mascara smeared over one cheek. Her bra was gone now too, and she had folded her arms behind her head.

Dino motioned for her to hold on and put on a worried face. Pacing up and down the room, he nodded a couple of times. "Geez, that's really bad... Yeah, I do have insurance, but I'll call them later... Shit... Okay, I'm on my way." He briskly terminated the fake call.

"So sorry, Sam, but there's an emergency."

"Who the hell was that in the middle of the night?"

"My neighbor," he improvised. "Looks like there's some major flooding at my house. He says the water is gushing out the door. Probably a burst water pipe. Not what I need right now." He gave a big sigh. "Look, I'm so sorry, but I gotta run."

"Why don't you stay for a while?" Samanta begged. "You can always fix that tomorrow."

"Look, my house is under water. I can already see the alligators playing in my living room. I must take care of it, now. This is serious. Sorry, Sam, but…"

"Can I go with you?"

"Not a good idea," Dino said. She was too drunk to even sit in the passenger seat. He watched Samanta as she flopped back on the sofa with an exasperated sigh.

Dino strode toward what he thought must be the master bedroom, opened the door, and went straight up to the bed. He pulled off the bedspread, carried it to the living room, and gently covered her with it. "Take a nap. I'll be back soon."

One last glimpse over his shoulder before he left the house—Samanta still lying on the sofa, eyes closed, breathing slowly. It would be dawn before he was back. He flipped the light switch off and pulled the door shut.

Time for a nighttime excursion to Tomato Land.

40

DINO

Dino drove back to the restaurant and parked his sport sedan, then got into Samanta's car. Fortunately, he had bagged her car keys before leaving her house. If she missed them, he could always say that he wanted to return her car to her house out of courtesy.

He had first considered driving to Sementina Springs in his own car, but then changed his plan. If somebody working late, or, worse even, a security officer, caught a glimpse of an unknown car parked in front of the building at 2 a.m., it would definitely raise more suspicion than if they noticed a familiar car with a license tag belonging to one of their key employees.

As he arrived at GR&S, he parked Samanta's car at the rear of the research building. He carefully pushed the door shut, eager not to make a sound that would blow his secretive arrival, and stood next to the car for a few minutes, motionless. The lot was deserted at this hour. He'd halfway expected a motion-activated floodlight to go on, but the research building remained dark.

None of the keys he'd snarfed from Samanta worked to unlock the main door. *Shit.* He bit his lower lip. How would Samanta normally access the lab building? Maybe she had a key card or some other electronic device. Dino wished he'd searched her wallet.

As he played with the key ring, trying to decide what to do next, he rubbed the plastic tomato mascot between his thumb and index finger. Suddenly an idea struck him. He held the gadget against what looked like a badge reader next to the door.

A distinct *click* and the door unlatched. Of course. There must be a chip inside the plastic tom. Clever design. He slowly closed the door and dug for his cell phone. The phone's torch light would show him the way. Recollecting the shortest way to Samanta's office and lab, he tiptoed along the dark walls, his pupils wide open, his senses on high alert.

In the corridor, he looked for surveillance cameras but couldn't spot any. If there were any cameras, they were likely mounted on the outside of the building. Few visitors were granted access to the research building, and those who did get inside were strictly accompanied by an employee.

The third key he tried opened the door to Samanta's office. Now came the difficult part of his unauthorized expedition: where to find the key to the high-security research lab? She had been extremely vague about this, and he didn't want to pump her for fear she might become suspicious.

He scanned the office for any clue, but it looked like any ordinary researcher's office. Probably tidier and better organized than most. A large white desk with a huge computer screen. A neatly stacked pile of documents and papers. A book-shelf with lots of reference books and proceedings—mostly about plant genetics. A cabinet stuffed with hanging file fold-ers. On top of the cabinet were two plastic trays, one labeled *IN*, the other one *OUT*.

Not exactly like my office, he thought. No empty coffee cups, no junk piles, no old, curling yellow Post-it notes lying around. Even the trash basket was empty. On closer inspec-tion, though, her office had absolutely no personal touch. Lifeless, sterile, like a showroom in a furniture store. No pic-tures or photographs on the walls, no flowers. If someone had to make a tangible profile of the person who worked here, they wouldn't be able to do so.

Dino sat down on the swivel chair. He opened a drawer

of her desk and rummaged through it. Folders, writing pads, printer cartridges... Pens, mints, scissors in another one. A Happy Birthday card depicting two clinking glasses of champagne. He opened it and looked at the signature: *With heartfelt wishes for another exciting year—Chuck.* Who was Chuck?

Still no keys. Maybe the clothes closet... He reached into the pockets of the two green lab coats. Slid his hand along the shelves that were too high for him to see. Checked the briefcase sitting on the windowsill... nothing.

Suddenly he felt nervous and broke out in a cold sweat. He was prying around in someone else's office, looking for a key to a secret lab that might unravel the Grand Captiva mystery, but he hadn't found anything yet. This was a unique opportunity—his only chance—to gather evidence. It wouldn't be easy to sneak in here a second time, plus, Samanta could be waking up anytime, looking for him, realizing that her office keys were gone...

Dino flinched at a sound in the corridor—or was it his imagination? He switched off the light and waited a couple of minutes, his ear glued to the door. Then steps. He had been right. Distinct footsteps growing fainter, and then the remote sound of a door slamming shut. Silence again. *Shit.* Someone else was in the building at two on a Sunday morning.

His anxiety stepped up a notch as he slowly opened the door and peeked out. The corridor was dark, except for a shaft of light across the hallway from a room about twenty yards away. The door was ajar. This probably meant that whoever walked away from that room would be coming back.

Dino had to act fast. If that person had gone, say, to the bathroom, Dino had only a few moments to cover his tracks and get away; if the person went to work in a lab, Dino would have more time, but he couldn't take that chance. He tiptoed to the lighted office and glanced through the crack. Apparently, there was no one inside. The doorplate read: *CLAYTON HARROD, PhD.—Molecular Genetics.*

Dino remembered the awkward time he had spent with Harrod. He took a deep breath, plucked up his courage, and gently pushed open the door.

The room was empty. Articles, papers, notepads, books, memos everywhere. How on earth would he be able to find anything useful in this mess? Dino had to be extremely careful now lest he blow his mission.

A huge poster on the wall, entitled, "*GENOME OF SOLANUM LYCOPERSICUM*," caught Dino's attention. He knew enough to understand that this was the scientific name of the tomato plant. The poster was crammed with compact biochemical information and symbols. Could be interesting, but there was no time. He probably wouldn't understand it anyway.

It took a lot of gumption to break into a corporate building in the middle of the night in the first place, but to have the guts to search an office, knowing that the owner could be back any moment, was just insane. Dino had a bad case of the jitters. No doubt, he would have to get out, *now*. He had no choice.

Harrod's computer was on, but there was no time to mess around with it. Dino took a last look at his desk to perhaps find a clue, some hint, even a remote one. He was clearly clutching at straws. What had Harrod been reading just before he left his office?

Dino stared at the title of a scientific paper on Harrod's desk. His jaw dropped, and he started to breathe heavily. He snatched the paper, fingers trembling, partly from anxiety, partly from a sudden flash of inspiration. He grabbed the article, lifted his head, and listened intently, like a deer grazing in an exposed area.

Then he spotted the red ribbon.

His heart pounded as he reached for it and pulled up the credit-card size white plastic badge. In fine print, at the top, Harrod's name and a long number; at the bottom, *RESEARCH 2—BARRIER FACILITY*. No doubt, an electronic key card for the DNA greenhouse. *R2*.

Dino let the card glide into his pocket and sneaked out of the room. His sneakers never made a sound as he sped down the dark corridor.

Outside the building, Dino leaned against the main door and exhaled deeply. Damn, he'd been lucky. He couldn't see any vehicle parked in the front lot. Strange. Did Harrod work and sleep here? Did he ever sleep at all? No time to worry about that.

He skulked around the building, staying as close to the wall as possible. A memory flashed through his mind—his father telling him that mice and rats always ran close to the walls and rarely ventured out into open spaces. That's why they'd always placed the mousetraps near a wall.

He tucked the folded research paper he'd filched from Harrod's office into his shirt pocket and walked to Samanta's car. He pulled the door shut as quietly as possible, leaned back in the seat, and closed his eyes for a few seconds. What he needed now was a moment to pull himself together.

With the headlights off, he pulled out onto the main road, checking the rearview mirror again and again. Everything looked quiet.

Dino slapped his thigh with the palm of his hand. He had done it. His heart was still racing, his shirt soaked with sweat. A second later, a powerful wave of anxiety crested overhead. He had broken into a corporate building and stolen a key to a high-security, possibly top-secret facility.

There was no turning back now.

41

HARROD

"C'mon..." Clayton Harrod tapped a wild rhythm on his desk with the fingers of his right hand while he waited for someone to take his call.

"Hi, it's me. This is urgent. Got a newsflash for you."

The voice at the receiving end was doughy with sleep. "You know what time it is?"

"Yeah, I know. I'm sorry. It's past five. But this is rather important."

"It'd better be. Okay, shoot."

"Someone's been in my office, snooping around. Last night. I mean, just a few hours ago."

"Who was it?"

"Not sure, but I have a hunch."

"Anything gone?"

"Yes. Not good."

"The gene sequence?"

"Maybe. A flash drive with some backup files that I kept in a drawer is gone—luckily it's encrypted. The computer itself hasn't been touched. And some of the papers on my desk have been ransacked, and one of them is missing. But what's worse..."

"Jeez, just tell me what they took. Okay?"

Clayton sighed. "My key card is gone. The one to the R2 lab."

"No shit—are you serious?" The voice at the receiving end had shaken off all its sleepiness. "How could that happen?"

"Hey, it was two o'clock on a Sunday morning. Not a soul on the premise. I had to go to the washroom. Only took a minute. So, I left the door to my office open and..."

"What the hell did you do?"

"I'm not allowed to pee anymore?" Clayton's voice grew louder. "I was alone for cryin' out loud. Had no clue anybody was lurking around in the dark, just waiting for me to—"

"You said you think you know who it was. Who?"

"That quirky guy from Lee County Hospital. Stampa."

"Stampa?" A raspy laugh escaped on the other end of the line. "Give me a break. What makes you think he was the one?"

"Caught him sneaking around the greenhouse the other day. He must have come with Martinez tonight. I saw her car parked outside. I've seen them with their heads together, twice now."

"Martinez's new boyfriend?"

"Don't think so. Think he's trying to get buddy-buddy with her from what I saw the other day. She's pretty naïve."

"Who?"

"Samanta. Martinez—aren't we talking about her?"

"Don't be so damn testy, Clayton."

Harrod didn't say anything. A long moment passed, then he sighed again. "Okay, tell me what I should do now."

"This sucks, Clayton. He probably can't figure anything out, but we can't take any chances. You need to recapture that flash drive. And we have to silence Stampa before he gets to the bottom of everything. We've invested too much time and resources in this project to let him ruin everything."

"Fully agree, but we shouldn't underestimate the dude. He's smart. Looks like a slouch, but he's damn smart."

"That's right. So, set a honey trap for him. And inform me immediately when he rises to the bait."

"You betcha." Harrod stood up as if to finish the conversation and to see someone off in person. "I'll keep you posted. Sorry for waking you."

He heard a grunt. Then the line went dead.

42

DINO

His throbbing headache had only allowed Dino to sleep a couple of hours on Samanta's couch. When he returned from his nightly excursion, he'd found her sound asleep in her own bed.

When she woke around nine, she was apparently still miffed about how their romantic evening had ended, but, after a few cups of strong black coffee, she was less short with him.

"So, how bad was it?" she asked.

"How bad was what?"

She frowned at him over the rim of her cup. "The pipe."

Dino remained silent for a few seconds, then his face lit up. "Oh, the pipe. Not as bad as I expected. Turns out it was a minor leak. Most of the water leaked outside of the house. The neighbor must have mistaken it for something bigger in the dark. But I'm really glad he called me."

Samanta shot him a peevish look. "Any carpets or furniture ruined?"

"No. Nothing. I was lucky, I guess."

"Who did you call, your insurance agent?"

"No. Had to call a 24/7 emergency plumber."

"I'm sure that wasn't cheap. Weekend, and in the middle of the night. How much did he charge you?"

"Can I treat you to breakfast? An omelet or pancakes? I'm starving."

She shook her head. "I look a mess and want to shower first. I'm not that hungry." She tilted her head and looked at him with narrow eyes. "Since you were at your own house in the middle of the night—why did you come back here at dawn and sleep on this uncomfortable sofa? You could have slept in your own bed and had a nice shower and shave and come over later. Or you could have joined me."

Dino touched his scratchy cheek. *She just doesn't give up, even when she's badly hungover.*

After more coffee, he managed to talk Samanta into throwing on some grubbies and letting him take her back to her car without waiting for her to shower. He'd left her car in the restaurant's lot after coming back from his foray to GR&S. Dino had made sure to return her office keys to her blue shoulder bag before she woke up.

They drove in silence for a while. He glanced at her out of the corner of his eye. She caught his glance and held his gaze for a few moments. Did she get any of it, that his story was all bullshit? Probably not. It was all his strained nerves.

Dino tried to recall some details. Had he locked the door to Samanta's office behind him? No, he ran down the hall and out the door... A bad blunder.

He pulled up next to Samanta's car and killed the engine. She remained seated, looking straight ahead, not saying a word.

Dino cleared his throat. This sober sendoff was awkward, but not nearly as disconcerting as last night's hanky-panky that resulted from too much alcohol. "Well, I guess that's it," he said. "I'll see you around."

"Thanks for the ride. Have fun with the clean-up at home."

"Sure." He was about to open the door and walk over to her side when he felt Samanta's hand on his arm. A firm grip this time, not a gentle touch.

"Wait," she said.

"What?" He certainly was in no mood for anything more than a quick bye-bye. He clacked the door shut and looked at her, hoping she wouldn't try to schedule a follow-up date. He was ready to pretend that he was simply swamped with work for the next few days and already booked in the evenings.

"I got a call on my cell phone at 3 a.m. from a colleague at work." Her voice suddenly struck a combative tone. "He said he'd seen my car parked in front of the research building and wondered if there was a problem. When he got to my office, it was unlocked, but no lights were on, and nobody was in the room. Strange, huh?"

He didn't know what to say. Remaining silent equaled admitting guilt, or at least knowledge. He had to say something. "Crazy guy, calling you in the middle of the night. Does he think you're the only person on the planet who owns a blue Hyundai? There are dozens of these cars in this area—"

"But probably not many with a bumper-sticker with a red heart that reads, '*I LOVE ORGANIC TOMS.*'"

Dino swallowed.

"There's something else," she said. "While you were asleep on the couch, I couldn't help noticing what you'd chosen as bedtime reading."

Dino was convinced that Samanta could see him blushing to the roots of his hair. He instinctively touched his breast pocket where he had stuffed the folded article he had swiped from Harrod's office. The paper was still there.

"A paper from the *Journal of Opioid Research*," Samanta said in an acerbic tone. "Gripping and suspenseful, I'm sure. A real mystery thriller, right?"

Dino's hand dashed to the side of his pocket.

He could feel the key card.

Samanta scrambled out of his car, her own car keys dangling on her fingers. "Thanks for the ride, Dino. Talk to you later."

He watched her slam the car door shut.

He had made a mistake. But all was not lost.

43

DINO

Certain opioids are small proteins. The sentence hit him like a powerful blow.

The paper confirmed what he'd suspected.

Dino remembered having learned a long time ago that the human body produced its own opioid-like substances—*endogenous* opioids they were called. These naturally occurring substances were different, though, from the opioids used as therapeutic drugs or drugs of abuse. And yes, those endogenous opioids were small proteins—peptides, small chains made by individual amino acids. They interacted with the same opioid receptors in the body that opioid drugs did.

Endorphins.

He thrust a fist into the air. Had he hit pay dirt?

Was it possible to use gene-altered tomatoes to generate a certain peptide, a small protein, that would elicit opioid-like effects if ingested by humans? Powerful effects? Had he unlocked the secret?

But then, suddenly, he had his doubts. The structure of these endorphins was well known. They wouldn't have the dramatic effects he had seen. And one couldn't just take them by mouth and wait for pleasant effects to kick in. No, that wouldn't fly.

He paced up and down his kitchen, trying to put things together.

After a short while, he shook his head slowly. His shoulders slumped. No. Wrong track. Being proteins, such tomato-generated opioids would be digested when eaten, losing any effect. And, if heated up, such protein opioids would be destroyed. They'd coagulate like an egg white in a frying pan.

Yet on both occasions when he'd fallen seriously ill and almost kicked the bucket, he had *ingested* tomatoes. The second time, in the form of cooked tomato sauce. No way this could have been due to a poisonous protein.

He was tracking a cold scent.

He vowed he'd find out how they did it—for all the people who had died. No way he could just let it go. Not now.

Dino put his head in his hands. He felt lost, like he was tilting at windmills. This whole thing was out of his league.

He decided on impulse to talk to Cat. They were no longer on speaking terms, but this was getting ridiculous. He would defy the one-sided severance of communication.

He reached for his phone and sent her a text.

I miss you. Can we talk?—D

***

Dino was stretched out on the light-colored love seat in his living room, his feet on an ottoman, a cold beer in his hand, trying to marshal his jumbled thoughts.

Whose side is she on? That was the million-dollar question.

Obviously Samanta knew much more than he had thought she did. After that awkward situation in the car, he'd had no choice but to call her and admit everything—that he'd pilfered her office keys, driven to GR&S in the wee hours of the morning, and sneaked into her office.

She was livid. When she pressed him for an answer, he didn't have one, at least not a plausible one. She had told him to his face that she was disappointed that he didn't trust her and accused him of deviousness.

Dino rolled his shoulders several times to relieve the tension that had built up in recent days. He snatched his cell phone from the coffee table, hesitated for a couple of seconds, then thumbed through the *contacts* list. His face was taut.

"Hello, Dino." The answer came immediately, like she had been waiting for his call.

"Hi, Sam. Is this a good time to talk?"

"Any time is a good time when it's you calling," she replied, but her voice sounded flat.

"Listen, I want to apologize again," he said meekly. "I was a total goofball the other night. I—"

"Yes, you behaved like an idiot. Like a criminal. You know it's a serious offense to break into a corporate building? We could report it to the police."

Dino swallowed. He already knew that.

"Sam, I'm calling because I want to... caution you. You may be in danger. I think there are people at GR&S who are after your gene-editing technologies. I believe they want to use them for dubious purposes. Harrod is one of them."

"After *my* technologies? What makes you think so? We share everything. We're a team." She paused. "One more time, Dino. What did you want in my office?" Her question had a curt touch.

Dino scratched the back of his neck. He wasn't out of the woods yet.

"I was in Harrod's office. Wanted to find out what he was doing with his gene-altered tomatoes. Then I heard sounds, clear signs that someone was coming. I didn't want to get caught, so I sneaked into your room."

"So you heisted my keys from my purse and took them with you, just in case someone might show up in the middle of the night, so that you could hide in my office? Really. This won't wash, Dino."

He shrugged, even though she couldn't see it. He was strolling down a dangerous path.

"You're in deep shit, Dino. You know why?"

He clenched his jaw.

"You could've asked me. See, the problem is, we have surveillance cameras. All over the place, the entire research building. Your face is on video."

"No way. It was dark. I didn't flick on the lights. No way someone can identify me—"

"Where've you been living for the last twenty years, Dino? In a cave? Have you ever heard of infrared cameras, motion-activated video cameras that produce a perfect picture even when it's pitch dark?"

Dino stiffened. Admittedly, he hadn't thought of that. He inhaled sharply but didn't say anything.

His mind had suddenly wandered off in another direction.

"Why don't you just tell me what you hoped to achieve during your disingenuous nightly visit to GR&S?" she insisted. "I still don't get it. You could've asked me. It's as simple as that. I just don't..."

"I'll explain my theory. Later, I mean. Not now, not on the phone." Her mention of the video cams had triggered something. His eyes wandered across the room, scrutinizing the TV rack, the bookshelf, the low coffee table with the glass top, the pictures on the wall, the hardwood console with the purple orchids, the large blue pot on the floor with the indoor palm tree... Yes!

"Listen, can we talk another time?" he said hastily. "Just thought of something I need to do, urgently. Sorry."

"I hope it's not another leaking water pipe," she said. Her voice was soft but laced with sarcasm.

The pot. The pot with the Areca palm.

Dino stepped over to the plant and studied the strong stem, the long, light-green, feather-shaped fronds with the narrow leaflets. He bent down and looked at the base of one of the fronds.

For a split second, he didn't know whether to rip the thing out or leave everything in place.

There was no doubt that he had just spotted one of those miniature cameras that he had seen in movies. They were readily available through the Internet. Small, black, with a tiny lens. No bigger than an olive.

They were spying on him. But who exactly were "they"?

Dino took a few steps back. That was the second reason the two fake contractors had paid him a visit while he had been at work. Not to paint the walls, but to remove what they thought were the Grand Captivas, and to install a spy cam. Maybe even several of them. He shuddered at the thought of someone sitting at a desk, watching everything he said or did.

He wondered if there might be a cam in the bedroom too.

Dino clenched his jaw. He felt naked and defenseless. Duped.

44

DINO

There it was again, that searing pain in his stomach. Dino's consumption of antacids had sharply increased over the past days and weeks. Stress, anxiety?

He had sweet-talked one of the receptionists at the hospital's ER into sharing Cat's work schedule with him. She confided to him that Catherine Gillespie had taken ten days of annual leave. This information reduced some of the tension and alleviated his heartburn, if only temporarily. At least he didn't feel he had to alert the police. He would have made a fool of himself... *Hi, I had a minor argument with my girlfriend, and now I can't find her. Please pull out an APB on her and kick off an international search.*

Dino's worries about the whereabouts of Cat and Mia gradually turned into a deep sense of frustration. She'd just gone away and left him in the dark. Eventually, a wave of anger took over. *Bite me.* But deep inside he felt differently. He knew he couldn't live without her, and he didn't want to.

He had been tired and distraught in the past days and avoided contact with neighbors and friends. One thing was clear to him: he was not ready to start a romance with Samanta Martinez to worm his way into her confidence and gain access to top secrets. He was not in a fucking vintage spy movie. Too much was on the line. He was positive Cat didn't want a clean sweep, that the separation was only temporary.

But the waiting was painful. He couldn't eliminate Samanta from his thoughts either. *Femme fatale?* She was attractive, without a doubt, but his infatuation blurred his perception. His brain cortex reminded him that he'd probably photoshopped into Samanta some traits he liked to make the picture more appealing.

Dino's shoulders tightened. Strangely, he was also afraid of her. Despite the attraction he felt for her, he did not trust her. And yet, he'd called her again and arranged for them to meet.

He was playing with fire.

***

The *Coffee Shoppe* corner in the large bookstore was filled with the usual chattering and discreet smooth jazz in the background. Dino spotted her and jumped up from his chair as she walked toward him.

"Sorry I'm late," Samanta said, out of breath.

"You look great, Sam."

She pushed her sunglasses higher up on her hair and smiled that seductive smile of hers that always enchanted him. The small jewels on her ear lobes sparkled, and so did her dark eyes. "Thank you," she said, cocking her head slightly.

"You wouldn't believe what happened if you didn't hear it from me," Dino said, giving their conversation a clear direction.

"That's not imperative. What is it?"

"Someone bugged my place—at least three spy cams I've found so far. One in the living room, one in the den, and one in the kitchen. Tiny, wireless devices like you see in thriller movies." He paused for emphasis.

Samanta frowned. "Really. Who? I mean, why on earth—"

"I'm not kidding you. Probably they tapped the phone too."

"Are you sure?"

"Sure as hell, and I have a hunch who did it."

"Your jealous girlfriend? Or should I say, ex-girlfriend?"

"Cut the crap, Sam. Do you know how it feels to be snooped on, to realize that almost everything you do is being taped and watched by someone sitting in a dark room? It's creepy."

She smirked and winked at him. "Who wouldn't get a kick out of watching Dino Stampa eating breakfast or watching TV?"

"I think they're after me because they're looking for something that's in my house, but they don't know where it is. I have no other explanation."

"Really? Any idea what it could be?" Samanta sipped her latte and glanced over the rim of the cup.

"Can I get you a pastry?"

"That's a non-sequitur. I asked you a question."

"Beats me."

She shifted her eyes away from him. "Sorry, but we have to cancel our dinner on Friday," she said in a casual tone.

"Kind of disconnected this morning?" he said, waiting for her to elaborate on the cause of her abrupt withdrawal. "Did I say something wrong?"

"No. I have a meeting in Chicago that I absolutely have to attend."

"Sounds wonderful. What kind of meeting?"

"Oh, technical. Plant genetics. All the big shots will be there."

"Will you have to give a presentation?"

"No, not this time, but I will participate in a panel discussion. Quite important."

"Well, I wish you success," Dino said. "How long will the meeting last? Will you be back on the weekend?"

"No, probably not. The meeting officially ends on Tuesday. Don't know yet when I'm coming back. I'll call you."

"I can call you before that," he demurred. "Which hotel are you staying at?"

"Don't know yet. Finding accommodations in Chicago is always a problem, especially this time of year, but I'll find something. Don't worry."

"I'll miss you." He wasn't sure how much of this was true

or whether it was just purposive.

She checked the clock on the wall over the counter, but remained silent.

"Can I take you to the airport? What time is your flight on Friday?"

"Actually, I'm leaving tonight. Thanks, but no thanks. I'll leave my car in long-term parking. No problem."

He sagged against the back of his chair and nodded. Strange—why couldn't he just ignore her formal tone or acknowledge that she was in a hurry? Normally, he wouldn't even think twice about someone speaking tersely. Something was strange about her. One moment she could be charming and seductive and soft, and the next she could be unapproachable, gruff, and cold. But the question was, why did it affect him so much?

Her smile was back, albeit a bit forced. A plastic smile. Her eyes weren't part of it. "Maybe I should leave. I've got last-minute stuff to do."

It felt strange, but Dino had a genuine desire to keep her there, sitting next to him, and prolong the moment. She looked so assertive without being complacent. A natural, elegant, and classy air. She had a sense of humor, was sharp as a tack, and her figure was mind-blowing.

He leaned in and touched her hand, then pulled it back. At this moment, he was no longer sure whether he wanted to see Samanta because he had planned to acquire some key information, or he genuinely had the hots for her.

45

DINO

Dino's new position at the hospital was interesting but demanding. One of the things he wasn't accustomed to yet was the enormous time pressure—they were dealing with patients, after all, and oftentimes risky decisions had to be made fast and based on his analytical results. His old job at Rainbow BioLabs had been different; although Jason Goodlette had always been a bit pushy, the deadlines set by the government were usually very generous.

A sharp knock on the door roused Dino from his daydreams.

"Dr. Stampa?" Laurie peered in from the lab.

"It's *Dino*." *Useless.* She still addressed him formally. "Come in. What's up?"

"I just did a pilot run on the sample you gave me earlier this morning. I think you should see the results."

Dino jumped up from his chair. All his deliberations and doubts had vanished in an instant. He was on red alert. "Good or bad?"

"Very good, I think."

Dino rubbed his hands.

Early that morning, he had stepped out onto his lanai to check the growth status of his tomato plants. It was always an exciting moment to take stock of his fertile fosterlings. He smiled with contentment at three more of those small, green, spherical, cherry-sized fruits that would soon look like real tomatoes. One already exhibited a hint of light orange, almost like a faint maquillage. But the really good news was the single red, mid-size fruit that was, well, an almost perfect and

179

near-ripe tomato. They looked so innocent, these mystical Grand Captivas, camouflaged and labeled as heirloom tomatoes from the garden center.

Dino had picked the first fruit.

"Not a word about this, Laurie. Promise?" Dino's demeanor signaled unmitigated bluntness, but also a sense of shared confidentiality. Now they were in cahoots.

"Sure, I'll keep mum." Laurie gave him a skeptical look. "I understand these analyses are important, but why do you treat them so secretively?"

Dino wasn't ready to disclose the truth. "Politics. Internal competition. You know, it's important that I not divulge my research until it's complete. That way we avoid rumors and speculation."

Laurie nodded, but it seemed clear that she didn't believe him. Ever since she had found him unconscious on the floor the other night, she seemed to be giving him a wide berth whenever possible.

"Will you have more samples for me to analyze?"

"Most likely, in a couple days. Why?"

"Because I'm way behind with my routine work. Someone from Internal Medicine inquired about the urgent patient samples. They actually called twice."

Again. Dino blushed from embarrassment and anger. "Let the suckers wait. This has highest priority." The moment he uttered this, he knew he shouldn't talk to his technician like this. "Sorry, didn't mean it the way it sounded. You didn't hear that."

Laurie shot him a glance, shrugged, and went back to work.

Dino spread the results sheets across his desk and was instantly immersed in them.

A hit, finally...

The Grand Captivas contained an abundance of a unique

protein that was not present, not even in trace amounts, in the other tomatoes.

Dino's ears burned and he was oblivious to everything around him. When his phone beeped, he didn't pick it up. He glanced at his office organizer—a staff meeting was scheduled in ten minutes, but he decided to ignore it. He could always pretend he'd been swamped with work.

He poured through the datasheet again. Like any protein, this Grand Captiva protein was made up of individual amino acids, the building blocks of any protein, lined up like beads on a string. Identifying this mysterious protein was the next step.

Dino took a deep breath to vent his impatience.

He consulted online databases, trying to compare the sequence of the amino acids in his sample with sequences of known proteins. After trying three different programs, including the most updated version of the best software available, he had to concede defeat. No match. This protein was not only absent in a normal tomato, but it was also a compound that was unknown to the scientific community. Something new, undefined.

Dino felt his head spinning. He sighed heavily. Defeated.

There was only one way to learn more about this unknown chemical. By studying its effects on a biological system. Probably on cell cultures first. Maybe on a lab mouse next. Perhaps even on humans too, but that was a bit risky.

Someone had to be the guinea pig...

Dino had been staring at the ceiling for a long time when his desk phone buzzed.

"The Chief Medical Director, Dr. Herring, wants to talk to you," one of the administrative staff announced. "It's quite urgent. Tomorrow morning, eight o'clock."

"What's it about?"

"He wants you in his office, tomorrow, 8 a.m. sharp." The phone went dead.

Dino was having *déjà-vus* of his encounters with Goodlette, his former boss. This could only mean trouble was brewing.

46

DINO

At 8:07 a.m. the next morning, Dino entered the anteroom of the sacred halls of the Chief Medical Officer.

"You're late."

"Oh, am I? I thought the meeting was for eight," Dino said.

The Chief's secretary looked at Dino over the rim of her thick black glasses. "Correct. The meeting *was* set for eight. But it's almost ten past the hour."

Dino shrugged.

"Dr. Herring is waiting for you." She motioned for Dino to enter the CMO's office.

"Thanks," Dino said and knocked on the door.

Dr. Nathaniel Herring was a middle-aged man with a pudgy face and thinning hair. He wore a white coat that he kept open in the front, revealing a boring red tie with white dots that was way too long and bulged over his paunch.

With a gesture of dominance, Herring pointed to an uncomfortable-looking chair and stared down as Dino squeezed in between the two metal bars that served as armrests.

"Thanks for coming on such short notice, Dr. Stampa," the CMO said. "I know how valuable your time is."

Dino wasn't sure he heard a touch of sarcasm.

"How is everything going down there in your lab in the basement? All settled in? Any problems encountered? Any needs? Getting along with the staff? They are wonderful people, I hear."

Too many questions at once. Dino took a deep breath.

"My team is fantastic indeed," he said. "Great people, hard

working. Yeah, I really like this place. Great to be here. Terrific job." He immediately felt that his feedback to the CMO was weak and generic. He could do with a higher budget and they would soon need a more modern GC/MS unit—but this was certainly not the time to broach those subjects.

"That's good to hear," Herring said. He cleared his throat. "Would you like some coffee?"

"That would be great, thanks." Had Herring really summoned him up here to ask how he had adjusted to the not-so-new-anymore job and chat nonchalantly over coffee? Not a chance.

Dino was starting to feel uncomfortable. He felt an urgent need to say something.

Herring straightened himself and put down the cup. "The reason I asked you to come to my office today is, well, a rather unpleasant affair. I don't like what I must tell you, but since you're reporting to me, I need to be straight with you. Even brutally honest." He fixed his eyes on Dino.

"Is it about the recent drug OD? Phantom opioid cases? They're keeping us busy."

Herring hesitated for a second, seemingly puzzled, but then regained focus. "No, it has nothing to do with the phantom opioids. Rather—it's about you. It has been brought to my attention that there is a problem in your lab—with your job performance, to be specific."

"What?" Dino was alarmed at this sudden turnaround in their discussion. "By whom? Scuttlebutt about me?"

"Look, a number of people have complained—independently of each other—that there are serious flaws in the way you handle the daily routine analyses. The results come back to the wards way too late. There were two incidences where the sampling had to be repeated because of a mix-up of data or something. This is absolutely unacceptable, Dr. Stampa. This is a highly renowned hospital with the highest ethical standards and a flawless reputation. All the biochemical analyses must be performed in a timely manner with the utmost accuracy and reliability. Your staff oftentimes is misinformed. The lines of communication are not up and running as they should be."

Dino swallowed and wanted to say something, but Herring raised his hand and cut him off.

"I know, you are relatively new here, but you must realize that this job demands the highest level of professionalism. The honeymoon is over. You hold a highly senior position, and you must exercise your responsibility accordingly." He paused. "But there is more, and you won't like it. It's about your personal behavior. Again, I got this from several independent sources—"

"Who the—" Dino interjected, but then stopped short.

"When people try to reach you by phone—during office hours, mind you—you don't answer. You don't return their calls or answer voice mails. You disappear from your office or lab without notifying anyone. I'm not talking about coffee breaks, I'm talking about your being AWOL for entire half-days, sometimes entire days."

Give me a break, Dino thought. *You're not checking attendance, are you?*

"I have to travel sometimes, or visit other labs, or go to meetings or conferences, both locally and out of town. I guess those duties come with a certain senior position?"

"I understand," Herring continued. "Obviously. But did you really have a dozen different dental appointments in a two-week period? Did you genuinely have a whole slew of family emergencies that forced you to take a day off? How many times can a grandmother die?" He snorted indignantly.

"With all due respect, sir," Dino said, "you're not micro-managing my calendar, are you? You must have more important things to—"

"Don't get smart, Dr. Stampa. I have to make sure this hospital runs smoothly. That all the values, rules, and regulations of LCH are adhered to, especially the medical aspects."

Herring rubbed his nose.

Dino wasn't sure what to reply. The MCO acted like he was head of human resources. If only they could talk about some clinical stuff. Or science.

"Last but not least," Herring went on, "I need to report back to you, unfortunately, that some of our staff at the hospital complained about your personal behavior toward them. I'm not implying sexual harassment, or racial comments, or verbal abuse or offenses, but I'd say it was pretty damn close to it. Be careful. We don't tolerate any of that here. We expect our doctors and other academics to be role models for all our staff."

Dino sighed. How long would this harangue continue?

"Take this as a warning, Dr. Stampa. A serious warning. Do you understand me?"

"Sure, I understand you."

"Fine. Thank you for your cooperation, I appreciate it. That's all for now." He rose abruptly and walked around his desk. There was a faint smile around Herring's eyes. Maybe a sign of relief.

As Dino walked toward the door, he felt Herring's hand on his shoulder.

"All the best to you. I know you can do it. Let's not be so formal. May I call you Dino?"

"Sure. What should I call you, sir?"

"I'm Nate."

They shook hands.

As he walked back to his office, he wondered who had finked on him.

Strange that Herring hadn't mentioned the recent incident with his, Dino's, own medical emergency.

47

DINO

Dino cranked up the A/C in his Chevy to full power, put on his sunglasses, and slowly pulled out of the parking lot. He had left a terse "I'm leaving early today" message with his lab staff. His face was set in grim resolve as he touched the side of his slacks and felt the key card through the fabric. *Free and painless access to R2.*

The westbound drive to Sementina Springs seemed shorter each time, although he took the same route. He remembered that the entire GR&S premises were dispersed over a huge area and had only a sketchy idea of where the high-security research buildings were located.

Several roads branched off the main highway. He deliberately overlooked the big sign that read, *PRIVATE ROAD—ACCESS FOR GR&S STAFF ONLY*, and pulled off the highway onto the second small, dusty road he came to.

A few hundred yards down the road, he encountered a group of farm workers walking in the direction he had come from. They all wore protective clothing and broad-brimmed hats against the blazing sun. Dino stopped and rolled down the window.

"Hey guys—you happen to know where the Research Building is?"

"*Hola… no entiendo,*" one of them said.

"Research. *¿Laboratório de investigación?*" Dino couldn't think of a hand sign that would unambiguously symbolize a researcher sitting at a lab bench, stuffing a piece of DNA into a tomato. "Oh, never mind. *Gracias.*"

He continued down the road, leaving behind a trail of reddish dust.

The building in front of him was a low concrete structure attached to an extensive wooden barn-like structure. Two black Silverados were parked near one of the entrance doors.

Careful this time. He needed to think twice before crashing this party. Despite his anxiety, he felt a hum of excitement.

He got out of his car and walked around the building. In his blue scrubs that he had borrowed from the hospital, he could easily be taken for a scientist working in the building.

Mosquitoes buzzed around him instantly. He slapped his face and neck. An insect repellent would come in handy, he thought, no matter its origin—natural or synthetic—as long as it kept these beasts away.

He didn't see anything suspicious, but it also struck him that he didn't know where he was. The sign next to the door read: *R1*. So, in all likelihood, *R2* must be nearby. The second, larger sign was more menacing: *NO TRESPASSING*.

He pressed his nose against one of the windows, trying to see inside the building, but couldn't discern anything in the glaring light outside. He continued his exploratory tour around the building until he had come full circle. A twinge of guilt and fear suddenly seized him. Sneaking around like this certainly would arouse suspicion, and if—

"Hey, you!" someone shouted with a reedy voice. "Watcha doin' here?"

Dino spun around. A tall man in a red T-shirt stood in front of Dino's car, arms akimbo.

"Howdy," Dino said. "Looking for building *R2*. Can you—"

The man stepped closer. "You work here?"

"Occasionally." Dino tried to assume an air of importance. "We're collaborating."

"Where you from?"

"ImmuneTherix." His improvising was risky. Very risky. He swept a hand across his forehead. He felt his leg muscles tightening, ready to run.

"You got an ID?"

"Sure, it's in my car."

"You been here before?"

"My colleague has. For me it's the first time."

"Everything all right, Al?" someone shouted.

"Sure, no sweat," Al replied. Then he turned back to Dino. "And what's your name again?"

"Spino."

The man scratched his head. "R2 is a bit further down the road." He gestured eastwards. "But you won't be able to get in there. Strictly forbidden."

"Oh, someone's expecting me there. Thanks."

"No prob," Al said.

In the rearview mirror, the baffled face disappeared in a cloud of dust and dirt.

***

Building R2 looked similar to the other one but much smaller. The entire building was shielded by a tall, heavy-duty wire mesh fence. *KEEP OFF—STRICTLY NO ENTRY.*

What a warm reception.

Dino realized that it would be next to impossible to climb that fence. It might even be electrified. Maybe there was a pack of Dobermans inside...

All flimsy excuses. Chickening out now when he was so close? He felt the sharp sting in his stomach again as he stepped up to the iron gate that led into the courtyard. Locked, of course.

Next to the door jamb he spotted a small white device, its bright control light blinking at him in commanding red. The key card reader.

He fished the key card from his pocket and glanced at it once more. *RESEARCH 2—BARRIER FACILITY* was written at the bottom. At the top, a long number, and on the left, a name. *SAMANTA MARTINEZ*.

Dino was convinced she had no clue that he had her card. When he had gotten back to her apartment that night, he had found her card in her handbag, a yellow ribbon attached to it. He had hastily exchanged her card for Harrod's card and made sure to swap the ribbons with the different colors as well. No doubt, as soon as Harrod realized his key card was gone, he would alert security, and his card would be blocked. Samanta would assume it was her card with the yellow ribbon sitting in her handbag.

Deep breath. He held the card against the electronic card reader...

The red light switched to green without a hitch, and the latch on the gate released with a *click*.

Dino shut the gate behind him without a sound and strode up to the building.

He prayed the same card worked on the main door. Any additional safety feature, such as a passcode he'd have to punch in, or a fingerprint or iris-reading device, and he'd be at the mercy of—

Whoosh—the door opened. Right guess.

Nobody was in the dim hall. No human voices to be heard, only the humming sound of the A/C system.

The nearest door that stood ajar led him into an anteroom. He took in his surroundings in a second—a small plastic table, a chair, a computer, a phone mounted to the wall. On the side, a bench, a pile of freshly pressed and neatly folded green lab coats, a carton with blue plastic booties, others with nitrile gloves, white surgical masks, and blue caps. A bin on the floor for the used gear.

Dino stopped, balancing on a wire's edge, teetering between going ahead and calling the whole thing off. Was all that stuff provided to shield the precious plant seedlings against unwanted dirt from outside, or... to *protect the personnel*? From toxic chemicals, or worse even, microorganisms, foreign DNA...

A cold shiver ran through him.

He donned a mask and pulled the rubber bands over his ears.

In the back of the room, another door led to a corridor from which Dino could peek across large glass windows into the rooms behind. One resembled a tropical greenhouse in a botanical garden, except artificial light flooded the windowless room, and the greenhouse contained rows of mostly small tomato plants. The other room looked like an ordinary chemistry lab.

He decided to peek into the laboratory. Would the keycard work here as well?

The green light flashed invitingly.

Laboratory equipment, microbalances, shelves with chemicals, cabinets with glassware, computers jammed the immaculately clean room. Nothing stood out to him as strange. Except...

A faint odor, despite the fresh circulating air coming in through slits in the ceiling. He sniffed, like an animal scenting danger in the wind. Sweetish, but vile. A nauseous touch. He scanned the bench, the shelves, the floor, for something that might—

An instant later he spotted it. A small white rat next to the trash bin was dead. Stiff, its back hunched, its eyes glazed over, the mouth open in a snap-frozen shriek, its long yellow incisors grotesque.

Dino held his breath and turned away.

48

SAMANTA

Samanta strode up to research building *R2* to do some last-minute things before heading to the airport. She checked her watch— not much time to spare.

She stopped in front of the iron gate and fumbled in her pocket.

She pulled the keycard by its yellow ribbon and presented it to the magic eye, the card reader—

The wailing howl of the alarm siren was deafening. Overhead, the flash of a large red headlight pulsating.

Samanta jumped as if a bomb had exploded next to her. She covered her ears, trying to protect them from the noise. She tried the key card again... maybe she could stop it. It was then that she saw it.

What the fuck was going on?

At the top, on the left side of the card, a name. *CLAYTON HARROD.*

It took her only a second to put two and two together. Dino. This guy thought he was smart. But she would outsmart him.

The most urgent task now was to prevent him from entering research building *R2*. She hurried back to her car.

49

DINO

Dino's head shot up. He waited for a few seconds, listening. His heart pounded. What the hell had he done? Why did the alarm go off?

He bolted out the door, yanked the gate open, and ran to the remote spot where he'd parked his car. He floored the pedal and sped off, tires squealing.

His excursion had not ended the way he'd planned, but at least he had acquired crucial evidence. Had anybody seen him? He hoped he could make it to the main road before—

Dino strained to see what was in front of him. A white sedan parked sideways blocked the small road, obstructing any traffic.

A jazzy green SECURITY logo unmistakably identified the vehicle.

Dino jumped on the brakes. "Damn it," he muttered.

A man came around the car. Athletic frame, white shirt, aviation sunglasses, hair cut short, mysteriously talking to the heel of his left hand, then using his finger to twist something in his right ear. Paragon of a bodyguard, if not a secret service agent.

The guy stretched out his right hand; there was no mistaking the authority in his gesture.

Dino gripped the steering wheel, knuckles going white.

"Hi, officer... I think I'm lost—"

"Can I see your license, sir?"

"Of course," Dino said. The Spino alias clearly was no longer an option. He had to show his colors.

"What were you doing up there at that building?"

"I was looking for research building *R2*. I was supposed to meet a colleague."

"At *R2*?"

Tomato Secret Service Agent turned his head away from Dino and had a conversation with his wristwatch while glancing at Dino's ID. "Dye-no Stam-pa, yes—Sierra-Tango-Alpha-Mike-Papa-Alpha. Yes... roger that."

Dino's heard was pounding.

"This is a clear offense, Mr. Stampa. You're trespassing on corporate property, although it is clearly indicated that there is no access for unauthorized individuals. You set off the alarm."

The officer walked around Dino's car and tried to sneak a peek through the windows.

"What were you doing near the research facilities?"

"I was looking for Ms. Martinez. Samanta Martinez," Dino said. "She works here."

The security man eyed Dino suspiciously. "Martinez? What do you want with her?"

"Well, I know her. She works in the research building, and I was supposed to meet her there—"

"You got an appointment?"

"Sure."

Tomato Secret Service Agent crossed his arms across his chest, legs wide apart. "Are you giving me a ration of shit?"

"I'm serious, officer, dead serious. She knows me. You can ask her."

The security guard pulled out a cell phone, stepped back a few yards, and talked in a low voice. He listened for a while, nodding from time to time.

"You follow me in your car. I'll go ahead. Take you to another building. Someone will meet you there."

Someone? Sam?

The officer's eyes flicked back and forth, and he furrowed his brow. He turned away from Dino and spoke a few words that Dino didn't understand into his wristwatch. Then he opened the door to his car.

"I know where she works," Dino said. "No need to lead the way. I can find her by myself." The minute he had said this he knew he'd made a mistake.

The security guy swiveled around and took a few steps toward Dino's car, bringing his face to within inches of Dino's. "If you knew where Ms. Martinez works, why did you look for her in the wrong building?"

Dino stiffened, searching for the right answer. "Because she told me to meet her there."

"I could have you arrested for snooping around private corporate grounds, if you'd prefer," the man huffed. "Follow me."

Dino made an appeasing gesture, then jumped into his car, slammed the door, and followed the security car.

A man waited outside the main building for them. Elderly, a bit heavy. Definitely not another Secret Service agent.

The security guy opened the driver's door of Dino's car and led Dino toward the entrance.

The two men exchanged a few words, then the security officer got back to his car without saying anything to Dino and leaned against the door, talking into a phone.

The elderly man took Dino by the arm. "This way. Let's go inside." He went ahead, walking with a slight limp.

He shielded his face as he followed the man down the corridor to a large office. Dino wished he had a large paper bag to pull down over his head.

"Not good, Mr. Stampa," the man said as he ushered Dino into the office. "You owe us quite a few explanations."

"I can explain, sir—"

"Do you know who I am?" He stared at Dino, his callous knuckles propped on the wide desk, ape-like.

"No, sir."

"I'm Chuck Kuzminski, CEO of GR&S." Chuck waited.
Samanta's boss.

"You were here before, snooping around. We know you.
You have quite a vivid imagination. You used false names,
gave us deceptive information, pretended to work for imaginary companies. I'd like to know why." He crossed his arms,
tilted his head. "Just tell me—what is it you're after?"

Dino's head was spinning. He needed to find a way out of
here. Unharmed. If that was still possible after all he'd done.
He'd screwed up—bad this time.

"Well?" Kuzminski pressed. "Or I can have you arrested for
industrial espionage."

"Ms. Martinez can explain. I know her. We're friends."
Dino said. A glimmer of hope. "You can call her."

"I was informed that you told security she was expecting
you? At the research building?"

"That's right, sir. 6 p.m."

Kuzminski's retort boomeranged instantly. "Don't take
me for a fool." His eyes were flinty, his nostrils flaring. "Ms.
Martinez left earlier. She's out of town."

Dino swallowed hard.

A knock on the door. A uniformed policeman appeared.

Kuzminski nodded to him, then turned back to Dino. "Just
one more thing. Almost forgot." He reached out his hand,
palm upside. "We'd like to get the key card to the security
greenhouse back. Dr. Harrod's e-card."

Without a word, Dino held up the flat card, its red neck
strap dangling off the side.

"Take him, officer," Kuzminski said.

"Turn around," the cop said, nudging Dino's shoulder.
"You're under arrest, sir."

The handcuffs snapped into place with a painful *click*.

50

DINO

Dino's wrists hurt. The chair was uncomfortable, the room hot and sticky, the swirling ceiling fan grated on his nerves. The wet, dark patches on his shirt grew bigger by the minute.

He was at a police station somewhere in Sementina Springs, waiting for... what? He had been unable to reach his lawyer, but he would try again.

Arrested for trespassing, for industrial espionage, Kuzminski had said. Ha! Dino didn't believe it; he could explain. Kuzminski no doubt must have realized by now that the key Dino had returned was not Harrod's, but Samanta's. Samanta was the pivotal person who could save him from... a hefty fine? From going to jail? The mere thought of that made his spine freeze. But Kuzminski had said she was out of town.

Rivulets of salty sweat trickled down Dino's face, burning his eyes.

He was jarred from his thoughts by an officer sticking his head through the open door. "You've got a visitor."

Detective Roberson slowly shook his head as he entered the room, implying without saying it: *What in the world have you done now?*

Dino let out a sigh of relief. The detective for sure was on a rescue mission rather than backing up the police force. On Dino's side, not against him.

"Dino," Roberson said.

"Can you get me out of here?"

"Tell me what happened." Roberson eased himself onto a chair. He sniffled and blew his ruddy nose. No getting away from the allergies.

Dino told him. Almost everything.

"You've done a stupid thing," Roberson said. "Time to stop this bullshit."

"Can you get me out of here, please?"

Roberson loosened his necktie. "Look—I could if I were sure that you..." he hesitated, reflecting. "I admit you've been cooperating with us nicely so far."

"Detective, please," Dino said in a quiet but desperate tone. "Can you... get me out?"

Roberson rubbed his chin. It looked as if he were weighing the options.

"I'm proposing you a deal," Dino ventured.

Roberson arched an eyebrow.

For an instant, Dino thought he detected the touch of a grin on the detective's face. He leaned forward. "You get me outta here—I'll give you something you might be interested in. Information, evidence—"

"You have some secret information, evidence for me? May I gently remind you that it's an offense to withhold information in connection with a crime? Deal or no deal, same difference." Roberson's eyes bulged slightly in disbelief.

"Okay, okay. Don't forget—I'm on your side, Detective."

Roberson gave him a deadpan look.

51

SAMANTA

The following day, Samanta Martinez dropped the magazine she was reading and glanced at her buzzing cell phone. Her immediate reaction to answer it showed that she considered the call important.

"Got a minute? Have an important update for you."

"Joe?" Samanta said, frowning. They had agreed to use cover names. "What's up? Something go wrong?"

"Unfortunately, yes. He spotted the tracking devices. He blocked the cameras, all three of them. He also stopped making phone calls from the house, except for silly things like scheduling dentist appointments. He actually rescheduled four times, can you believe that?"

She already knew. "He's fooling us, of course. He knows that someone is eavesdropping on him."

"All I know is that we're still ahead of him. We can monitor wherever he drives."

Samanta thought she picked up a stifled yawn from the deep voice on the other end of the line. "Joe, you okay? You sound tired."

"Pulled an all-nighter."

"Voluntarily, I'm sure," Samanta said, grinning.

"Yeah, right."

"Anything else?"

"Yup. Our subject got an email from a certain Pascal Gaudreau, biochemist and researcher at Analgesix, a small company in Raleigh, North Carolina."

"And?" They were used to keeping their messages short,

curtailing their comments, and keeping explanations to an absolute minimum.

"Looks like our man sent him the tomato protein. They seem to know each other well. Gaudreau's some kind of opioid guru. Apparently ran a functional test and confirmed that... let me read it to you: *Your protein exhibits extremely high affinity in the... MOR binding assay and potent response in the isolated... vas deferens and... antinociceptive tests.*" Joe was struggling with the technical terms. "He also included some tables with a lot of numbers and abbreviations. I have no clue but thought you might find it interesting. What the hell does it mean?"

"In a nutshell—a positive response," Samanta said. "A strongly acting opioid. Will explain more when we meet next time. You think it was the *Red-O*?"

"Not a hundred percent sure, but my guess is yes."

Samanta lowered her voice. "What are we gonna do? I'm still out of town. We need to act quickly."

"Is Operation Thunderbolt still on, as planned?"

Samanta startled. "Yes, sure. We have a Plan B?"

"Of course."

"So we move in for the kill?"

"Yup."

"Good luck. Keep me in the loop, okay?" He had already hung up.

52

DINO

Dino pumped his fist.

Not only had he been released from the police station the day before, after Detective Roberson made some phone calls and completed extensive paperwork, but Dino found excellent news in his in-box.

His friend Pascal Gaudreau informed him that Sample One, which was the code name for the Grand Captiva protein, was positive in the functional test for opioid activity, while Sample Two, which had normal tomato controls, was negative.

Dino called him immediately.

"A huge, I mean a *huge* response," Pascal had said. "Much stronger than morphine."

In other words, the arcane protein in the Grand Captivas not only bound to the opioid receptor in cells, it also elicited a powerful effect.

"Fantastic!" Dino shouted. "Can you also predict whether this works in the brain as well?" He remembered the euphoria the tomatoes had caused him, but more vividly remembered the nausea, his disorientation... and waking up in the hospital.

"Can't tell at this point. That depends on whether the body degrades the protein rapidly before it can reach the brain. Second, and this is important, it depends on whether this protein can actually cross the blood-brain barrier—"

"The protective wall that shields the brain from noxious compounds?"

"Exactly," Pascal said. "Molecular border control, if you will. But, again, I can't tell. All I can say is that your protein is a hell of an activator of the opioid system."

Dino offered a thumbs-up, although Pascal couldn't see his triumphal gesture through the phone. A shoo-in.

"Pascal, you think e-mail is a safe way to communicate?"

"Sure, why not? Don't worry, your data won't get lost."

***

Two days later, Dino called Samanta. She was back from her conference.

"How was Chicago?"

Dino was prepared to hear an enthusiastic torrent of new ideas, about opportunities for collaboration, novel insights into scientific problems, making new friends. Instead, Samanta's answer was lame.

"It was nice." Period. Absent any kind of verve.

"Anything new in the field? Any major breakthroughs?"

"Not really. You know, just a few methodological details. How about you? What did you do while I was in Chicago?"

Oh, nothing, Dino thought. *Only got arrested for breaking into a high-security building and identified a new protein in a tomato that someone engineered to have an extremely strong opioid activity.*

"Not much, I'm afraid," he said. "You promised to call, but never did." Dino tried not to sound too reproachful.

"Oh, you know how conferences are. Endless meetings, social obligations, official dinners, etc. Not much time for anything else. No bad intentions."

Really? It takes five minutes to call.

"I understand. Which hotel did you stay in?"

"The Sheraton."

"Downtown? On Magnificent Mile?"

"Exactly. Great shopping there."

Time for shopping?

"How was the weather?"

"Windy and rainy. They don't call it the Windy City for

nothing." Samanta's voice sounded tired. Gone was the bantering undertone. "But it didn't matter. We were cooped up all day anyway."

Dino was confounded but didn't show it. He had monitored the weather forecast for Chicago; it had been a sunny, warm, and pleasant week. He tactfully changed the subject.

"You know, we had a few new cases of opioid ODs at LCH. Bad outcome. Two people died."

"That's terrible." The casual way she said it sounded distant, not matching her words of dismay. "Can we talk about something on the brighter side? Like what you're doing this weekend?"

That sounded more like her. She was such a tease—but also playing a dangerous game with him. Hiding something, probably even lying to him. She was damn hot, but she also had an ice-cold side that he didn't understand. She was clearly making use of him—the same way he was making use of her. And they both knew it.

Cat sprang to mind as she always did when Sam was dallying with him. He visualized her happy laugh, the way she threw her hair back, her warm smile when she looked at him or kidded around with Mia. When she was serious and listened to him. When she lay next to him. That's where he really belonged.

The ten days Cat had taken off from work were over. She must be home by now. He longed to hear her voice.

As soon as he and Samanta finished their call, Dino called the Sheraton in downtown Chicago. He asked the operator to connect him with Ms. Samanta Martinez. They couldn't put him through. Nobody with that name was staying there. Maybe she had already checked out? No, nobody with that name had stayed at their hotel in the past few days. And sorry, they could not give him any detailed information about their guests on the phone.

Why did Samanta hide things from him and, worse, warp the truth? Vagaries?

Dino rubbed his temples with his fingers. His head ached, and his stomach cramps were back.

53

DINO

On his way home from work, Dino wondered why Cat still had not replied to his earlier text message. Where on earth was she?

He pondered whether he should call her mother, but then dismissed the idea. Cat had never been on the best terms with her mother. She had often told him that she felt her mother had never really been emotionally attached to her, and as a child Cat had often been left alone.

He decided to check on Cat's house instead. His hope of seeing her evaporated as he drove around the small lake toward her place. The short driveway was deserted, and he didn't see anyone on the front porch or on the lanai. The pool was undisturbed. The water looked smooth, almost oily, under the darkening sky. He couldn't make out any lights inside the house. He knew before he rang the doorbell that nobody would answer.

Back at his house, Dino arranged the food on the coffee table in front of the TV. He popped an antacid and a painkiller and washed them down with a glass of beer.

Still restless, he got up again and walked over to the side table where he had placed Cat's birthday present. He had bought her an aquamarine-colored necklace. It hadn't been cheap, but it was worth the price. Sadly, he would not be able to celebrate with her on Sunday, but he would give it to her later. He still needed to gift wrap it and compose a loving phrase for the carefully selected card.

He reached into the box and held the handmade jewelry

in his fingers. Beautiful and eye-catching, it would complement her blonde hair. The individual beads were not all the same size; the ones in the front were larger, gradually becoming smaller toward the back of the necklace, where a delicate golden lobster clasp joined the ends together. The necklace would look absolutely stunning on Cat, emphasizing and embellishing her beautiful eyes.

Dino's dreamy look morphed into an intense gaze as he grasped the full meaning of what had just gone through his mind.

The necklace... the beads... lined up like the individual amino acid building blocks of a protein, like pearls on a string, joined together at their loose ends into—a ring.

The opioid protein had to be a ring structure. No loose ends, just an endless loop. That's why the digesting enzymes were unable to find the first or the last amino acid that they could cleave off. That's why the whole protein was so stable. The string was probably cross-connected by strong bonds, holding it together, shielding the spherical structure from outside influences. A perfect cyclic opioid peptide.

He ran to his home office and opened his laptop. It took him less than five minutes to find what he wanted.

Cyclic peptides, also called cyclotides, not only existed naturally in plants, they were being developed in a few laboratories around the world as potential new pharmaceuticals. Plants could be genetically engineered to become factories for these cyclic peptides. Plant-made pharmaceuticals. That was the true meaning of the PMPs, plant-made pharmaceuticals.

Someone had hijacked this technique to program tomatoes to produce a novel cyclic peptide that acted like an opioid drug once taken by humans. The perfect drug factory. Clever. Ingenious.

It was up to him now to find out who exactly was the mastermind behind all this. It was of paramount importance to accomplish this before they found out that he was tracking them. No time to lose.

As if coordinated with Dino's deliberations, his cell phone chirped. He stared at the text message for a second, then a wave of joy and relief flooded over him.

Returning tomorrow. Can we meet on Sunday? TTYS—Cat. P.S. Love U.

54

DINO

Cat's birthday cake from the Danish bakery sat on the back seat of Dino's car. He had read meaning into the *"P.S. Love U"* that appended Cat's short text message to him. She must have taken time to reflect on their relationship because the time-out seemed to be over. She had taken a vacation, made up her mind, and returned with a proposal for a new start. Probably she would attach conditions to the continuation of their relationship, and he would willingly comply. Yes, he had behaved like an idiot, and failed in many ways, but he'd put it behind him. He was certain she would forgive him.

Whistling, Dino went upstairs to take a shower. He would pick Cat and Mia up at their house in twenty minutes or so, and they would go out for a nice brunch. It was Cat's birthday, after all. It touched him that, after that endless period following the abrupt termination of contact, she wanted to spend the day with him. Time to reestablish domestic peace.

He hadn't felt so excited on his way to a date for a long time. Okay, he had been aroused when he went out with Samanta, but that was different, and those moments seemed far away now. The current wave of exhilaration that seized him was deeper, more meaningful.

Deep inside he wished Samanta would leave him alone— but he still needed her for his purpose. Until the mission was accomplished.

As he exited Brown Pelican Cove and headed toward the Heron Bay area, Dino pondered for a moment what to say and what to keep to himself, at least for the moment. He would certainly not address upfront his strange adventure with Samanta.

It wasn't an affair after all, even though it had come close. He would also skirt his recent hassle with Nate Herring. Cat wouldn't approve of Dino having created problems at work again.

He decided not to confront her with *why-didn't-you?* comments. It would sound too reproachful. Instead, he would tell her that he loved and cared for her deeply. When their major discord had escalated, Cat had criticized him for not making any commitment and for never telling her about his feelings. He had replied that he was an emotional person, but he simply didn't express his emotions openly.

He was ready to change or, at least, make a stab at changing. Himself, not the world. Apparently, Cat was also making efforts toward a reconciliation. Earlier on the phone, she had lifted the veils of her secret behavior. "I took a one-week yoga and meditation workshop for calming mind and body," she'd explained. On Hilton Head Island, South Carolina. Mia had stayed with Cat's sister. "As a corollary, I've come to grips with my jealousy issue." She'd sounded proud, but slightly embarrassed.

He smiled.

***

Dino wasn't ready for what came next. As he drove around the curve of the lake toward Cat's house, he sensed that something was wrong.

A white Collier County Sheriff patrol car was parked in Cat's driveway. Her car was nowhere in sight.

An officer stood next to the car, talking into his radio mic. As Dino came to a halt on the road in front of the short driveway, the officer looked up at him, then motioned him on.

Dino pulled to the curb one house further down and jumped out of the car.

"Is there a problem?" he said as he approached the patrol car.

The officer stepped toward him and stretched out his palm, as if directing traffic. "Who are you, sir?"

"My name's Dino Stampa. This is my friend's house. What happened? Where is she?"

"Who are you looking for, sir?" the cop said still trying to keep Dino at arms-length.

"Catherine Gillespie. Do I need to draw you a picture? She's my lady friend."

The officer's face reddened. "I need to see your ID."

I don't need this. He handed over his driver's license. The cop kept the license in his hand and gestured toward the front door. A second officer appeared in the doorway.

"I wanna talk to Catherine," Dino said with a defiant undertone and took a step in the direction of the house.

Before the officer could intercept him, a loud cry emanated from the house.

"Dino!"

Cat squeezed by the officer and ran into Dino's arms. Her hair was rumpled, her face wet with tears, her freckled cheeks smeared with mascara. She was breathing heavily.

Dino hugged and squeezed her. "What happened? Why're all these—"

She struggled to get free and stared into his face.

"Mia. They kidnapped Mia," she sobbed.

"Who kidnapped Mia?"

"We don't know."

Dino held her tight and gazed at the officer in disbelief.

The officer nodded, returned the license, and motioned for them to get inside the house.

55

CAT

The *Amber Alert* went out five minutes later. Their cell phone revealed a description of a gray Ram pickup truck, Florida license tag, featuring the Sunshine State sign.

There were a million gray pickups on the roads, and it was likely that the kidnappers, whoever they were, would change vehicles as soon as they could.

Cat had composed herself enough to tell Dino what happened. Her pale face twitched, and she gasped a few times. He brought her a glass of water and held her hand as she tried to explain. One of the cops stood idly by, listening closely to what she said, while the other one stepped outside to communicate with headquarters.

Her mind drifted back to the moment it happened.

She had just come back from South Carolina. She and Mia had stopped at the Bougainvillea Point Mall in Naples. They came out of the grocery store and loaded the paper bags into the trunk of her car. As always, Mia insisted on steering the empty shopping cart back to where the other carts were lined up in front of the store, just a short distance from the car. Cat waited for her in the car. In the rearview mirror, she saw Mia pushing the cart into place. Cat glanced at her cell phone to read an incoming text message. When Mia did not yank open the back door, Cat got out. "Mia," she called, turning in circles. "Mia? Where are you?"

Cat scanned the crowd of people milling around the parking lot. Why would Mia walk away without telling her? Should she get security? Her daughter knew where they had parked the car. Same area, as always. Surely, she wasn't lost.

"Did you see my little girl?" Cat shouted to two women standing near the store entrance. The escalating panic in Cat's voice was evident. "About this tall..." she extended her hand, "short, blonde hair, blue jeans, white tee?"

The two women looked at each other. "I saw a girl that fits your description," one of them said. "But I thought she was with her father. It might have been someone else." They described two young men briefly talking to the girl, and then one of them grabbed her by the arm, not very gently, and heaved her into a gray pickup. All of it happened quickly.

Cat ran the few yards toward the place where the women said they'd seen Mia and the men. She looked around frantically. No Mia, no gray pickup truck.

Cat sobbed while Dino hugged her. The police officer took over the narrative, facing Dino.

"Store security called 9-1-1. We went through the surveillance video and found the right frame quickly. Looks like a child abduction. We have the license tag of that Ford pickup, and some nice shots of the two alleged kidnappers. Next, Ms. Gillespie identified her daughter on the video. And then, Amber Alert issued—you saw it yourself."

He turned to Cat. "Don't worry, ma'am, we will get your daughter back."

Cat watched as the officer handed Dino his card. "We will get back to you, and hopefully soon. If you think of something that y'all think is important, call." He tugged on Dino's arm, stepped back a few steps and lowered his voice, but she could still hear it clearly. "In case someone contacts you..." he said, then hesitated.

"The kidnappers you mean?" Dino's voice was a whisper.

"Yes—call us immediately. Don't do *anything*. We'll take care of the rest."

56

DINO

The next morning, Dino showed up late at the office. Concentrating on work was impossible.

He wiped his face with his hand, unable to quiet his mind. He had hardly slept the previous night. Cat was devastated about the abduction of her child, and they had been up almost all night, talking with the police, trying to come up with a strategy—but there really wasn't much the two of them could do. Around four in the morning, he convinced Cat to take a sedative. After that, he'd been able to close his eyes for a few hours.

He clasped his hands behind his neck, staring into the distance.

By all accounts, Samanta must be involved in all this. She sure as hell made common cause with Harrod. The two of them were partners, collaborating on the same dark project. She had withheld information, or given him misleading information, or lied to him, like the Chicago farce. Or playing ignorant about the Grand Captivas.

He had given her way too much information, Dino realized. He'd been too naïve. He had trusted her, blinded by his goals, by his tenacious desire to know the truth, and, sadly, by his simmering lust for her.

His phone buzzed. The display read, *UNKNOWN CALLER.*

"Hello?"

"Can I talk to Mister Dino Stampa, please?" Dino didn't recognize the voice. Male with a thick Latino accent.

"Speaking." He waited for the caller to identify himself.

There was a crackle in the line. "You need to listen to me

carefully," the voice said. It sounded distorted.

"Who's calling?"

"That's not so important now. Listen to me, and don't hang up. The little girl is okay, she's fine."

The kidnapper.

"Mia?" Dino jumped as though he'd been punched in the gut. "Where is she?" Dino said through clenched teeth.

More crackling. "Listen. I don't have much time. You do what I say, the little girl will be fine."

"What the hell do you want?"

"I want you to stop messing with the tomatoes. No more visits to Sementina Springs."

"Hey! You! I'll do whatever you say, but give us back the girl," Dino shouted. He realized that the door to his office was wide open.

"I will call you again. But in the meantime, don't call the police. You will regret it. Wait for further instructions. And leave the fucking tomatoes alone, okay?"

"Hey, listen. Is it money you want? Hello... hello?"

The line went dead.

Dino wiped his forehead. His face was covered with pearls of perspiration. He thought of Cat—he needed to call her immediately.

Why had the abductors contacted him, and not Cat?

Because it had nothing to do with Cat. They wanted to blackmail *him.*

Dino squeezed his eyes shut. He gave in to his anxiety, his whole body trembling.

Ten minutes later, Dino had composed his features. Slouched in his chair, he mulled over the latest events. His first instinct had been to call the police right away, but then he'd changed his mind. Better to wait. Who knew what the kidnappers would do if they found out; they had explicitly warned him not to call the cops. Maybe they were watching him. Maybe they had wiretapped his phone and could monitor where he drove his car.

He had tried to call Cat at home, but she didn't answer. She was possibly still asleep. That soporific she had taken the night before had been a killer dose. He decided not to leave a voice mail. Better to talk to her in person.

Laurie looked up as he brushed by her. She had donned protective goggles and was pipetting organic solvents in the laminar flow cabinet. She glanced over her shoulder. "Can't hear you," she shouted, trying to drown out the swooshing noise of the airflow.

He came closer and leaned toward her, pointing to his watch. "Doctor's appointment. Will be back after lunch." Nobody would believe him anymore if he continued to use the dentist as an excuse for his frequent absences. He had only twenty-eight teeth, after all, with the wisdoms all gone.

Out in the parking lot, Dino walked around his car. He kneeled on the pavement and inspected underneath it, as much as the inadequate lighting would allow. While nothing struck him as suspicious, he realized he had no idea what a modern miniature GPS tracking device looked like.

He drove south on US-41, pleasantly surprised that the traffic was flowing smoothly. It was past the morning rush hour and before lunchtime. He stopped in Bonita Springs at the Italian deli shop. As he pulled into a parking space, he realized it was the same slot he'd been parked in before when someone had smashed his front window. He dismissed the idea of parking somewhere else. After all, he was not super-stitious.

He ordered a double espresso and enjoyed the hot, thick-flavored dark coffee. It would put some life into him. He tried again to call Cat, just to let her know he was coming home. No details of that ominous call he had received. Not now on the phone.

This time she answered. He paid and stepped out into the blinding sunlight.

Dino saw it when he turned on the ignition.

As he lifted the windshield wiper and grabbed the folded piece of paper, he knew it was no advertisement. Someone with shaky handwriting had scribbled a message in black ink.

SHE'LL BE SAFE IF YOU DO WHAT WE SAY. NO TRICKS. WE WILL CONTACT YOU AGAIN.

Dino spun around but saw no one except a few shoppers with plastic bags. He cursed and crumpled up the piece of paper. On second thought, he smoothed it out again. One never knew; this might be a piece of evidence. He had been in the store for seven, eight minutes, max, so whoever targeted him couldn't be far. He scanned his surroundings again, the shady areas under the trees, the side entrance to the store.

He hopped in his car and sped away, his attention fixed on the rearview mirror. He changed lanes frequently, randomly turned right or left at major intersections, and then made a U-turn at the next light to get back on US-41. As he approached the neighborhood that led to his gated community, he took a deep breath and released the air slowly, trying to calm himself. He hadn't caught sight of anything that would indicate someone was following him, but Dino's knuckles were white from clenching the steering wheel, the collar of his business shirt soaked.

Even if he couldn't identify a tail, he knew that *someone* was watching him. On the road, at home, and possibly at work. Everywhere, all the time.

***

"Cat? It's me," Dino shouted as he opened the door.

He found her on the couch in the living room. Her eyes were swollen, and she looked feverish. He hugged her and sat next to her, holding her hand.

"Any news from the police?"

"They called, but they haven't found her yet. They said they have a few leads, that they are doing their best, and that

I should be patient." Cat started to sob. "*Be patient...* as if I were waiting for a delayed plane at the airport."

Dino gently pressed her arm. "They'll hunt them down, Cat. The police have excellent tools. They'll find those bastards."

She stomped her foot. "All I care about is my daughter. I want her back."

"They'll find her, Cat. I promise."

"The police told me that, thanks to the Amber Alert, they found the gray pickup, not far from the mall. The kidnappers must have parked another vehicle there."

"Or someone picked them up."

"Whatever. The cops told me that forensics has been scrutinizing the truck for any traces of evidence, and they are making progress."

"Good. You know, their modern methods are extremely sophisticated. I'm sure they'll be able to tell the identity of every person who was in that vehicle. And then grab them by the throat."

"They should get Mia first."

"Of course. Listen, Cat," Dino cleared his throat, "I was contacted by one of the kidnappers, by phone—"

"And you're telling me *now*? Did they say anything about Mia?"

"I didn't want to tell you on the phone. Too dangerous. Listen, I think—I know—they are eavesdropping on us. My phones are tapped, yours may be too." He took Cat gently by the shoulders and looked into her eyes. "Listen, they said that Mia was fine."

Cat gulped down a sob. "How do we know that's true?"

Dino sighed. It was hard for him to veil his frustration and anxiety, but he wanted to appear strong. Concerned, yes, but determined and strong. "You know what? They obviously want something from us. If they harm Mia—God forbid—they know they won't get it. So, they will take good care of her."

They had gone through this before, the previous night, over and over again.

"What do they want, for heaven's sake? Money?"

"I don't know," he said, the look on his face grim. He pulled a package of soft tissues from his pocket and passed it to Cat.

"Did you already call the police?"

"No. The creepy guy on the phone told me to keep mum. He left no doubt that, otherwise, something would happen to—" Even before the words were out of his mouth, he regretted them. They just slipped out. "That I would be in trouble. I think we should heed his warning."

"I think we should call the police."

"Calling them would only ratchet up the situation to a new level. I will inform the police, believe me, but I cannot use my phone. Nor yours, to be on the safe side. But I will talk to them, just leave it to me. I must be very careful now and watch every step I take. But we'll get there." He checked his watch. "Geez, I gotta run. Have to get back to the hospital. Just wanted to see you. I'll come by right after work."

Cat pressed his hand. "Thanks, that's sweet of you. I love you."

Dino looked surprised. He tried to kiss her, but she pulled away.

"Just one more thing. Dino, honestly... while I was away, did you double-cross me?"

"Double-cross? What's this got to do with—"

"You know exactly what I mean. Were you on the make with that woman?"

That was not exactly what he needed right now. A jealous girlfriend in the middle of this mess. He stalled for time. Why did she rekindle this again, right now?

"No, Cat, I wasn't. I missed you. I know where I belong." This was not mendacity, this was the plain truth. He hadn't longed to tell the truth so badly in a long time, even if it was not to his advantage. "Look, I've made mistakes, lots of mistakes. I shouldn't have gone out with Samanta. I regret it now. But believe me—there was nothing between us."

Cat shot him a questioning look. She had lost some of her crestfallen mien.

Dino stood up. "Listen, I really have to split. They will kill me at LCH if I'm not back on time." A few minutes later he was on the Tamiami Trail, heading north.

57

DINO

Dino watched Laurie as she carefully placed a multi-well plate into the autoanalyzer. He waited until the machine started to automatically retract the platform with the samples.

"How's everything going?" he asked.

Laurie turned and looked at him through her plastic goggles. "Okay. But I'm still behind with the analyses."

"I can ask someone to help you, if you wish."

"That's okay. I'll just work a bit longer today. I think I can catch up."

Dino gave her the thumbs-up sign. Co-workers like Laurie were rare. His lab seemed to be running without a hitch, despite Herring's arguing the converse.

At least Dino's workplace was one of the few sane places in his current upside-down life.

And he was safe in his lab. Unlike in his house. Or Cat's house. Or his car...

Dino nodded at her and turned away. At the far end of the lab, Gavin, one of his senior technicians, was busy with the UPLC-MS machine. When he spotted Dino, his face lit up.

"Oh, Dino," Gavin said. "I have an FYI for you."

Gavin loved abbreviations, although it was a matter of luck as to whether or not he used them correctly.

"A woman was asking for you. Around noon."

"And what did you RSVP to her?"

"That you weren't in but that you would be back in the P.M."

"Who was she... what did she want?"

"Didn't tell me her name. Said she had a sample for you

that needed to be tested for opioids."

"Any work order come with the sample?"

Gavin shrugged. "I've no clue. She insisted that the sample be frozen immediately, and she followed me to the minus-eighty-degree freezer. Struck me as kind of strange, as if she didn't trust me."

"A nurse? A technician?"

"I don't know. She was in a long green lab coat. Maybe from the surgery department..."

"A long green lab coat, you're saying? What did she look like?"

"Stunning." Gavin gave a short, self-conscious laugh. "Beautiful. The kind of woman that turns men's heads on the street."

Sam? Following an impulse, Dino strode to the super-cold freezer in the back of the lab. He didn't bother putting on the protective cold-proof gloves. He yanked open the heavy door and opened the compartment where he had placed the tomato samples, unmistakably labeled with date, content, initials...

Dino let loose a string of curse words. He banged a fist against the freezer in disbelief and frustration.

The frozen tomato samples were gone. The rest of the tomato sauce, the bag with the first ripe tomato from his Grand Captiva plant on the lanai—all missing. Vanished.

"Describe the woman," Dino commanded.

Gavin looked flummoxed. "Uh... maybe in her thirties... tall, like me... couldn't see the rest because of her wide lab coat."

"Her face? Olive skin? Large, dark eyes?"

"Yeah."

"Short black hair?"

"Yup."

"Sam," Dino mumbled, grinding his teeth.

It must have been her who came to visit him in his office. And her request to freeze whatever sample she'd brought with her was a false pretense to be able to see where he kept the tomato samples in the lab. And then to take them.

Dino was breathing heavily now. The light dawned. She had stolen the evidence.

"Shit." Dino slammed the door to the freezer shut with a powerful kick.

Gavin threw him a disconcerted look.

Dino locked his office and walked up to Laurie. "I'm sorry we have to postpone the lab discussion we had scheduled for later," he said, scratching his cheek. "I have to attend an improvised meeting, sort of a last-minute thing. I hate this. Management calls, and you have to drop everything and run. I'll be away a couple hours, I guess, maybe even more."

He wasn't sure whether Laurie's snicker was genuinely innocent or because she saw through his humbug.

***

At the first light, Dino took a right turn, and then a left. Then he drove around the block. He hadn't detected any suspicious car following him. But he had no experience with this cat-and-mouse game either. For now, it didn't matter much anyway because he was driving to Cat's house, and they would probably assume he would do so.

When he arrived, Cat was doing okay, considering the circumstances, but she was in no mood to report to work yet. She planned to go back to LCH the following day, she said. Sitting around her house worrying was no good. There wasn't much she could do to help Mia at home. Work would distract her, and it would kill the long hours with nothing to do but sit and wait, hoping.

"Be careful," she said.

"I will, don't worry," Dino said, grabbing the car keys.

He drove north on US-41 and turned right on Vanderbilt. After a mile or so, he turned into the driveway of the Pelican Marsh community and waited outside the main gate for five minutes. Then he made a quick U-turn and sped away. Nobody seemed to be following him.

He turned left on Livingston and took a right on Sementina Road, heading east. At this time of the day, traffic was smooth. For the past couple of miles, he had spotted a red sedan behind him that didn't pass him even when he slowed down. As Dino started to worry, the red sedan turned right onto a local small road. The other driver most likely had been looking for an address or something.

As he drew closer, his plan was clear. He would barge in on Samanta, the same way she had barged into his own office earlier.

PART THREE

Red-0

58

DINO

Dino kept his speed down as he drove down the small residential road off Sementina Road that led to the tall condo complex where Samanta lived. He pulled into one of the visitor parking slots and strolled toward the entrance.

He pushed the button on the intercom but stood away to the side in case there was a video system connected to it. It took a while before he heard the buzz.

"Yes—who's there?"

The good news was she was at home. The bad news, she might not let him in.

"Express courier delivery for you," he said, trying to change his own voice to a higher pitch. "You need to sign to confirm receipt."

There was a long pause, then the front door lock clicked open. He stepped inside and rode the elevator to the sixth floor.

The door to Samanta's condo was ajar. Dino knocked twice and put his right foot across the threshold. "Hello—anybody home?"

"Jesus, you startled me," Samanta said. "What the hell is going on here?" She shot him a deprecating look. "I didn't expect you. In fact, I was getting ready to head out."

She was dressed in a white robe, her hair wet and disheveled, a towel around her neck. In the background, he could hear a TV and Dino could see a glass with a pink-colored drink on a console in the entrance area. It didn't exactly look as if she were on her way out.

"Sorry to disturb you. Are you alone?"

225

"Yup."

Her eyebrows twitched upward just a little as she opened the door and stepped aside.

"Look, we need to talk," Dino said. "May I come in?"

"You should've called. I'm kinda busy right now."

"Your date can wait. I want you to be straight with me." He stepped into the apartment and pushed the door shut. "Your duplicity has to stop. Right now."

"Hey, hey, Dino, what's wrong with you? What's all this rigmarole about?"

"Oh, it's not rigmarole at all. I'm dead serious."

"Geez, relax, buddy." Samanta rolled her eyes.

Dino stabbed a finger at her. "Where's Mia?"

"Pardon me?" Samanta looked slightly amused, shoving any visible flare of anger aside.

"You heard me. *Where. Is. Mia?*"

"Mia who? I honestly don't know what you're talking about."

"Cut the innocent scientist act, Samanta. I know who you are. Game over." Dino inched toward her.

Samanta looked over her shoulder as if checking to see if someone else was listening to this escalating conversation. Then she turned her head back and locked eyes with him. "Dino, honestly, I think you've lost it." She stretched out both palms and took a step back. "Please, don't come any closer." She had raised her voice.

"Look, it's useless. I know everything. In fact, I suspected it for a long time, but now I know for sure. Why don't you turn yourself in to the police before it's too late? That's my best advice to you."

"What the hell are you talking about?" Samanta took another few steps back. Her face had lost its color. "This is too much. First, snooping around at GR&S and then heading down to my apartment and harassing me. Stop this shit. Leave. Now."

Dino showed no inclination to leave or to stray one inch from his accusations. "I know you and Harrod are in cahoots. I won't leave until you tell me where you and your friend are hiding Mia. It's that simple. If you're not willing to tell me, then you will certainly have another chance to do so. I'm sure the police would like to hear it from you."

"You're nuts, Dino. Get out of my house, or I'll call the police."

"No need to call. They're on their way. I've placed an automatic call, giving them your address. Unless I cancel the whole thing, they will be here shortly."

"You're bluffing, Dino. I know you. You've been a liar, a cheater, a friggin' weasel, and a damn idiot. I don't believe you, and I don't trust you anymore."

"What a coincidence. I don't trust you either."

Dino had obviously gotten under Samanta's skin. This was perfect. If she was in a rage, she would be less in control than normal and more likely to let slip a secret. He had the edge. She stood there, her face ashen, her arms crossed in self-defense.

"I know everything, Sam," he said calmly. "Drop the pretense. No need to hide behind a mask." Dino paused to let the words sink in. "You've been developing methods to express a new drug in tomatoes. A cyclic protein with high binding affinity to the human opioid receptor, causing potent effects in people. Clever, very clever, I must say. You buddied up with Clayton Harrod. An excellent research team indeed, complementing each other. The perfect couple. He the molecular geneticist, you the plant specialist who knew how to use a tomato as a cheap and safe factory to crank out high amounts of a weird protein."

Samanta stared at him. She stood there, frowning, obviously dazed from the flood of accusations, but she remained silent.

"That's when Timberlake came into the game." Dino was

shouting now. "He collaborated with you and Clayton on the technology to produce therapeutic protein drugs, antibodies, for treating his cancer patients. He did not know, at least initially, that your major goal was to generate extremely potent opioid drugs. Drugs hidden in a tomato. A product existing naturally in those tomatoes. The perfect distribution system. Perfect for shipping. Perfect for a huge market. By selling and feeding these toms to people, you'd cause them to become addicted to opioids. You and your buddies would have them hooked without raising any suspicions." Dino's eyes sparkled with excitement.

"You're mad, Dino," Samanta said calmly. "This is a bunch of crap."

"There was an unexpected snag though," Dino said, ignoring Samanta's protests. "A small problem with your strategy. Turns out Timberlake got suspicious. He found out about the real purpose of your research and tried to put the kibosh on your plans. He wanted to go public. Big mistake. He paid with his life for his imprudence."

"This is ridiculous," Samanta said. "You don't have a shred of evidence that would support your fantasies. It's... it's outrageous."

"Just wait, I'm not finished. You also wanted to insinuate yourself into my confidence. You tried to get me into bed with you, hoping you could extract something useful from me. You wanted to find out what I knew about your fraudulent activities. You wanted to find out the details of it and whether these cyclic opioid peptides could be identified in a tomato with routine analytical tools."

If Samanta had been rattled before, she appeared to have recovered her poise. "What you're saying is so off the wall that I won't even try to vindicate myself." She took the towel off her neck and pulled at it with both hands. "Dino, I frankly believe you're in deep shit. You have maneuvered yourself into a dangerous position, and it'll be hard to extricate yourself."

Dino was ready to go in for the kill. He felt a bit shaky but decided to go for broke. "When you and Harrod realized I was on to you, you wanted to silence me. First, by smashing my car, slipping warning notes under the windshield wiper. Then, by attacking me in front of my house. Not you personally, of course, nor Harrod—you two would never get your hands dirty—but one of your hitmen. When you realized that none of that worked and you could not keep me from unraveling your dark deeds, you decided to blackmail me. At the same time, you tried to eradicate all incriminating evidence, such as the sprawling Grand Captivas on my lanai. And you swiped the tomato samples from my lab freezer."

Samanta's eyes widened. She opened her mouth as if she were going to say something, but just gasped for air.

Dino stepped forward, pointing a shaking finger at her. "The ultimate thing that you and your accomplice did was to abduct an innocent little girl, who you know is my girlfriend's only child, who I care for a lot. This is your worst act of cowardice—an ugly crime for which you're going to pay a heavy price."

Dino was breathing heavily now, his eyes narrowed to slits. He wasn't sure whether what he'd just heard was the elevator ping in the outside hallway, but he focused his full attention on his opponent. "For the last time—where is Mia?" He put one foot forward and lowered his upper body, swaying slightly, like a fighter in attack position. He was facing Samanta with his back to the entrance.

She glanced at the door for a second, then reeled backwards.

"You fucking bastard," she hissed. "You spoiled everything—"

Dino sprang forward with his arms stretched out, aiming for her throat. Samanta uttered a heart-piercing cry. She brought down her arms and hit his forearms heavily. He stumbled, flailing for support, and collided with the wall.

"Stop—freeze—don't move, Stampa!" a loud, shrill voice commanded from behind.

Dino recoiled and slowly turned his head. He had not heard anyone come in.

He stared into the scowling face of a burly young man with shaggy black hair and a bushy mustache. He'd never seen this man before, but apparently the newcomer knew who Dino was.

"Are you all right, Samanta?" the man asked, his gaze fixed on Dino.

"I'm fine. But our friend has gone postal. He's moved to the offensive. So glad you came at the right moment. He was just about to assault me."

"Hold it. I can explain," Dino said with a bleak smile, raising his hands.

"I said, *freeze.*" The man raised his outstretched hands.

Dino was staring into the muzzle of a gun.

59

DINO

"Hands against the wall. Step back, feet wide apart." The command was biting, unmistakable.

Dino obeyed. Despite the grave situation—he had never been held at gunpoint before—or maybe because of it, he was trying to cling to his sarcastic humor, which always had been a source of hope. He was terror-stricken, but he was convinced the less he'd let his opponents know about what was going on inside him, the more invincible he would appear. "Nice to meet you too, but I didn't quite catch your name."

The man remained silent. He reminded Dino of the bad guy in the old western movies, a *forajido*, an outlaw.

"I should've known you were expecting a gigolo," Dino said, turning his head toward Samanta.

"Shut up, asshole," Forajido said, frisking him. He took Dino's cell phone, put it in his own pocket, and glanced at Samanta. "He's clean."

"Sorry I ruined your nookie," Dino said, "but feel free to continue as soon as I'm gone. I wish I could join you for the gum party, but—"

Forajido's face had turned red. "Don't try my patience, Stampa." He looked over his shoulder. "Don't worry, we'll have lots of time to talk about Red-O." He took a couple of plastic ties from his pocket, yanked Dino's arms back, grabbed his wrists, and zip-tied them together.

"These are really comfy," Dino said. "Much nicer than the metal chinkers, if you ask me." Dino was scared to death, but he made a huge effort not to show it.

"We're going for a ride now. Move your ass, Stampa."

"Where we going?"

"You'll see soon enough."

"Oh, a surprise party, I see. Listen, there's no need to pull a black bag over my head and knock me out with a sedative. I'll be just fine with a silk blindfold."

"I think I'll get dressed," Samanta said. "I'll be ready in a minute."

"Need a hand, honey?"

"Shut the fuck up," Forajido yelled. He turned to Samanta. "Take your time. We're not in a rush. In the meantime, I'll have a little conversation with our friend here."

***

"Where we heading?" Dino asked. It was more of a rhetorical question as he doubted he'd get an answer.

Stony silence.

"I love surprises."

"You'll soon be laughing out the other side of your ass, Stampa. Now shut up, for cryin' out loud."

"Would you mind taking off my handcuffs? Or at least loosening them a bit? They hurt like hell."

"As soon as we get there."

They had put him in the back seat. Dino's mind raced, searching for a way out of this scary situation unscathed. It was best not to provoke them further. He could wreak revenge on this smug blowhard later, but for now it was best to comply. Samanta hadn't said a word since they left her apartment. Forajido was driving, but his eyes were riveted on the rearview mirror, watching Dino more than the road ahead of him.

Dino thought of Cat waiting for him, desperate to hear anything new about what had happened to her daughter. And he was worried about Mia. He considered for a moment whether they would take him to the place where they were keeping the girl, but then dismissed that possibility. No, that would be too risky for them. Beads of sweat broke out on his forehead. He'd never felt so vulnerable and defenseless.

Forajido took the left lane and waited at the red light at the US-41 intersection. They merged into the rush hour stop-and-go traffic and crept southward.

Dino's shoulder and neck muscles ached. A sting of conscience hit him for having maneuvered not only himself, but Cat and Mia too, into this scary situation. He pulled at the plastic ties around his wrists, but it only made them hurt more. If only he could get some relief for a few moments, move his hands, let the blood run into his numb fingers again.

"I hate to disrupt this nice ride, but I'm afraid I gotta find a men's room. Soon. Very soon." He glanced in the mirror for the guy's reaction.

"I'm sure you can control your urge for ten more minutes. How stupid do you think I am?" Forajido refocused his attention on the traffic.

"But we're not moving at all. It's bumper-to-bumper. Look, I'm bursting. Oh, well, if something happens—it's not my car. I warned you."

The man seemed to ignore him. He drummed his thumbs on the steering wheel as his jaw muscles bulged out rhythmically.

"Why don't we stop somewhere?" Samanta said, speaking for the first time. "If he has to pee, he has to pee."

A human reaction, at least, Dino thought. But this could also mean the ride would take a lot longer. He still wondered where they were heading. They had just gone through Old Naples and were now moving southeast. Did that mean that they would drive all the way across the Everglades, heading for Miami? They had just passed Davis Boulevard on the left.

Dino's frustration was rising as he evaluated his current situation and his chances of escaping. They were two against one and he was severely handicapped with his hands tied behind his back. Waiting for an opportunity was probably the best thing to do. Comply, act cooperative, remain calm, if not submissive, and then, when the right moment came—and he was positive it would—he would use surprise to his advantage and get away.

Forajido ignored Samanta too.

"Okay, I get it," Dino said. "Tell me what you want from me. I have no clue. I'm ready to talk, but you need to at least give me a hint."

"Don't worry, soon you'll have all the time you want to talk. Maybe more."

Dino swallowed hard, his heartbeat racing.

Forajido suddenly pulled over to the right into a driveway. Ahead of them was a large L-shaped one-story building that bore little resemblance to a mall or a grocery store, but rather looked like an official building. They pulled into an empty slot in the wide parking lot.

The man got out of the car and yanked open the back door. "Get out. No tricks. Not that you would get very far."

They walked toward the building, sandwiching Dino between them.

A man stepped out of the building, letting the heavy glass door shut behind him. The writing on the door read, *COLLIER COUNTY SHERIFF'S OFFICE, NAPLES, FLORIDA.*

60

DINO

"The zip ties were a bit of overkill," the deputy at the sheriff's office said, glancing at Samanta and her companion. "A bit gung-ho, but that's okay. Let's take them off."

Dino shook his aching arms and blew up his cheeks. He looked at his swollen hands and the red marks on his wrists. "Thanks. Where's the men's room?"

"Right down the corridor, first door to the right."

Dino shot Forajido a triumphant look. In the hallway, he looked back and saw him throw up his hands, while the deputy made a reassuring gesture.

Dino felt safe now, although he still wondered why Samanta and her buddy had brought him to this place. Why would they expose themselves by stepping into the danger zone? They must be pretty confident about their roles.

He almost bumped into a man coming out of the restroom.

"Oops—a near miss," the guy said.

"A near hit, I'd say."

Dino looked around. There were no windows in the room. He let cold water flush over his wrists and carefully dried his hands. He took a deep breath. Eager to learn what was going on, he returned to join the others.

Another man had joined the group. He stretched out his meaty hand as he saw Dino approaching. "I'm Detective Griffin from Narcotics. Mr. Stampa, I assume?" He squeezed Dino's fingers.

Dino flinched. He felt as though his hand would fall off. Griffin was a big man, completely bald, with gray piercing eyes and a clean-shaven face. He looked friendly, but he was the type of man you wouldn't want to mess with.

Griffin looked at his notes. "Let's go this way," he said, pointing down a corridor. He gave Dino a soft but unambiguous nudge on the shoulder.

"Where we goin'?" Dino asked, confused. "How about the others?"

"Don't worry, they're fine. We don't need them anymore."

Dino's hopes for getting out of this impasse were dashed. He turned his head. The officer was still talking with Samanta and her buddy.

"You'd better be careful with those two, Detective," Dino said in a low voice. "Especially the woman. She's involved in some dirty drug business. A case for you, I think. Don't let them escape."

"Thanks for the tip, sir, but leave it to us to enforce the law."

"*See it, say it, make-the-call.* Isn't that what you keep telling citizens all the time? Well, guess what? I *did see* something, and now I want to *say* it, that's all."

"What a coincidence," Griffin said. "We want to hear what you have to say. Now's the time." He opened a door that led to a small, plain room with just a table and a couple of time-worn chairs. One of the walls was made of non-transparent glass. Like in those interrogation rooms where a bunch of agents listen on the other side of the glass and read meaning into every word you say. They watch you, but you can't see them.

Griffin pointed to a chair. "Have a seat, Mr. Stampa. Want a glass of water?"

I want to get out of here, that's what I want, Dino thought. *I'm in the wrong movie.* "No, thanks, I'm fine. Please tell me what this is all about. I've been abducted by two criminals, kept at gunpoint, handcuffed, and carried off, and you want to make pleasant conversation? While the two mobsters step out of the building scot-free and walk away just like that? While an

DEAD NATURAL

innocent little girl has been kidnapped and is being held cap-
tive in a remote place, scared to death, and her mother is desperate?"

"Look, we are asking the questions here, okay?" Griffin
retorted. "You can help us a lot if you just answer them. Got it?"

"No, I don't get it. Am I under arrest or what? If so, on
what grounds?"

"Sit down now, sir," Griffin said. He waited for Dino as he
lowered himself slowly onto one of the wooden chairs. "No,
you're not under arrest. You may be, eventually, depending on
how things develop, but for now you are, let's say, merely 'a
person of interest.'"

"What the hell does that mean?"

"You may be involved in a criminal investigation, but you
have not been charged with a crime, and you are not being
arrested. You are free to go after we finish talking."

"Why can't I leave right now? I have things to do," Dino
snapped.

"Because you don't want to be charged with obstructing
a criminal investigation, right? Please clearly state your full
name, home address, and date of birth," Griffin said.

"Uh? Am I being recorded?"

"Do you mind?"

"I guess not."

How fast things can change. A short while ago, he had
thought he had apprehended two criminals—now he seemed
to be the one having scrapes with the law.

"You currently work at LCH as supervisor of the clinical
chemical lab, right?"

"Head of Analytical Services, yes, correct."

"You are familiar with GR&S, the company in Sementina
Springs?"

"Of course, I am. I went there several times. That's where I
first met Sam—Ms. Martinez."

"What was the purpose of your repeated visits to GR&S?

They produce tomatoes, after all." Griffin folded his arms across his chest and leaned back. He gazed at Dino with narrowing eyes.

Dino understood that this was the turning point where the tough questioning would start. The small talk before was just a warm-up.

"In the beginning, I was just interested in some of the methodological details they had developed. You know, plant genetics and the like."

"Why would a chemist working at a hospital be interested in plant genetics?"

"GR&S's research labs have adopted certain techniques that are well known in the field for heterologous expression of proteins in plants. Tomatoes, to be specific. And—"

Griffin's facial expression told Dino that this had gone right over Griffin's head.

"Using their techniques, one could turn plants into chemical factories that synthesize and crank out a foreign protein. Made possible by inserting the blueprint for that foreign protein—a piece of DNA encoding for that particular foreign protein—into the plant's own DNA."

"Why would they do that?"

"The plants? Because—"

"No, the people at GR&S."

"Oh, I see. To genetically modify their vegetables into something superior. For example, increase their nutritive value or make the plants resistant to natural enemies—insects or mold or what have you."

In a split second, Dino had devised his strategy. If he could baffle the detective with enough scientific details that he would not completely understand, he could shift the focus of a previous question to another area. The ploy seemed to be working.

Griffin nodded pensively, cocking his eyebrow. "There's

one thing I don't understand. Why would a clever and successful businessman and CEO invest a lot of resources—brainpower, time, and money—to genetically modify a tomato, with the sole aim of getting higher levels of nutrients? You can buy that stuff, I guess, in any health store, probably at CVS and supermarkets, as dietary supplements."

"I'll tell you why—as a marketing strategy. An advantage in the competitive field of vegetable and fruit farming, nothing else. Why do you think 'organic' produce sells so well? Marketing message. *All natural*. That's all." He made a sweep with his hand.

"If you were so interested in these techniques," Griffin said, "why didn't you simply ask the researchers at GR&S to discuss them with you? Why did you have to break into their research building at night?"

Uh-oh. The ploy had worked, but only for a second. Griffin had psyched him. "Good question," Dino said, pointing a finger at Griffin, his standard reply when he needed to gain some time to think. He cleared his throat. "I got into their research building the other night because I had some plausible evidence that a small group of researchers at GR&S did not only plan to use these gene-modifying techniques to have the tomatoes produce higher nutrients but also to have them generate harmful compounds. Opioids. Small cyclic peptides that act as opioids."

Griffin listened carefully. He got up, paced back and forth, then sat down on the edge of the table, looking down at Dino.

"What exactly do you mean by *plausible evidence*?"

Dino thought a faint smile played on Griffin's lip. "Long story," he said. "First, on one of my visits to GR&S, I snatched a couple of tomato seedlings, a new variety that they call Grand Captiva. They are—"

Griffin stopped him with a wave of his hand. "I know what Grand Captivas are. Move on."

Dino was astounded to hear this, but he tried not to show

it. "All right, then. I took some tomato fruit from this plant and analyzed it in my lab. And guess what?" He looked at Griffin and paused to increase the suspense.

"You found Red-O, a cyclic opioid peptide," Griffin said. "We know." He looked down at his notepad. "'With high affinity to the *mu* opioid receptor,' whatever that is. 'A hundred-fold more potent than morphine. Almost as potent as fentanyl.'"

"How... how did you know that?" Dino said, caught off guard. He hadn't expected to hear this from the detective. "I mean, I kept the analytical results locked in my office. That's hot stuff."

"Hot stuff indeed," Griffin said grimly. "Look, what do you take us for?"

Dino's head was spinning. There must have been a leak somewhere. Who, that was the big question. Laurie? No, she was loyal to him. Samanta? Unlikely. She was too deep in this mess.

Griffin jolted him out of his speculations. "You should've gotten back to the police immediately. We don't appreciate your rookie methods, Mr. Stampa. You have no idea how dangerous this is." He sat down on his chair again. "You just said, long story... what is the other evidence you have?"

Dino's mind reeled backwards. The shooting of Miguel... Harrod, Somporn, and Chuck Kuzminski... the hospitalized patients with clear opioid OD symptoms... the repeated assaults and warnings he had received... and finally the kidnapping of Mia. But how did all this tie together?

"Hell-o?" Griffin leaned forward. "I asked you something."

"Hmm?" Dino pulled himself together. "Yes. One day, I got to know one of their researchers a little better—Samanta Martinez." He made a move to get up from his chair, bumping the table with his knee. "She's the one out there. Get her before she gets away."

Griffin took Dino's arm and gently but firmly pushed him back into the chair. "Easy, man. We know who she is."

Dino gave him a puzzled look. "Why don't you arrest her then?"

Instead of an answer, Griffin just smiled. "Tell me what happened."

Dino sighed. "She acted really strange. One day she was friendly, sometimes even too friendly, if you know what I mean."

"Were you intimate with her?"

"I didn't sleep with her, if that's what you mean, but yes, at times it was close. She invited me to her apartment, and we went out several times. On other days, she would be aloof and act unsociable, even slightly aggressive. To be honest, I utilized her to find out more about their plans with the opioid tomatoes. I thought that after a few drinks she would loosen up and reveal things that I wouldn't hear otherwise. I couldn't squeeze out too much useful information from her though."

"Martinez is a very attractive woman. Did it ever occur to you that things could be the other way 'round? That she might have used *you* to gain access to information? That she used her feminine charms to lure you into a false sense of romance and make you talk?"

Dino stared at Griffin with wide eyes. "No, actually not. Never thought about it this way."

"You said you couldn't get any useful information out of her, so where is the other evidence?"

"Okay. Harrod, Dr. Clayton Harrod. Samanta's colleague, or should I say, accomplice. He is a molecular geneticist at GR&S. A clever fellow, highly intelligent—a little nerdy." Dino shrugged. "Don't let him escape. At least you can't blame me for not telling you. Big mistake, I think."

"Cut to the chase, Stampa."

"He's the guy who's behind the fraudulent research. I made it into his office once. Okay, I admit, I was trespassing." Dino raised both hands. "I found documents on opioids. He's also the one who works in the middle of the night, probably doing illegal things. You should also have a look at the CEO, Kuzminski. The two of them could well be in bed together. It's possible." Dino gasped for air. He brushed his hands through his hair. The damn situation was so complicated; he didn't really know how to sort it all out.

"Look, this is all pretty speculative, isn't it?" Griffin said. "Not much evidence. Not many hard facts."

"How about my chemical analysis of the tomatoes?" Dino said, flaring up.

"I agree, that's hard evidence, but we had that piece of evidence long before you started planting tomatoes in your own backyard."

Dino was flabbergasted. *How did they know? How could they know?*

Griffin got up from his chair. "I think it's time to get to the root of the matter." He stopped short, placed his hands on the table and gazed at Dino.

"What?" Dino said, turning his palms up.

"We know everything you've told us so far. Nothing new in your story."

"You know it from whom?"

"Martinez."

"Samanta? You're kidding me. Don't tell me she turned herself in."

"I'm not sure you realize who Ms. Martinez is. That's not her real name, of course. Yes, she's a scientist. You're right in that regard, except she doesn't work for GR&S. She works for the DEA."

Dino's mouth fell open. It took him a few seconds to regain control. "The Drug..."

"Yup, Drug Enforcement Administration. Department of Justice. In close collaboration with the FBI."

"Sam's a cop? Really? Are you pulling my leg?"

"No, I'm not. They placed her there as sort of an under-cover agent, but I guess her mission has been completed." Griffin stepped back a few steps, folding his arms across his chest. "The Red-O secret has been lifted."

Dino stared at the table in silence for a moment. He needed to digest this before he could rethink his actions.

"She's still a bitch."

"Careful," Griffin said, smiling. "She's one of us."

"How about Harrod? He's also...?"

"I'm not commenting on other people at this point in time," Griffin said. "But we're close to busting a big drug ring." He paused for emphasis. Then he stood up. His eyes had an intense focus. "Until we catch those responsible for this mess, and until we have the big fish, the wirepullers, I'm asking you—no, I'm commanding you, to stay out of it. Understand?"

Dino suddenly thought of Cat. "How about Mia, the kid-napped girl? Has she been found yet?"

"Unfortunately, not yet, but we are making progress. That's a different story. We'll keep you and Ms. Gillespie posted." Griffin's voice grew tenser. "But, again, I urge you—go home, mow the grass, play golf, but keep your nose out of our inves-tigation."

Dino tapped his hand on the tabletop. "Detective, can I ask you something? What exactly are the police doing to find Mia? The girl?"

"They are doing the best they can, believe me. They search the area where the kidnapping took place, they look for wit-nesses, and a forensic team is all over the place. After the Amber Alert, they got quite a few tips and hints from the public. Not all were equally useful, but some were. I cannot go into detail, as you understand. Now it's even in the media. So, we're making progress. I certainly understand what you and especially the girl's mother must be going through."

Griffin stood up and reached out his hand. "Thank you for your time."

Dino grasped that this marked the end of their conversation. "Can I leave now?"

"You may," Griffin said. "Do you need a ride? We'll be happy to get you out of here."

61

DINO

"Cat, they said they're making progress. Whatever that means," Dino said.

"That's what they always say. The police, politicians, negotiators, all alike. They're always making 'considerable progress,' and they are always 'optimistic.' You know what? It's a euphemism for admitting that they are stuck. They can't just say, look, we are groping in the dark and we have no clue. In fact, we're in deep doo-doo. They never say that." Cat got up from the armchair.

"You should eat something," Dino said. "I know you feel lousy, but you can't go on for much longer without eating or sleeping."

He sighed. Despite the heavy load on his shoulders, he wanted to help her, support her, comfort her—but he realized there wasn't much he could do. He looked at her. Her eyes had lost their sheen, her shoulders sagged.

They sat down again and remained silent for some minutes, each immersed in their own thoughts.

"So, if that Martinez woman is not what you thought she was—the mad scientist gone rogue—who then is the real bad guy?" Cat asked.

"Good question. To be honest, I don't know."

"But I'm sure you're making progress. Considerable progress, right?"

For the first time in days, Dino thought he detected the faint arc of a smile on Cat's face.

Dino's phone buzzed. He thumped his glass down on the coffee table, on red alert.

UNKNOWN CALLER.

He switched to speaker mode, nodding to Cat. "That's him," he whispered as he took the call, although he wasn't sure.

"Dino Stampa, please."

"Speaking. Who's this?"

"We talked before."

Dino immediately recognized the husky voice with a marked Latino accent. He planned to extend the conversation and get as much information from the mysterious man as possible.

"I talked with a lot of people before. Who's this?"

"It's not important. Just wanted to let you and your woman know that the *chica* is fine."

Cat winced with obvious pain and held out her hand as if to say, give me the phone, I want to talk to them myself, but then it looked as if she apparently relinquished her plan.

"I want to talk to Mia," Dino said sharply.

"I don't think she wants to talk to you right now. She's busy playing. I told you she's fine." The Latino accent was more pronounced now.

Cat jumped to her feet and clutched at the phone. "I wanna talk to Mia," she screamed.

Husky Voice chuckled. "You seem desperate. Okay, but only for a minute."

Cat snapped the phone. "Mia?"

"Mom! When can I come home?" Her voice was an uncontrollable whimper.

"Mia, darling. You'll be home soon, very soon. How are you? Everything's all right with you?"

Incomprehensible stammering. Sobbing.

"Where are you, darling?"

"Dunno... I'm scared. Please, Mommy, come and get me?"

"Be patient, Mia. We'll get you soon. I miss you." Cat wiped away her tears. "Are they treating you nicely? Got something to eat?"

"Mmh..."

Cat exchanged a glance with Dino. He was listening with the utmost concentration. "Where are you? Inside or outside? What do you see?"

"In a room. Mom, imagine, I saw Sandy today. Sandy talked to me again—"

"Who's Sandy?" There was a rustling sound on the line. Mia was gone before Cat could say anything else to her.

"What do you want?" Cat screamed into the phone. "Why are you doing this? Please, bring my baby back," she sobbed. Her entreaty was met with silence.

"Stampa? I wanna talk to Stampa," Husky Voice said.

"I'm here. Tell us what you want," Dino snarled. "Give us the girl back. Is it money you want?"

"No, I don't want any money."

Dino threw up his free hand and rolled his eyes. "I'm listening."

"Stampa, we need that flash drive that you snatched from Harrod's office."

"Flash drive? I don't—"

"You know exactly which one I mean—the one with the encrypted data. We know you have it. So, if your girlfriend ever wants to see her *hijita* alive again, you need to give up that drive."

"I don't know what you're talking about," Dino said, desperately wanting to be believed.

"If you ever want to talk to the little girl again, maybe you will suddenly 'member what you did with it, *que no*? Look, I give you time until tomorrow 6 p.m. Someone will call you in the evening and tell you when and where to deliver it. If all works out, we'll release the *muchacha*. *Comprende*?"

"I still..."

"And one more thing. You're an intelligent man. Don't be so stupid as to inform the cops. Or play any other trick. You will really regret messing with us."

"Can you be a bit more specific? Hey!" Dino shouted. "I

have no clue what you're talking about. Can you... hello? Hey!"
But Husky Voice had hung up.

***

Cat acted as if she'd been rousted from sleep. The lethargic
sadness was gone and had been replaced by a bout of energy
and determination. Dino had not seen her like this since the
actual kidnapping took place.

"Let's pull it off," she said. "Tomorrow is the day. We'll do
what they say, deliver the decoy, which will lead us to Mia.
The police will do the rest." Her cheeks were red, her eyes
shiny again, and she looked like she had finally found a silver
lining. "We will catch those thugs."

"I fully agree that we should involve the police, despite
them threatening us that the deal will fall through if we do.
In fact, I told Griffin everything—you know, that detective at
the Sheriff's HQ in Naples. I will call him—with this." Dino
fished for a small phone in his pocket. "A burner. Griffin gave
it to me. He insisted I should never use a landline or my smart
phone to get in touch with him."

"I wonder where on earth Mia is? I hope she's okay. She
sounded so... terrified. We know there must be a woman
involved, at least one—Mia mentioned her. But I don't know
what she meant by having chatted with Sandy."

"She didn't say they had a chat. She said she *saw* Sandy,
and that Sandy talked to her."

"What do you mean? What's the difference?"

Dino sat down on the armrest of the sofa. "It means that
she *heard* Sandy. By the way, Sandy could also be a man's
name."

"Doesn't help us much. Forget it. Your speculations are for
the birds."

They were silent for a few moments. Then he startled. "For
the birds!" Dino snapped his fingers. "Jesus, how could I ever

248

forget? You remember? Mia called him Sandy. The bird."

Cat raised one eyebrow. "I don't get it."

"Of course not... you're thinking of a sparrow or a wren. Think big."

She slowly shook her head, then it must have dawned on her. "The stork? That loud stork with the red cap?"

"Exactly. Actually, it was a crane. A Sandhill Crane with a red crest. The one that made those really loud rattling calls. Remember, Mia called him Sandy. Sandy, the Sandhill Crane."

"Yeah, could be, but—isn't that a bit far-fetched?"

"Maybe," Dino admitted, "but it could still give us a hint. Maybe Mia recognized where she'd seen the bird last time."

"That big swamp? The nature preserve we visited a few weeks ago with her?"

"Exactly. Corkscrew Swamp Sanctuary—Gateway to the Everglades. Where we saw all those animals."

"Why would these guys take Mia to an alligator swamp?" Cat sounded incredulous.

"To hide her. Nobody suspects a nest of chickenshit bastards in an alligator swamp."

They locked eyes with each other. Dino was determined to go all out to get Mia back.

62

SAMANTA

Mid-morning, Samanta stormed by the receptionist straight to Kuzminski's office. She knocked briefly and opened the door without waiting for permission to enter.

Chuck Kuzminski was half sitting, half lying in his executive chair, feet on the large desk, talking quietly into his phone, a broad smile on his face. It was apparent that he was involved in a relaxed conversation rather than negotiating a tough business deal. He waved Samanta in and motioned for her to sit down.

Samanta hesitated, then closed the door behind her and sat in one of the armchairs around a low coffee table. She knew from experience that Kuzminski would continue to talk and could easily ignore her for five to ten minutes. She had never been sure whether this was carelessness on his part or a deliberate demonstration of superiority, or both.

Kuzminski shot her a glance, then swiveled his chair away from her, facing the large window. He talked even lower now, then laughed. The usual game. She checked her watch and tried to bury her frustration.

"Talk soon," he finally said and turned his chair around.

"Sorry to intrude like that," Samanta said, getting up from her seat, "but it's important."

Kuzminski motioned for her to stay seated. He came around from behind the desk and stepped over to the visitor nook. As he plunked himself down onto the sofa, the leather creaked as if someone had crumpled a plastic foil. "Important call," he said. "So, what's cooking?"

"Look, it's becoming a tight squeeze. The past few days

have been crazy. We must be extremely careful now, or we'll spoil everything. The cops will be all over the place as soon as the bombshell drops. We have to secure all the evidence." Samanta was breathing heavily.

"Whoa, whoa, whoa, one thing at a time," Kuzminski said. "Where's Harrod?"

"He's busy in the lab. I don't think he has a clue about what's gonna happen."

"Sompy?"

"Same."

Kuzminski grunted. "How about Stampa? What is he doing now?"

"That's exactly the point—the sore point," Samanta said with an incipient frown. "The sheriff interrogated him yesterday, but last I heard they turned him loose last night. Lack of evidence, they said. He's on the loose again."

Kuzminski's initial gleeful looks had morphed into a morose expression. "Damn it. What do you think he's gonna do?"

Samanta shrugged. "I don't know. He is rather cunning."

"And unpredictable."

"I agree."

Kuzminski cupped his chin in his hand and stared at the floor. Then, suddenly, he stood up and paced the room. "He could bring down the entire company. In one second, he could ruin everything I've spent decades building."

Samanta bit her lower lip. "I realize that the stakes are high, Chuck. For all of us. Not just for the company. Just give me some more time. I'll get there."

She got up. "Anyway, just wanted to inform you that the lull is over. Time for action now."

"Take care, Sam. Stay safe."

Samanta threw back her head and gave that soundless laugh, lasting three seconds. Then she was dead serious again. "Don't worry, I'll be safe. Did you forget? I'm trained to do that."

On her way out, she let her fingers slide into her pocket, gently touching the smooth surface of the device, making sure the flash drive was still there. She would put it back on Harrod's messy desk, from where she had snagged it earlier, at the earliest opportunity.

63

HARROD

Clayton Harrod drove by the pool and pulled up to the curb, some fifty yards away from Dino's house. He'd had easy access to the gated community by tailgating the car in front of him, although the sign clearly said, *ONE CAR AT A TIME*. Nobody seemed to have noticed his car slipping through the gate.

He walked briskly up the quiet street until he was directly in front of Dino's house. So far, he hadn't encountered anybody on the street.

Harrod's plan was simple. He would ring the doorbell first. If someone was home, he would invite himself in under a lousy pretext. In case nobody answered, he would use the remote for the garage door that he had snitched from Dino's car a while ago. Harrod had figured that Dino might think he had misplaced the remote and gotten the spare one; things like that happen all the time. This would give him access to the garage, and he could just walk into the house from the garage. Nobody would see anything, and there wouldn't be any traces left. No break-in. Dino wouldn't even notice. By then it would be too late.

Harrod peered around the corner of the house and glanced at the screened lanai. Nobody was out there. As he walked toward the main door, he had a fluttery feeling in his stomach. He had never done this before. He kept telling himself it would only take a minute, and then he'd be out of there.

He pressed the doorbell button and waited. Nothing. Once more. Again, there was no sound or any indication that anybody was home.

Harrod glanced up and down the street. Except for a couple of schoolkids in swimming gear who were heading for the pool area, nobody was out. He unzipped his fanny pack and reached for the remote.

The wide door to the double garage rattled open sluggishly as Harrod broke out in a cold sweat. It seemed like Dino had procrastinated an overhaul of the garage door opener—but the neighbors surely were used to it and probably didn't even register the jarring noise.

There was no vehicle in the garage, and Harrod felt immediate relief. He whizzed inside the garage and pressed the remote again. It took forever for the damned door to close.

He removed his sunglasses and baseball cap and gave his eyes a few minutes to adjust to the change in light. He grabbed a pair of vinyl gloves from the fanny pack—the kind of soft protective gloves that they always wore in the lab—and groped his way through the almost dark room, bumping against a trash can that he had not noted before. Finally, he found the door connecting the garage to the inside of the house. He took a deep breath and turned the doorknob as slowly and quietly as possible. He had been right. The door was not locked from the inside.

He was in the house.

The air felt hot and sticky with the A/C set to power save mode. Harrod stepped along the corridor toward the messy kitchen and living room area. He found boxes, journals, papers, and junk mail dispersed on the tables and shelf spaces, but he marked all of it as nothing of importance to him. The master bedroom was tidy, and the bed seemed untouched.

A French door, halfway open, allowed him to peek into the den. A large wooden desk covered with more books, articles and paperwork, left barely enough room for a modern, ultra-flat desktop computer. Bookshelves jammed with binders and heavy textbooks completely covered one wall. Probably the most promising area to search for what he needed.

He opened the blinds just enough to allow him to search the office for valuable material. He went through drawers, bookshelves, cabinets, and looked under piles of papers, between rows of books, momentarily forgetting about the time. His search had been fruitless so far, and Harrod increasingly felt that his assurance of success was being allayed.

He startled at a strange sound that seemed to originate from inside the house, and froze. It was probably nothing. He was too taut; all tensed up. So far, no success, but he knew he had to find the flash drive with all that sensitive data on it, whatever the cost.

Where would one keep a USB stick? Where would someone try to hide it?

He closed the blinds again and stepped back into the master bedroom. The only place he hadn't examined yet was the walk-in closet.

A musty smell hit him as he entered the stuffy closet, crammed full of clothes, sports equipment, shoes, and a few large, empty boxes with the original Styrofoam pads. He immediately spotted the shiny safe sitting on a low console. It was firmly attached to the wall, probably fixed with screws from the inside, with heavy bolts and an electronic security lock. He didn't have any tools with him, and they would be useless anyway. Beads of sweat trickled down his face as he tried to focus on a strategy to get out of there, with or without what he had come for. He was pretty sure that the valuable drive was securely locked away in that safe and that he had no way whatsoever to force it open.

There was that noise again. Unmistakable this time. Coming from somewhere closer. Harrod froze, rooted to the spot. *Someone was in the house.*

His eyes that never seemed to blink winked in quick succession.

64

DINO

Dino had been asked to give a brief presentation to hospital management on the status of the Analytical Services Lab, stressing the current strengths and weaknesses since he took over as head. The meeting at LCH was scheduled for 1 p.m., but he wasn't properly dressed for it. There would be hell to pay if he missed it.

He left his car in the driveway and fumbled with his house keys, making a mental note to order a new remote for the garage—he must have lost it somewhere. He had spent most of the morning at Cat's home but planned to drop by his house to get a fresh shirt and a tie before heading out for work.

The minute he stepped into the master bedroom, he sensed something was wrong. He couldn't put his finger on it; whether it was a faint musky smell, or that something had been moved. He couldn't tell. Just strange vibes...

He steered toward the walk-in closet and opened the sliding door. As he reached into the closet to grab a shirt, he caught a shadow out of the corner of his eye. A row of clothes swayed back and forth, and he instinctively turned around.

After that, everything went too fast. The blow to the midriff hit him with full force. Dino's knees gave way. He was gasping for air. A man stood in front of him, half hidden by the hanging clothes. The next punch was aimed at his chin, but Dino was able to whip his head to the side so that his right shoulder absorbed the impact, cushioning the blow. The guy stumbled.

Dino settled on his target and kicked his adversary in the shin full force. There was a scream of pain as the man went down, sweeping a bunch of shirts off their hangers and down on top of his head. He struggled with both hands, like a drowning man, trying to free himself from the clothes.

Dino, still panting heavily, stared at the man lying on the floor. "Har... Harrod!" he yelled. His first impulse was to kick Harrod in the groin to immobilize him, but for some strange reason he just couldn't do it.

"What the fuck are you doing in my house?"

Instead of an answer, Harrod stretched out his left palm in a soothing gesture.

Dino didn't know what to do. Hit the bastard? Although he'd taken a few bad hits himself, he simply didn't have the heart to do it. Call the police? Harrod would certainly not wait next to him, twiddling his thumbs while he did that. Lock him in the bedroom? No, the guy could escape through the window.

The best thing to do was talk to him. Gain time. Make time to think by buttonholing Harrod.

Harrod moaned and got to his feet. He stretched out both palms and fixed Dino with his piercing dark eyes. "Look, I can explain."

"I can do without your weak ass explanations." Both men were standing a few feet apart, facing each other, bent forward slightly, bouncing from one foot to the other, hands in front of their faces, like two boxers in a ring gauging their opponent's next move. Harrod was taller by a head but much scrawnier. Dino was sure that if it came to a fight, he could take him.

"What do you want, Harrod?"

Harrod flinched but didn't say anything.

"Your flash drive, right?" Dino ventured, remembering what the man on the phone had mentioned. "You could have asked me. Would've been so much easier than driving all the way out here, sneaking into the gated community, breaking into my house, and then being at a complete loss as to what to do and where to look for it."

"I don't know what you're talking about," Harrod said.

"Oh, do I seriously need to jog your memory? The files with all the information about Red-O, the wonderful opioid drug hidden in the Grand Captivas. Remember now?"

Harrod swallowed hard, slouched his shoulders, his arms going limp. His dark eyes darted left and right, as if assessing his chances of escaping. The fight posture had made way for the flight mode.

"You're looking at the wrong person," Harrod said. "Sam Martinez is the scientist who went rogue. Don't act as if you don't know."

Dino frowned. His posture had relaxed slightly. He didn't believe what Harrod said, and he needed to act quickly. In a split second, he decided to settle for a strategy—a risky one, but the only one he could think of. He needed to leverage Harrod's weakness. Harrod was an extremely sharp guy, but he was slow and a bit naïve, and Dino definitely out-muscled him.

"Look, Clayton," Dino said in a calm voice. "I'm proposing a deal to you."

"I'm not naïve, Stampa," Harrod said, as if he'd read Dino's thoughts.

"I know that you're smart. That's why I am suggesting this deal. It's a win-win."

Harrod narrowed his eyes and cocked his head, his pose a combination of fear and curiosity.

"Look, let's be honest. I know that you didn't break into my house to take a nap in my bedroom. You want something from me. I want something from you. Why don't we simply exchange—"

Harrod interrupted him. "What could you possibly want from me?"

Dino took a few steps back, blocking the door with his back, all the time keeping tabs on Harrod.

"Mia. The little girl. In exchange for the flash drive."

"I don't know what you're—" Harrod said lamely.

Dino raised his voice to a threatening level. "Don't play me for a sucker, Harrod. You're intelligent, but you're a damn lousy liar." He jabbed his finger at Harrod. "We have an agreement. Your charming buddies and I. We've agreed to exchange the USB drive with all those explosive files for Mia. So, why don't we take a shortcut and do it right now, instead of waiting for tonight? Let's go for a prisoner swap."

Harrod's face clouded for a few moments, then brightened. His ashen skin had turned a slight pink. "So... you admit that you do have my electronic data?"

"Yup."

"How do I know you didn't copy the data?"

"You know better than me that the flash drive is copy-protected." A bold assumption, but Dino could read by the tacit admission on Harrod's face that he guessed right.

"How do I know that you're not bluffing? That you're not simply luring us into a trap with a decoy?"

"How do I know that you'll return Mia to her mother?" Dino asked, shaking his head. "Look, we both mistrust each other, but without a little bit of mutual trust we won't get anywhere. We'll gain nothing. Neither your side nor mine."

Harrod didn't argue the point. Dino took his lack of protest as a sign that he was involved in Mia's abduction, or that he at least knew where they had hidden her.

"Where do you keep the flash drive?" Harrod asked again.

"Where are you hiding Mia? Look, we are locked in a stalemate. I'm asking you one more time, do we have a deal?"

Harrod remained silent for a few moments. It looked to Dino as if he were weighing all his options. Then, suddenly, the look of bewilderment on Harrod's face changed to one of sly comprehension. "Deal," he said.

Dino couldn't trust him, of course, but he had a plan. He had to act smart, though, and swiftly, and he had to be extremely careful not to put Mia in more jeopardy.

"The drive is in my safe. In fact, right over there." Dino pointed to the black safe on the console. "I'm sure you were toying with the safe before I interrupted you. I could've told you it's tamper-proof."

Dino walked over to the safe. "I'm gonna open it now—but no tricks, Harrod. You stay put over there against the wall."

He shielded the input screen with one hand and punched in his code. He shot Harrod a triumphant look, reached deep into the dark compartment with his right hand and slowly retracted his arm. Instead of a thumb drive, Dino whipped out a black, shiny pistol and pointed it at Harrod.

"Just FYI, Harrod, it's loaded. It's a .38 Glock with eight bullets. Please don't give me an excuse to use them."

Harrod gazed at the weapon in disbelief, then at Dino. "You... you blowhard. You're gonna regret this."

"I don't think so," Dino said. "The safe, that's where I usually keep my gun. You know, to lock it away, especially when children are in the house. Like Mia, for example. But once in a while, such a shooter comes in handy."

"That thing makes me nervous, Dino," Harrod said. "Don't point it at me. We can close our deal without the gun."

"I'm afraid I'll have to use it if you defy my instructions." He motioned for Harrod to move. "Let's go and find Mia. You go ahead, nice and slow, out the front door. No tricks, my friend. My index finger is kind of twitchy."

In the hallway, Harrod turned around suddenly, making Dino jump. "Look, we can settle this," Harrod said. "You let me go and I'll tell you where Mia is."

Dino narrowed his eyes and exposed his teeth, like a snarling dog. "Harrod, I warn you. One false move and I'll kneecap you. Both legs."

Harrod's lips were covered with beads of sweat and he was visibly trembling. He teetered toward the door.

"Open it. Nice and slow," Dino said, pressing the muzzle into Harrod's side. He snatched the keys from the console in the hall and followed close on Harrod's heels down the hall and slammed the front door shut behind them.

Dino looked up and down the street. He couldn't see anybody. A white convertible drove by the house slowly. A woman he didn't know waved at him; Dino returned the salute.

"You want me to sit in the back?" Harrod asked, pointing to Dino's car on the driveway.

"Nice try. I'm driving, and you can whack me on my head and run away. Excellent idea, except it won't work on me." He looked up the road and pointed with his chin to the gray Nissan that was parked at the curb. "That your car over there?"

"Yes."

"Give me the keys," Dino said. "*You're* driving." He grabbed Harrod's keys and followed him to the car, making sure the man was still aware of the gun that Dino held in his right hand.

Dino tossed the keys on Harrod's lap. "Let's go."

"Where we going?"

"I thought we agreed on that," Dino said. "Mia's hideaway."

The game plan was to force Harrod to drive to the Collier County Sheriff's HQ in Naples. Dino would hand Harrod over to the cops, and then they would make him spill the beans and disclose Mia's hiding place.

But then a sudden wave of panic seized Dino. Although he had the advantage of holding a gun—what would he do if Harrod didn't follow his commands? He couldn't shoot him once they were driving on the highway; he would wind up killing both of them.

Showing no sign of weakness was imperative now.

"What are you waiting for?" Dino said, noticing at the same moment that Harrod was looking into the rearview mirror, blinking with his right eye. But it was too late.

Before Dino could see the danger coming, two strong hands squeezed his throat. He let go of the Glock, and both hands instinctively flew to his neck, struggling to get free from the powerful viselike grip. Harrod's buddy, who must have been waiting in the car, shot through his mind. A sharp pain jolted through his head. He gasped for air, and his movements slowed. Everything around him started to swim in a sea of color and sound, pulling him into a whirling funnel.

65

HERRING

Dr. Nathaniel Herring glanced at his watch—1:17 p.m. He drew in a deep breath and shook his head. *Where the hell is Stampa?* he thought, fuming. Most of the senior members of hospital management were there, waiting for the speaker. They all had tight schedules and hated to waste time.

The large conference room had been set up for Stampa's formal presentation. An administrative officer was ready to take the minutes. Coffee and cookies were lined up, but Dr. Dino Stampa, the new director of Analytical Services, was nowhere in sight. *VIP airs?*

Everybody had engaged in small talk across the large conference table, had helped themselves to coffee, and finished last-minute phone calls. Gradually, the jokes and laughter trailed off. People were beginning to express their concern and vent their growing impatience.

"Nate," Dr. Enfield, the hospital director, shouted across the table. "Seriously? What are you going to do?" He pointed to his watch.

Herring, who had organized the meeting, said, "Give me a minute." He felt his frustration rising. He fished out his cell and was thumbing down the *contacts* list when the door flung open, and one of his administrative officers burst into the room. She stepped up to Herring and whispered something to him.

"He's not in the lab?" Herring asked. "And nobody knows where he is? Did you try his cell?"

The woman nodded.

263

Herring stood up. "Colleagues," he said with a stern expression, "unfortunately, we're unable to locate Dr. Stampa at this time. He had left a note in his office that he'd be late this morning, but he hasn't checked in yet. Under these circumstances, and in view of the time—" he checked his watch again—1:21 p.m.—"I think we have no choice but to cancel this meeting and reschedule it for another day. I'm terribly sorry for the inconvenience, but..." He didn't finish the sentence.

A no-show. Herring would summon Stampa to his office immediately. This time Stampa would have to bear the consequences of his behavior. He had been warned.

66

DINO

Dino's skull was throbbing like a jackhammer, and he felt nauseated. The goon in the car had choked him badly, his clasping fingers hard as steel. They could have easily put him away, but they hadn't.

The alarming thing was that they hadn't bothered to blindfold him. It could, of course, indicate that they were going to a place with which Dino was familiar, but more likely... that he wasn't coming back.

The sound of his own heartbeat pounded in his ears.

Dino didn't remember how he'd gotten onto the back seat of the car, but that's where he woke up. The goon who sat next to him held a gun in his hand while Harrod drove. They were heading east, then north on Sementina Road; Dino was almost sure their destination was GR&S. But Harrod took a left onto Sanctuary Road and drove down the narrow road until they reached an area with scattered bungalows. Behind those, Dino knew, would be the entrance to the Corkscrew Swamp Sanctuary, the place they had visited a couple of times, and where Mia had seen the Sandhill Cranes. His gut told him now that this must be the place where they were keeping her. The thought of being close to her banished his fear.

Harrod's guy motioned for Dino to get out of the car. Inside a ramshackle bungalow, he pushed him into a small room that was austerely furnished, the paint peeling off the yellow walls. All the blinds were closed, but light spilled in through the thin gaps between the white slats. They had told him to sit at the far end of a wooden table. The thug watching him sat at the opposite end, staring at his smart phone, probably playing some stupid game. He had angled his chair so that he could watch both Dino and the door.

"May I have a glass of water?"

The guy showed no reaction.

He tried again. "*Agua, por favor.*"

"Drop the bullshit," the goon said, returning to his phone.

Entering a conversation, establishing some sort of a relationship, was what he had heard would work in such dangerous situations. But Dino didn't really know how to win the man over. It could also backfire. He was no trained psychologist.

"How long you think—" he started, but his renewed attempt was interrupted by a rush of noise outside the room. Loud human voices.

The door burst open, and Harrod stepped into the room, a creepy smile on his face. "Now you can sing, Stampa. We're all ears."

"Where's Mia?" Dino said boldly. "I want to see Mia before you hear a single word from me."

"Really? I'm not so sure about that," a deep voice thundered. "I'm not so sure."

Dino startled. It sounded like... No, impossible.

A hulk of a man entered the room, followed by a shorter, leaner guy.

A cold shiver ran down Dino's spine.

"Look who's here—who would've thought that we'd meet again so soon."

"Jason," Dino stammered. "*You?*" Could it really be his former boss, Jason Goodlette?

Goodlette let out a guffaw. "You look like you've seen a ghost. Long time no see. How you been, Dino?"

Dino's thoughts whirled in his head. This must be a dream. He just wanted to get away from here, from this person. The panic that had seized him earlier came creeping back.

"So nice of you to come all the way out here, Dino," Goodlette continued with his unsavory nonsense. He sized Dino up. "But you look a bit ruffled today," he added, putting on an ugly grin. He smoothed down his own hair with his massive hand. "Anything we can offer you? Champagne, bourbon? Or something stronger maybe—more exciting?"

Dino didn't answer. He looked at Goodlette with a steady gaze. He needed to stick it out. This was a showdown. He was clearly outnumbered and needed to act carefully every step of the way and bide his time.

Goodlette turned to the watchdog who had jumped up from his chair when Goodlette entered the room. "You may leave now. *Puedes irte.*" He reached for a chair.

"Did you lose your tongue, Dino? I don't remember you being such a reticent man."

"Where's Mia?" Dino uttered between clenched teeth.

"That cute little girl is fine. She can't wait to get back to her mom, though. But in exchange, we'd like to get—"

"You bastard! You're a sneaking coward, that's what you are, Goodlette. Using an innocent child for your dirty tricks." Dino shot his former boss a contemptuous look. Then he realized that he needed to control his anger in order to think clearly.

Goodlette laughed again. "Check your offensive language, Dino. I don't know this side of you. You could be quite sarcastic, but I never heard you talk like this before."

A million thoughts went through Dino's mind. Goodlette, connected to this opioid-producing gang of criminals? Was he the boss? Or just another link in the food chain? All the time Dino worked at Rainbow BioLabs, there had never been the slightest hint of something going on behind the scenes...

Goodlette banged his fist on the table. His eyes had taken on a mean look. "Look, I can't waste any more time. Just tell me—where is the flash drive with our data? What else did you take?"

Dino was stumped. As many times as he'd tried to redirect the conversation to a topic away from the flash drive, the moment had come when he couldn't evade the issue anymore. If he told them he didn't have a clue what flash drive they were talking about, they wouldn't believe him and would likely adopt more drastic measures to press for the information—he didn't want to go there. Alternatively, if he continued to tell lies, he could only do so until they were on to him.

There was no way out.

Although the situation seemed utterly hopeless, Dino suddenly realized he had a trump card—he could use that imaginary flash drive as leverage. As long as they couldn't get hold of that device with the sensitive data, they wouldn't kill him. Scant comfort, but still...

"I'll tell you after you provide evidence that Mia is alive and well," he said in the calmest voice he could muster.

Goodlette turned his head to the man who had accompanied him. The guy nodded briefly and mumbled something into Goodlette's ear, covering his mouth with his hand.

"I'm afraid we cannot bring the girl in because she's not here," Goodlette said. "But we can certainly show you a snapshot of her. You'll see that she's alive and kicking."

"Yeah, right. How do I know that the pic wasn't taken days ago?"

"Oh, that's easy. We can let her hold something—a newspaper, or a tablet, for example, flashing today's headlines. For reasons you'll understand, we will inactivate the date and location recording on our smart phone, though."

"How clever of you," Dino said. "Okay. I want to see the picture, but I also want you to attach the photo to a text message and send it to Mia's mother. Catherine Gillespie, who—"

"Who happens to be your hot little slut. We know," Goodlette said with an ugly grin.

Dino shot up from his chair, his nostrils flaring, his neck corded. "Watch your mouth, Goodlette, or I'll—"

Goodlette's bodyguard jumped into position. "*Relájate*," Goodlette snapped and motioned for him to relax.

Dino took his seat again. He took a deep breath and exhaled slowly. "So, Jason, deal or no deal?"

"Deal." Goodlette turned to his bodyguard and spoke insistently to him in rapid Spanish. Dino's rudimentary command of the Spanish language was not sufficient to catch what he said, but Goodlette's hand movements gave it away. Outstretched thumb and pinky of his left hand held close to the left ear and mouth, then a rectangle formed with forefingers and thumbs of both hands, held in front of the eyes, and the *click* with one index finger.

So they would send a picture to Cat. But Cat knew—Dino and Cat had discussed it the other night—that the metadata of JPEG files contained a lot of additional information, including the exact geographical location of where it had been taken. The cops would have no problem locating Mia now. They had been waiting for such information, and they would clamp down the moment they got it.

All Dino had to do was stall. "You got her cell number?"

"Of course—you think we're amateurs?" Goodlette said. The goon, meanwhile, had left the room.

"Interesting stuff, the Red-O, I have to admit," Dino said, changing the subject. "Fascinating, really."

Goodlette flinched, then sat upright from his slouched position and thrust his chest out. His hands were tucked in his armpits, thumbs visible and pointing up. He had a proud gleam in his eyes.

"Potent, very potent opioid," Dino continued, "yet invisible. Doesn't show up in the routine screens for opioids. A heat-resistant protein that's not digested in the gut. Here's the best part. There's no need for a chemistry lab or a repurposed barn or basement to produce the stuff. Plants do all the work for you. Tomatoes. Toms—the perfect factory, storage container, and transmitter of the drug, all in one."

"Yes, the concept is brilliant," Goodlette said, as if involved in an interesting scientific discussion rather than talking to a deadly adversary trying to unravel a closely guarded secret.

"I agree. A very clever plan," Dino said. "Therefore, I guess it's not your own idea, Jason. Who designed it?"

Goodlette must have caught Dino's tone, but didn't seem to be offended. "Clayton, most of it. Clayton Harrod. He's a genius." He glanced at Harrod, who all the time had sat in the back of the room, seemingly detached, not saying a word.

"Really? All the time I thought it was Samanta Martinez," Dino said as cool-headed as possible.

"Forget her," Goodlette said. "She's too naïve. Too much buddying up with Kuzminski. She couldn't have done it, never." He sucked in a deep breath.

Dino watched him. If Jason knew about Samanta's real identity he didn't show it, unless Jason was an outstanding actor, which Dino doubted.

"Too bad the cops found out about all of this," Dino said.

"Timberlake did. The sonofabitch thought he was smarter than us."

"Why did he have to pay with his life?" Dino felt the blood rushing to his head.

"Meddling with us is never a good idea. A professional took care of it." Goodlette stared at the opposite wall with a blank look on his face, as if remembering the victim. After a pause, he gazed at Dino and jabbed a finger at him. "Timberlake made a mistake. His own fault. Like you, Dino. You made lots of mistakes. Although you got warnings. You know too much, way too much."

Dino felt the sweat trickling down his forehead. His mind had vacillated between hope and despair, but it looked as if Goodlette was capable of doing anything without remorse. If these brutal beasts eliminated everyone who stood in their way, they wouldn't hesitate to kill him too. It was true that he knew too much. Why would Goodlette tell him all these explosive details if he didn't plan to kill him? Dino felt the hair on his forearms rising.

As if Goodlette had been reading his mind, he said, "I assume you realize that we can't just let you walk away, Dino. Not now, after you know everything."

"Why not?" Dino said. "The police know the truth behind your deceptive practices. They're on their way. Give it up, Jason. Game's over."

As if trying to moderate an intemperate reaction, Goodlette squeezed the edge of the table with both hands and took a couple of deep breaths. He gazed at Dino with a piercing look. "You know what I'm beginning to think, Dino? That you're bluffing." He raised his voice. "You must be scared to death."

These psychological games were gradually wearing down Dino's resistance. He suddenly felt exhausted. He couldn't think of any way to outwit Goodlette.

The bodyguard entered the room and handed Goodlette a cell phone, pointing to the screen. Goodlette glanced at it, smirked, and stretched out his arm across the table for Dino to see the picture. "Have a look," he said. "There she is. Happy as can be."

Dino got to his feet and leaned forward. He stared at Mia, who had a sulky expression on her face. She was dressed in a triple-color-striped, short-sleeved dress and wore a barrette with smiling ladybugs clipped to one side of her blonde hair. He could tell that she didn't feel at ease, and he could see from her eyes that she had been crying. The snapshot was taken outdoors, on a dusty, unpaved, small road, with shrubs and tall grass in the background. It could have been anywhere in Florida.

Goodlette retracted his arm. "Wait," he said, blowing up the picture with two fingers. He stretched out his arm again. "Watch carefully."

The girl held a folded newspaper in her left hand, probably *Gator News Today*. The page facing the photographer was the weather forecast. It showed a row of cartoons with a yellow sun, black clouds, lightning, and raindrops. "*Today's Weather*," the headline read. Today's date.

"I can't read it... can you make it bigger?"

Goodlette zoomed in and again held the phone under Dino's nose.

Dino could clearly see her little hand holding the paper, and he had no problem reading the date. But he was much more interested in seeing what she was doing with her right hand.

Mia was holding a little plush toy in her hand, a cute ochre-colored bird with long legs, a long gray neck, a long, pointed bill, and, most conspicuously, a shiny red forehead that looked like a cap. The girl was stretching out her right hand a bit, as if trying to show the cuddly toy to whoever might look at this picture.

Dino wrapped his head around what he was seeing. *They sell those plush toys at the gift shop at Corkscrew Swamp Sanctuary Visitor Center.* There was no doubt about it.

It was Sandy, the Sandhill Crane, and Mia sending an encoded message.

67

DINO

They had shown him proof that they'd sent the pic to Cat's cell. This was hopefully a big enough trigger for her to activate plan B, as they'd discussed earlier. Cat had Inspector Griffin's contact details, and she would get in touch with him immediately. The cops would identify the exact location where Goodlette's thugs kept Mia and be on their way soon.

The only problem was that if Goodlette found out that a Southwest Florida police squad, armed to the teeth, was zooming in on him and his gang, he would immediately put the kibosh on the deal that he'd made with Dino and he, Dino, would be left to Jason Goodlette's mercy.

Dino's heart raced, he felt overwhelmed by an increasing dizziness. He was screwed. In all likelihood, he had two options for staying alive: playing for time or escape. The chance of either of these tactical steps succeeding was minimal. In fact, next to naught.

"The cops have had you in their sights all the time," Goodlette said. "I know this from reliable sources. They think you have something to do with the proliferation of some of the opioids in Southwest Florida. They don't have enough evidence to arrest you, but they are keeping tabs on you." He paused to let the words sink in. "Don't look so appalled, Dino. You know this is true."

Dino's bullshit gauge spiked. *That's ridiculous.* Nice diversionary step, but it won't work.

"So, I guess, since you don't need me anymore, I'm allowed to vamoose?"

Goodlette produced a contemptuous smile. "Very funny.

You haven't changed a bit, Dino. You're still the same schmuck I hired a while back. Get real. Time's running out. I have a plane to catch." He glanced at his golden watch. "I'm truly sorry it had to go this far, but it's your own fault. You've been sticking your nose too deep into our affairs. You have maneuvered yourself into this dead end. Sad that you'll end this way, but—you don't leave us any choice."

"What do you mean, end this way..." Dino said, his voice cracking. His mouth felt dry.

"We'll give you a little taste of Red-O. I'm sure you'll like it. And when the cops find you, they'll think it is another one of those opioid OD cases, just one in a long series of fatal ODs. We'll be long gone by then."

Dino's panic reached a new level. He looked around. There was no way he could escape from this room. He was clearly outnumbered. There were people in other parts of the house, maybe even outside. His chances of survival were close to zero. Of course, they had taken his gun and his cell phone. He thought of Cat...

Goodlette glanced at his watch again. Then he turned to the other man in the room and said something in Spanish. Dino didn't understand everything, but he could distinguish a few fragments; *tarde*, *llame*, and *aeropuerto*. Goodlette was late, and it was about a phone call and the airport. He had mentioned before that he had booked a flight.

Now or never. If someone is under stress, then they are more prone to make mistakes, especially when they aren't prepared for an unexpected situation.

"Going on a nice vacation, Jason?"

Goodlette didn't answer. He tugged on the goon's sleeve and gestured for him to get closer to Goodlette's face. He whispered something in the man's ear, pointing to Dino. This could only mean a horrible thing.

The goon nodded and left the room.

"Oh, one more thing I always wanted to mention," Dino

said. "I'm deeply grateful for what you did for me, Jason. Writing that strong recommendation for me. I'd never gotten my dream job at LCH without you." Dino shot him a quick glance. "But—why did you do it? I know you're a good person and a nice guy, but why?"

"I wanted to get you out of the way. I figured if you got a new, demanding job, you'd be so busy that you'd forget about what happened. You wouldn't have time to poke around in my business, search for hidden opioids in plants, and maybe find out things that you shouldn't. I guess I got it all wrong. Your tenacity is boundless."

Dino's shirt was sticking to his body, his hands trembling, his mind spinning. He needed to play for time.

"Was it you who suggested to Susan Farewell that the strange opioid-like symptoms could be due to pesticide residue?" Dino probed.

"Of course," Goodlette said, "to distract from the real facts."

So Goodlette had been the mysterious source of fake news. His outrage, a long time ago, had been fake. Dino's pulse was racing. Any moment now that gorilla would come back with a syringe and...

"Look, Jason," Dino said, holding on to the last glimmer of hope. "I'll make you an offer. I'm in deep mire, but you're also up shit creek without a paddle. Here is my offer: We team up. I get into your boat. I'll be on your side. We'll be a great team. I have a lot of knowledge in..." Dino's speech got weaker and slower as he spoke about his wish to become a renegade, until he stopped in mid-sentence.

"Yeah, right," Jason said in a languid tone. "Dino joins the mob."

The door flung open and the goon stepped back into the room. He nodded and said something to Goodlette. *Everglades Airways* was the only thing Dino understood.

Then the guy looked across the table, directly at Dino.

Dino's blood froze. *Red-O* was the only other word he was able to pick up, but it was enough.

68

SAMANTA

Samanta Martinez parked her Hyundai in the visitor parking lot at the Corkscrew Swamp Sanctuary. The park wouldn't close until later in the afternoon, so her blue vehicle blended in nicely with the other cars. It would be too obvious if she left it on the rural access road or one of its narrow side roads.

Dressed in camouflage pants, a matching long-sleeved shirt, and a camo cap, all purchased at Walmart, Samanta sat on the driver's seat, her legs stretched out across the open door, as she fought to get her waterproof combat boots on. She stood and checked all the pockets one more time, then zipped them up. She put her hand on the hidden holster and adjusted it a bit. Maybe she had overdone things by dressing up like this, all Rambo-style, but who knew where this could lead.

Samanta knew that a specially trained squad of the Florida State Police would soon be zeroing in on the house where the kidnapped girl was being held. It would probably be only a matter of hours until the kid was freed. While rescuing the girl was no doubt the most important mission, she had other plans for herself.

During her out-of-town meeting with a special DEA task force during the recent long weekend that she had billed as a scientific convention in Chicago, they had developed the necessary tactical steps in their long-term strategy to bust the Southwest Florida opioid ring, the Red-O mafia, as they called it. Her duty was to focus on Clayton Harrod and Dino Stampa.

She had been following Dino for the past several days. Not

in person, but thanks to the tracking devices she and her colleagues had planted in Dino's house, on his car, and even in some of his clothes, she always knew where he was. They had also secured several items that could be used as evidence later, like the transgenic tomato plants on Dino's lanai—how stupid to put them right there in plain sight—and some samples from his lab.

She took another swig of water and tossed the empty bottle on the back seat, then locked the car. Ready. Showtime.

She knew where Dino was. She suspected, but wasn't totally sure, that he was with Clayton Harrod, that bastard. Who else might be in that old house that they obviously used as some sort of a makeshift headquarters?

She felt unflustered and confident about fulfilling her mission. It would be fast, and it would be easy. Harrod and Stampa were scientists, not undercover agents like she was. They were smart, if not highly intelligent, but they were slow and clumsy, if not clutzy, inexperienced, top-heavy, and, basically harmless.

The situation was, however, compounded by the fact that she liked Dino. He had a good sense of humor and was quick-witted, well-educated, and civilized, although a bit arrogant at times. It had been a dangerous tightrope act these past weeks.

Samanta walked back along the access road, always careful to take cover so as not to be spotted by anyone in the scattered homes in the neighborhood. She walked either close to the trees and shrubs, or, for short distances, through the dense grassland. She had to duck down and walk along the bank of a creek for a few hundred yards.

She could easily have been mistaken for a birdwatcher, especially as she used her field glasses to observe the one particular bungalow she was interested in. On her way, a great blue heron squawked loudly, then made a standing jump, sailing away in protest as she had apparently invaded his space.

Samanta walked up closer to the house, making sure she maintained sufficient cover from the shrubs. What she saw was the backside of the house. Nothing suspicious, but in all likelihood, Dino was inside.

She walked slowly around the house, pausing behind a tree to reassess the situation. She was now about thirty feet from the driveway and the front entrance. A black, full-sized sedan was parked at the carport. It wasn't Dino's car, but there was no doubt that the second car, a gray Nissan, sitting askew on the driveway, was Harrod's.

Harrod was here. And at least one other person. No sign of Dino so far. She scanned the shabby, neglected house with her field glasses. All the blinds were down, and she couldn't see anything inside.

She focused her attention on the front door as a sturdy young man in a black T-shirt stepped outside. He could be Hispanic, but it was hard to tell from that distance. He was followed by a tall, broad-shouldered, barrel-chested man, dressed in a white shirt, sunglasses hiding his eyes. The older man heaved a carry-on bag into the trunk and got in on the passenger side, while his younger, darker complexed companion walked around the car and sat down on the driver's side. They drove slowly around the gray Nissan and down the narrow, unpaved road that connected the scattered houses with the main access road leading to Corkscrew Swamp.

Samanta sagged with relief for a moment, but then the tension returned. How many more people were in the house? No way she could sandbag all four, if not more, of them. Now, if she were lucky, there would only be two, pushovers both. Harrod, who was easy prey, and Dino, who would be so surprised to see her that she could overpower him. For a moment she weighed the idea of calling for backup, but then she abandoned it. It was too late, and the core of the available police force would be concentrating on moving in on the kidnappers and freeing the little girl.

She took a deep breath and ran toward the house, pressing her body against the exterior wall when she got there. She waited a few seconds for her heavy breathing to subside as she wiped away the sweat dripping from her forehead and eyebrows. The sun was no longer pounding down as it had earlier in the day, but the air was still steamy. She reached for her handgun and, holding it with both hands, muzzle pointing up, she tiptoed along the wall, making sure to duck down when she passed a window.

Samanta felt her throbbing pulse as another shot of adrenaline rushed through her body. It was foolish to try to accomplish this mission on her own. She would call the police as soon as she had Harrod and Dino, but nothing could hold her back now.

She'd decided to go for the front door. She could hide in the entrance hall, provided the front door didn't open right into the living room. Samanta took a deep breath and slowly turned the doorknob… it was unlocked. She opened the door a tiny crack and listened. Muffled voices in the background, one of them unmistakably Dino's. The other one was too low to distinguish anything specific. She slipped through the crack in the door and tiptoed along the wall.

"He tried to kill me," she heard Dino scream.

"You bastard—you're gonna pay for it." That was the other voice, and it belonged to Harrod.

Samanta booted the door with a heavy kick and jumped across the threshold. "Freeze!" she shouted.

What she saw took her a second to sort out. Dino was kneeling next to a man who was lying on his back, not moving, his arms spread wide apart. Dino held up his hands in defense. Harrod stood with his back to the opposite wall, aiming a handgun at Dino.

Her arms whirled around, and she focused on Harrod.

"Drop the gun, Clayton," she hissed. "Now. Or I'll shoot you."

Harrod looked at her with wide eyes, mouth gaping. "Samanta," he said with a fear-hoarsened voice. His hands were trembling. It looked as if she was the last person he was expecting. Instead of dropping the gun, Harrod slowly swayed his arm, pointing his shaking pistol at Samanta.

"Drop it!" Samanta yelled. She could see that Harrod acted indecisively, that he most probably didn't know exactly what to do. He didn't seem to be accustomed to using handguns. But he was also a dangerous, crazy guy.

Within a moment, an ugly grimace overtook Harrod's baffled face. "You bitch," he snarled. He stretched out his arm, cocked his head, and tried to focus the muzzle on Samanta's chest.

She had no choice but to pull the trigger.

69

CAT

Cat's heart was pounding as she answered the phone. She just knew that this must be either very good news... or very bad news.

She had been unable to reach Dino. He didn't pick up his cell, and he was not at his office. Someone from the hospital had told her that they had been trying to find him too, but that he'd disappeared. Cat could care less about the blown-off executive meeting at LCH. She wanted to be with her man, now, because the kidnappers would contact him again, and then—

"Hello," Cat said, her eyes welling up.

"Catherine Gillespie? This is Detective Roberson." He paused, waiting for an answer. "Hello, you still there?"

"It's me. What's happened to Dino?"

"I'm not calling about Mr. Stampa, ma'am. It's about Mia."

Cat's heart skipped a beat or two. She sank down in a chair. Her head was spinning. All her weariness came down on her in this moment. She swallowed.

"What..." she started, then her sobs drowned out her words.

"Ms. Gillespie," Roberson said. "Listen. We found your daughter. She is safe and in our hands. She's fine and unharmed. It's over. We will—"

Cat didn't hear the rest. She had a dry feeling in her mouth, and her ears started to ring. The phone, the table, everything started to swim, and her world drowned in a vortex of darkness.

70

DINO

Dino ran.

His ears were still ringing from the gunshot Samanta had fired. But he had only one thought—run for his life and escape, then get in touch with Mia's kidnappers.

When Harrod collapsed, cursing, holding his bloodstained right arm with his opposite hand, Dino knew that Sam had just put Harrod *hors de combat* rather than tried to kill him. He was temporarily out of action. When she moved toward Harrod, snapping the handgun he had dropped on the floor and checking his wound, Dino jumped to his feet. As Samanta knelt by the side of the unconscious goon, staring at the syringe—the needle still sticking in his neck, seemingly oblivious to everything and everyone around her, he had seized his chance and fled through the back door.

Dino still couldn't fully understand how he had been capable of prying the syringe away from the man who had tried to give him a fatal shot. Mortal fear, probably. He couldn't recap exactly how he had turned the syringe around and landed the needle in the man's neck. He didn't know what kind of poison the bad guys had drawn up into the syringe, but he assumed it was an opioid. Harrod, who had initially observed the scene with a look of utter bewilderment, woke up from his dreaming and, apparently, decided to stick a gun in Dino's face. Then, out of nowhere, Samanta had appeared... Weird, but somehow Dino was free.

He had no idea where exactly he was, but he knew he was close to Corkscrew Swamp Sanctuary. He had no phone and no car. He could ask for help at the visitor center. The problem was how to find the entrance to the sanctuary.

Dino ran across the grassland and soon came to a narrow, dusty road. He followed it for a few yards, then stopped. It was possible that this road merged with a wider road that eventually led to the sanctuary—but it could equally well lead away from it. Not a single house was in sight, only tall grass and some trees in the distance.

He was the only human soul for as far as he could see.

There were no sounds of civilization. Only the soft swishing of the knee-deep grass in the breeze, the angry squawking of a flock of birds, and the humming of bugs.

Dino hit the side of his neck with the flat of his hand. These damn gnats were out to get him. He cursed as he tripped on a bulging root of a large tree and rolled his left ankle. A sharp pain shot through his foot and up his leg.

He turned around, checking the position of the sun. It was late afternoon, so he guessed that the somewhat denser forest that lay ahead would be north, which meant that the sanctuary must be somewhere in that direction. He understood, with an ironic touch, why people felt desperate and said they couldn't survive without their most important body part—a smart phone. It would be so easy to use the compass and the map. And he could call Cat.

Dino realized, with a grim face, that it was not only impossible for him to make calls, he was also unable to take any calls. The kidnappers had announced they would call him this evening, and they had insisted that he follow their instructions. What would they do if, as they would certainly assume, he simply ignored their call?

He still couldn't fully believe that Goodlette was the mastermind behind this horrible abduction.

But Goodlette was gone. He had said he had a plane to catch. They had mentioned *Everglades Airways*. Of the four airports in the area, only the small Naples Municipal Airport offered chartered flights with Everglades Airways.

No doubt—Goodlette was heading for downtown Naples. To take off and save his bacon.

Cursing, Dino trudged through mud and waded through water at least a foot deep among the magnificent Cypress trees. Everything was wet, but he didn't care anymore. He had to find the boardwalk. Once he was safely on the boardwalk, all he needed to do was follow it and he would end up at the entrance to the sanctuary, where the parking lot was located. Where there were people. Human beings.

Walking through the swamp was not only dangerous but creepy. A snake slithered through the water near him. Was it a harmless water snake or a deadly moccasin? Dino had no clue, but he shuddered at the thought of it. His ankle hurt, but he had to stand it. The knees of the Cypress trees, projections from the root system sticking out into the air, looked to him like arms reaching up to grab him. It was getting dark, and he needed to get to the boardwalk before dusk. The mere thought of spending the night in this swamp raised his hackles.

Half an hour later, he thought he heard the faint sound of human voices. This could only mean one thing: the board-walk was close. He had lost all sense of direction; it could even be possible that he was going in circles. With the sun gone, hidden behind dark clouds, he had a hard time following a straight line. Then he saw it. About a hundred yards in front of him, the boardwalk with its planks and handrail, on stilts, winding its way across the swamp. It would be easy to climb up to the man-made, dry walkway. The problem was getting there.

A splash in the water startled him. He knew the swamp was infested with alligators. Corkscrew Swamp was a nature preserve, and this was their natural habitat. Except nature hadn't meant for visitors to go for a stroll in the swamp.

A few yards away in the smooth but now deeper water,

Dino spied rapidly expanding concentric ripples—a jumping fish, probably, or something that fell from a tree. Nothing to be concerned about. He continued sloshing through the water toward the salvation of the boardwalk. What looked like a thick log with deeply furrowed bark drifted in the water across a small flotilla of aquatic plants. It was only when the gentle V-shaped wakes and the prow slowly approached him that Dino's instincts kicked in, rooting him to the spot. He caught sight of the nostrils and the protruding yellow-rimmed eyes and knew instantly that the ten-foot log he had spotted was a gator.

He reached for a heavy, dead branch that had fallen from a tree and thwacked it on the water's surface, as far away as possible from where he stood.

The rigid critter shifted its track slightly to the left and continued to glide silently through the water. Dino slung the branch away from him. It landed in the water with a splash—and in the blink of an eye the water surface exploded as the languid log transformed into a torpedo, bolting for its prey, all snapping jaws and lashing tail. Dino stumbled and fell in his haste to get away from the gator. With his head turned to keep an eye on the gator, he struggled to his feet and strode as fast as he could across the sandy bottom in the direction of the boardwalk. The gator did not bother to follow Dino. The gator, an ambush predator, was not interested in the relentless pursuit of its prey.

Finally, Dino reached the boardwalk and pulled himself up over the railing, sprawling on the wooden planks in exhaustion. The swamp trek had been terrifying, especially the final leg of his journey.

Reflecting on his adventure once he was on dry land, Dino had to admit that the gator had actually been smaller than ten feet. Quite a bit smaller.

71

SOMPY

Somporn Wattanapanit wondered where everybody was on this late Tuesday afternoon. Samanta was not in, and Clayton Harrod was away from the office too. Did they know that it was close to the moment when the trap would snap shut? But then, why would they have even the faintest idea that something was going to happen? He and Kuzminski had been extremely careful not to give away anything that would cause suspicion.

The only person he could not bring in on the operation was Stampa, the snoop from LCH, who seemed to have a special relationship with Samanta Martinez. He had been openly sniffing around lately. It had been a bit too obvious that he was up to something. Was he a cop? Or was he cooperating with the others?

Sompy shook his head and blocked any suspicious thoughts from his mind. They needed to act quickly, as planned. They had enough evidence, and they needed to clamp down. He reached for his office phone and called Taneesha, the CEO's new assistant.

"Yes, Mr. Kuzminski is in," Taneesha said, "and yes, he has time to see you. He's expecting you in ten minutes."

***

"Sompy," Kuzminski said, and patted the visitor jovially on the shoulder. "Come on in, have a seat." He went around Sompy with his shuffling gait and peeked out the door.

"No visitors, no calls. For half an hour," he said.

287

Taneesha understood. "I won't disturb you."

Kuzminski carefully closed the door and sat in his executive chair behind the massive desk.

"So, seems like we're ready to make out move. We're ready, and our friends are in grid position."

"Except Harrod is gone. He didn't show up in the lab today. His office is locked—"

"Don't worry, Sompy," Kuzminski said, "he's probably busy somewhere." He thumbed down the *events* list on his smart phone calendar. "We have scheduled a meeting with him for tomorrow morning at ten. Why don't you join us? You may want to come a few minutes early."

He leaned back and laughed. "Let's ask everybody to come to the party."

"And we'll be the party poopers."

"You bet," Kuzminski said.

The phone on his desk buzzed and the green light flashed. Kuzminski gazed at it, inhaled as if to protest, then decided to ignore it.

A moment later, there was a shy knock on the door. Taneesha's head appeared in the crack.

"Didn't I tell you to leave us alone?" Kuzminski said, demonstratively upset.

"Mr. Kuzminski, it's—"

"Can't this wait? Is it so important?"

"Yes," Taneesha said. "The police are here. They want to talk to you. Now." She showed two men in, both dressed in civilian clothes.

Kuzminski stared at the badge that the big man who walked into his office flashed at him.

"Detective Griffin, Collier County Sheriff, Narcotics," the guy said with a stern face. His navy-blue tie was loosened, his collar unbuttoned. "And this..." Griffin pointed to his colleague, "is Inspector Acardi, Homicide."

"Homicide..." Sompy whispered, more to himself than anyone.

72

DINO

A blue Hyundai was the lone vehicle parked in one entire section of the Corkscrew Sanctuary parking lot. It was hard to miss. Dino walked around the trunk and spotted the signature bumpersticker. *I ♥ ORGANIC TOMS*. Samanta's car.

He still wondered why she had tried to keep him in check. Did she really believe he would have buddied up with Harrod and the others?

Across the trees, in a more remote section of the lot, he saw a blue-red-white strobe light flashing against the fall of darkness. Police—not exactly what he needed. If the cops were really after him, it would take forever for him to convince them that he was innocent, and by the time they believed him, Goodlette would be miles away, if not in the air already, heading toward a safe haven.

What could he do in this awkward situation? Wait until a car showed up at the sanctuary, and ask the driver if he'd mind giving Dino a ride to the Naples Airport? Dino looked as if he'd been tarred and feathered, except the tar was mud and the feathers were leaves and dirt and plant parts. Water dripped from his pants into his shoes. He wondered what kind of bugs and leeches were likely crawling around in his underpants—but he would have to leave that for later.

Time was running out.

"Need a ride, Dino?" a familiar voice said out of nowhere. A woman's voice.

Dino cringed, then turned around. A silhouette about twenty yards away stood out against the red evening sky.

Samanta.

"Quite a bit of a detour," she said. "You could've come with me on the road, but you chose to take that devious route through the swamp. Why work smart when you can work hard, right?"

Dino was stunned. As far as he could see against the back-light, Samanta was not pointing a gun at him. She just stood there, legs apart, hands on her hips. His first instinct was to run, to dive away somewhere, hide... He took a few strides, but his ankle hurt so much that he stopped. She would no doubt outrun him. He held up his hands in defeat.

"I'm unarmed. Please, be reasonable, Sam."

Samanta took a few steps toward him. "Don't run, Dino. I won't harm you. I made a mistake, a big mistake. Everything has been turned upside down. It's a total clusterfuck."

Dino walked in her direction until he was only a few yards away.

"Samanta, please listen. I need your car. I'll explain once we're on the road. But I need to find Goodlette. He's on the run."

It was as if Dino had uttered the key word that opened the magic mountain.

***

They were scorching down I-75, southbound. Everybody, it seemed, was going over the speed limit, so they didn't stand out from the other drivers.

"Here's your cell," Samanta said, handing Dino his much-missed smart phone.

Dino grabbed it from her hand. "How considerate of you. Thank you. I'm no longer cut off from the world."

"Be glad they took it away from you. Just imagine—the phone would be worthless if you'd dropped it in the swamp," Samanta said.

Dino ignored her mock sneer. He checked the *recents* list;

there were several attempts from Cat, but no call from an unknown number. It looked as if the kidnappers hadn't tried to call him, although it was way past six, the time they had said they'd contact him again. Something was wrong.

Dino speed-dialed Cat. He shot Samanta a glance, then turned away from her, looking out the side window. Cat answered instantly.

"Dino! Where've you been?" Cat shouted. "I've tried to reach you all this time." He had expected her to sound depressed, but she seemed to be in an almost boisterous mood.

"You wouldn't believe what happened this afternoon," Dino said. "I was—"

Cat cut him short. "Dino—imagine... Mia has been released. She's free. And she's fine."

Dino swallowed and blinked away a gush of tears. "What? What are you saying? Where... where are you, and where is Mia?"

"We're at police headquarters in Naples. Everything's fine. Oh, Dino, I'm so happy..." Cat's voice choked with a mixture of joy and relief.

"How is she? She's all right?"

"Yes, yes, she's fine. Right now, she's undergoing a medical exam, but she's in excellent spirits. They will give us a ride home soon, I guess."

"What a brave girl," Dino uttered a big sigh of relief as he pressed his palm to his heart.

"Are you coming home too? Where the heck are you?"

"I'll be home in a little while. I'm on the interstate right now with... uh... a policewoman. Everything's fine, but complicated. Will tell you the entire story when I'm home. Right now, it's a bit difficult."

"Understand, you can't talk," Cat said. "See you soon. Love you."

"Love you too, Cat."

Dino finished the call and drummed his feet on the floor

of the car. His eyes drifted to the left. Samanta was looking straight ahead.

"So, I'm *a policewoman*, right? You're still afraid to tell her the truth?"

"She's free. Mia, our little girl is free," he said in a calm voice. He felt an increasing sense of happiness. Dino pumped his fist. His earlier fatigue was gone, and a new boost of energy had kicked in.

"To tell you the truth, Sam, I didn't believe it when the cops told me you were a DEA agent," Dino said.

"But you believe it now?"

"Absolutely. I had no clue. The entire time."

"And to tell you the truth, I didn't know at first exactly what your role was, Dino. You seemed harmless and innocent, but at times you acted so weird that I got suspicious."

"But you know now whose side I'm on? I hope you do. Gee, I almost got killed. First, that goon aimed a poison-filled syringe at me, then Harrod brandished a gun under my nose, then you barged in, adding to the general brouhaha. It's a miracle I got out alive."

"I know now," Samanta said tersely.

Dino figured that her scanty comments about his heroic escape were not a reflection of her being upset, but rather a result of her trying to concentrate on the crazy traffic and changing lanes constantly.

"Would you do me a favor and turn down the A/C a bit? I'm cold," Dino said. "After all, I waded through a swamp. I'm soaked." He tugged on his shirt and pants with a disgusted look.

"You're shivering. I could stop somewhere and you could—"

"Forget it, Sam. I can change my clothes later. We have to catch Goodlette first."

They continued for a few miles without saying much, both lost in thought.

"You sure the cops will be there?"

"Dino, you've asked me that three times. The answer is *yes*. They will wait for us at the entrance to the terminal. Discreetly, without raising any suspicion."

"I still don't understand why they can't just shut down the airport and catch the guy."

"I told you why. They cannot shut down an airport, even a small one, just because one person—you—surmises that, maybe, a criminal may board a plane, maybe at this airport, maybe at another one. They don't even have an arrest warrant."

Dino gave an angry snort. "Goodlette is not just a criminal. He's probably the head of a large drug gang. The *honcho*. Who, as a side job, directs a bioanalytical company in Fort Myers. A company that I happen to know quite well."

Samanta just pursed her lips and shifted to the right lane.

"Take the next exit onto Golden Gate Parkway," Dino said, pointing to the large sign ahead.

"If you hadn't acted in such a stupid way, we could've worked together. From the beginning. It would've been so much easier," Samanta said. "But, since I didn't know for sure who you really were, I had no choice but to keep my real identity hidden."

"Come on," Dino said. "I'm not such a mystery man. Cat keeps telling me that I'm so transparent and so predictable. Don't pretend you didn't know." He shook his head. "There was no need to sic the cops on me, really."

A few minutes later, she swerved onto Airport Pulling Road, then made a right turn onto North. They had finally arrived at Terminal Drive.

WELCOME TO NAPLES MUNICIPAL AIRPORT, the sign read.

Welcome to Showdown City, Jason.

73

GOODLETTE

"To Nassau, sir?" the young ticket agent at the check-in desk asked, but he was not really waiting for an answer. He was tapping away on his keyboard.

"Yes. Is the flight on time?" Goodlette asked.

"It should be. There is a storm front coming in later, but I think we should get you out of here before the thunderstorm closes in." He smiled and closed his eyelids slowly before opening them again in slow motion, like a sleepy owl, reassuring the passenger that everything was just fine.

"Checking any bags?"

"No, just have a carry-on."

"You may want to check it, sir. There isn't much room on that plane."

"I'd rather hold on to it," Goodlette said, pressing the telescoping pull handle as if someone might try to take it away from him. "I'll hold onto it."

The agent threw an appraising glimpse at the bag and nodded. "Okey-dokey, no prob. Traveling light tonight?"

"Uh-huh."

"Let's see, about your seat..." He was drumming his fingers on the desk. "The Bahamas are nice. A short vacation, I guess?" He pointed again at the small, black carry-on.

Goodlette hated it when employees commented on his trips or his baggage. Especially when he was under time pressure. And tonight, he felt enormous pressure. He needed to get away, before it was too late. He nodded.

"Here we go," the agent said. "Returning on... Friday. Already.

Gee, that's a very short vacation." The printer spit out his boarding pass.

"It's a business trip," Goodlette muttered, hoping that the idiot would stop with the small talk. He wouldn't need his return ticket, though, but he had assumed it would raise suspicion if he bought only a one-way ticket.

The ticket agent smiled from ear to ear. "You're all set, Mr. Henderson. And thank you for flying Everglades Airways."

Goodlette grabbed his passport and boarding pass and walked away from the check-in counter. He scanned the hall; not many people around. Just a handful, mostly airport employees, and a few passengers, businessmen like him.

He wiped the pearls of perspiration from his forehead with the back of his hand. This damn blond wig was making him sweat like a pig, and it itched. So did the fake, red-blond goatee. He pushed the thick-rimmed glasses up on his nose. Getting out of the country wasn't a big problem. Coming back would be different—but he didn't intend to return. Getting to the Bahamas was his first goal. Then he would catch a flight to Recife. How long he would stay in Brazil would depend on a number of variables... but he would decide that later.

For now, he just needed to board that plane and leave.

The trickiest part was right ahead of him. After that, things would be a breeze. He wheeled his carry-on toward the security check area and handed his passport and boarding pass to the officer, trying to affect a poker face. His heart was racing, but he hoped the guy wouldn't notice.

The officer studied the passport issued to one Ronald Henderson, looked Goodlette right in the eye, studied the date, flight number, and scribbled something on the boarding pass.

The security officer handed Goodlette the documents. "Have a safe trip," he said, his eyes already on the next passenger in line.

Goodlette threw his loafers, belt, and light jacket in one of the plastic boxes, heaved the carry-on onto the conveyer belt, and waited for the green light. An officer waved him through the scanner. Almost done.

As he stood on the receiving end of the conveyer belt, barefoot, holding on to his pants that had already slipped a few inches down on his belly, it occurred to him that he had forgotten to take his laptop out of the bag. He glanced at the young man and the more senior woman who were scrutinizing the contents of his bag on the screen. Why did it take them such a long time? Goodlette tried to put on a nonchalant air. He knew that the border security officers were trying to spot individuals who exhibited abnormal behavior, such as acting nervously, or people constantly looking over their shoulder. *I'm as cool as a cucumber*, he told himself. *I have nothing to hide. This is so boring.*

The young officer pointed with his gloved hand to the screen. They were whispering something. More staring. The woman glanced at Goodlette, then at the screen.

The sweat was trickling down Goodlette's forehead and nose. As he studied the conveyer belt in front of him, a few drops splashed on the black plastic.

The woman motioned for him to step over to a small bench. "That your bag?" she asked.

"Correct," Goodlette said. "Correct."

She lifted the bag onto the bench. "Please open the bag for us, sir," she said in a calm voice.

Goodlette turned the safety lock until he had the right combination. He zipped open the main compartment.

"Laptops must go separately," she snapped. "Please open your computer."

Goodlette flipped the top open and waited.

"Open it," the woman said rather impatiently.

"Oh, you mean start it up? No problem. No problem." Goodlette punched in his password to unlock the desktop, glancing left and right out of the corner of his eyes, praying for more privacy. He was sweating profusely now.

The young officer had arrived too. He rummaged through the shirts and underwear with his blue gloves, taking out a cell phone, a bunch of cables, and what seemed like other electronic devices, and putting everything separately on the bench.

There it was—the external hard drive with all the details. The blueprint. The most precious item in his baggage, but also the most explosive one.

"And what is this?" The woman took a brown paper bag, removed from it a double plastic bag that was tied in a knot, and held it under Goodlette's nose.

"Tomatoes," Goodlette said calmly. "Tomatoes," he repeated, as if it were the most common item people took on a vacation to the Bahamas.

"Small snack for the flight, huh?" she said. "Please open the plastic bag."

Goodlette's panic level ratcheted up a notch.

74

DINO

"Sorry, but we don't give out information on our passengers," said the Everglades Airways agent behind the check-in counter. He sounded peremptory.

Samanta rolled her eyes. She leaned forward, invading the man's space. "I'm from the DEA, Drug Enforcement Agency," she hissed. In her outfit, she looked more like a deer hunter than an agent.

"That's true," Dino threw in. He leaned on the counter with both arms. "And I'm—"

Samanta grabbed Dino's left arm with a firm grip and stopped him short. "Don't say another word," she commanded. "Leave it to me."

She's probably right, he thought. His hair spiked wildly in all directions, his face was covered with mud, and his clothes were still wet and dirty. He knew that there was no time to explain to the airline people what they wanted.

Samanta waved frantically across the hall until a man in a white shirt and a striped tie came running toward them, coming to help.

"Police," he said sharply, flashing his badge at the agent. "We need to see the passenger list for the Bahamas flight. It's an emergency."

"One moment," the ticket agent punched in a number on his cell. "Everglades check-in. It's important." Seconds later an airport security man appeared from nowhere, striding toward the group.

Both Samanta and the deputy county sheriff went down the printed short list of passengers that the airline official had handed them.

"He's not listed," Samanta said. "Shit."

Dino pressed his lips together. This was the last airline they had checked. Minutes ago, they had gone through the same procedure with Gulf Coast Airlines and BusinessAir, the only other carriers offering flights tonight. All of them had told them the same thing. There was nobody named Jason Goodlette on any of these flights.

"He might have got through with a false passport," Samanta said. She turned to Dino. "Describe to the airline guy what Goodlette looks like."

Dino stepped up to the counter. "Tall, big man... dark hair, combed back... loud voice... what else... You recognize someone who just checked in?"

The agent seemed to reflect for a few moments, then he shook his head. "No, not really. We have a lot of tall, big men. But—no. Can't think of anyone."

"He might be in disguise," Samanta said to the cop. She turned to Dino. "You would be the only one to recognize Goodlette, even if he changed his physical appearance."

Dino had a wry smile on his face. His eyes were glowing. "I'd recognize that fucker in a split second from ten miles away. Even against the wind. I worked for him for years."

The other policeman held up his hand. "One moment," he said to Samanta, listening, then nodding. "Thanks," he said, and finished the call. "Negative. Fort Myers International as well as Punta Gorda. No one under that name. And there is no code-sharing flight with Everglades Airways from either airport."

"Dead end, I guess," Samanta said. "Shit, shit, shit." She turned to Dino again and gave him a hard look. "You sure he said *Everglades*? One hundred percent sure?"

"Not one hundred percent, but with almost absolute certainty."

The cop rolled his eyes. "Scientists," he mumbled.

75

GOODLETTE

Goodlette flopped down in his window seat in the first row. He took a deep breath and released the air slowly. It would only be a matter of minutes and they would be up in the air. *Adiós, Florida.*

It had been a close call. The security guys had peeked into some of his files on the laptop—he wondered whether they were actually authorized to do so, but he didn't care. He had nothing to hide on his desktop. The real hot stuff was on the external hard drive. Then they had snapped one of his Grand Captivas and cut it in two, and, of course, found nothing. Then they had inspected the other tomatoes but obviously found no signs that indicated tampering. No injection sites, nothing. They had even run them back through the X-ray machine and carefully studied them. He got them all back. How stupid did they think he was?

"Something to drink, sir?" a flight attendant asked.

"Sure. Champagne, please." Goodlette could relax now. Everything had been taken care of. His partners would erase the last traces before they went underground themselves. He had gotten rid of Dino Stampa—poor guy. He was probably lying on his back in the morgue with a tag on his big toe by now—but it was his own fault. Had he minded his own business, he would still be alive. Harrod would send him an update soon on how things had gone.

He peeked back over the backrest of his seat into the cabin. The small plane was not full; maybe twenty, twenty-five passengers.

The captain's voice crackled a warm welcome above

Goodlette's head and an announcement that they would be out of there shortly, before the approaching thunderstorm could delay their take-off. Everybody should relax, lean back, and enjoy the flight.

Goodlette looked up as the flight attendant closed all the overhead compartments. His precious tomato seeds were still there, intact. Packed in their natural packing material, the tomato. Goodlette rubbed his palms together. He would start a new business in South America. He would rake in the money and become a rich man in no time. He would buy a hacienda, maybe even a palace, and he would have an armada of cars, servants, and bodyguards. He knew how to spend his bucks.

The captain's call to the cabin crew to prepare for take-off jolted him back to reality. The smiling flight attendant locked the door, stood in the aisle and gave the thumbs-up sign. Then she sat down and fastened her seat belt.

Goodlette checked his seat belt and pushed the knob on his armrest. He heard the jet propulsion engines slowly warm up and gain power. He realized that they would be taxiing toward the runway shortly.

He closed his eyes and waited. Life was not so bad after all.

Something crackled in the loudspeakers overhead, but he didn't understand anything in the general hubbub. He waited. He knew that once they were off the ground, he would be safe.

Goodlette opened his eyes. The pilot had cut back the engines and the only sound was the air condition set to max. It was still way too hot and stuffy on this plane.

The captain's voice again. "An urgent last-minute matter." They would have to open the door again for a moment. No worries. They would be in the air shortly.

Goodlette watched as the flight attendant fumbled with the door handle. He hated passengers who were late. *Why can't they be on time, like everyone else?* he thought. Must be a fucking celebrity. He closed his eyes again.

76

DINO

The cop with the striped tie stepped in first, peering at the passengers from the front rows to the back.

Samanta came next. She knew from Dino's description what Goodlette looked like. She shook her head.

None of the passengers spoke a word. They all stared at the front entrance, where the apparent latecomers talked to each other in soft voices. Meanwhile the pilot had opened the cockpit door and joined them. Samanta said something to the cop and waved Dino in.

Dino took a few steps so that he had a full view down the aisle. He tried to get the general picture, then slowly walked from row to row, looking left and right, studying the faces of the passengers.

"What's going on?" a middle-aged man asked. "Is the take-off delayed?"

"Looking for someone?" a young woman asked.

Dino ignored the comments. He joined the others.

Then he saw the big guy in the first row, in the window seat. He had a fuzzy blond mane of hair and a reddish mustache and goatee, as well as a pair of dark-rimmed glasses, all of which hid half of his face. Nothing unusual, nor especially conspicuous, but what struck Dino was the bulging eyes staring back at him. A deer-in-the headlights look. Frozen. Terrified. Panic-stricken, like a cornered animal.

"What the fuck... what the fuck?" the passenger said.

Dino launched into attack mode.

"That's him!" he yelled.

Both Samanta and the officer stepped forward, seemingly alarmed.

"No doubt. I'm positive that's him," Dino reiterated.

"Would you mind coming with us, please," the officer said quietly, assisting Goodlette out of his seat. "The less resistance you offer, the fewer problems you'll have."

"That your bag?" Samanta asked Goodlette, pointing to the black carry-on in the overhead compartment. She pushed his hand away. "No problem. I'll carry it."

"Growing a beard, Jason?" Dino said, grinning broadly. "You've changed beyond recognition, but goatees are so out these days." Then he turned around. "Sorry for the ballyhoo, folks," he shouted down the aisle. "Have a nice flight."

The flight attendant threw up her hands.

Dino felt a firm grip on his shoulder. It was the captain turning him around and gently but resolutely pushing him toward the exit.

***

The next morning, Dino's temples throbbed, his head still a humming beehive. He felt slightly feverish and the painkiller hadn't helped much.

During the night he'd been overwhelmed by a roller-coaster of feelings. First, the immense relief of having caught Goodlette after a tense and stressful evening, then the over-powering joy of being reunited with Cat and Mia, then a pang of horror as he recapped what had happened over the past days and weeks, and finally, the creeping fear that things might not yet be finished. Maybe some members of the gang were still out there looking for him, seeking revenge. He had fallen into a deep sleep initially, but then awakened around three in the morning—restless, fearful, anxious about what was coming next.

The police had summoned him to attend a meeting at

GR&S the following morning, set for nine o'clock. They wanted everyone involved to be there. He assumed there would be a lot of questions. Although he dreaded these interrogations, he hoped to gain clarity on many points that were still a mystery to him.

The next morning, on his way to Sementina Springs, Dino stopped at Panera's for a strong cup of coffee. While he sipped his double espresso, he received a text message from Nate Herring at LCH.

What's going on? Where R U? Call me ASAP.

Dino shrugged. He could picture the distinguished CMO fuming with rage. This time, Dino had a rock-solid excuse for his long, unscheduled absence from work. Much better than flimsy dental appointments. The county sheriff would explain things to hospital management, and he, Dino, would probably end up a hero. Dino decided to call Nate after the meeting. Maybe Detective Griffin could corroborate his explanations.

He finished his coffee in one gulp and grimaced. His stomach hurt. Before he could put the cup on the table, a coughing fit seized him. He wondered if he had choked on the coffee, but feared it might be the beginning of bronchitis.

He fished for his cell and texted a reply to Nate.

Have to testify w/ Collier County police in big opioid drug investigation. Will call you this PM—Dino

Dino smiled. He had assumed an air of importance. No longer a suspect, he was now a state's witness, a key witness, as an opioid expert.

77

DINO

Detective Morgan Griffin sat at the top of the conference table, the chairman's territory usually occupied by Kuzminski. Inspector Acardi was to his left, Detective Roberson to his right.

I know half of the cop squad in Southwest Florida, Dino thought as he looked at the familiar faces.

Kuzminski sat at the broad side of the long table, the window to his back. He was flanked by Taneesha, his secretary, and Somporn Wattanapanit. *Why are they still here, walking around free?* Dino mused. He glanced at the door; a police officer in uniform stood next to the exit, arms crossed. He seemed to be keeping tabs on the whole party. Nobody would be able to escape easily.

Samanta had taken a seat next to Dino. Several other people, likely senior GR&S managers Dino did not recognize, were present too.

"Where's Harrod?" Dino whispered to Samanta. "Don't see him."

Instead of an answer, she gave him a dig with her elbow.

Dino reached for the water bottle and the glass in front of him. He gazed at Samanta, raised his eyebrows, and held up the bottle. She shook her head. He poured himself a glass, drank all of it, and refilled it. He felt weak, hot, and dehydrated.

"Why don't we get started," Griffin said. He was obviously chairing the meeting. He looked down the table. "Thank you, Mr. Kuzminski, for letting us have this conference room for a temporary command center. Appreciate it. Thank you all," he looked into the audience, "for joining us this morning."

This looked almost like a formal business meeting to Dino. He assumed it would be an informal breaking-news info session.

Griffin cleared his throat. "Before we start, I would like to urge you to remember that everything we discuss here remains within these walls. Nothing leaks out, okay?" His piercing but friendly gray eyes shifted from one participant to the next. "I think we understand each other." Griffin patted his bald head. "There will be a press communiqué later this afternoon, and tomorrow we'll hold a press conference. But more on that later.

"The facts. Jason Goodlette, CEO of Rainbow BioLabs in Fort Myers, was detained last night at Naples Municipal Airport while trying to leave the country on a jet headed to Nassau, Bahamas. He's been arrested for playing a key role in a major illegal drug ring in Southwest Florida. Goodlette is also suspected of being closely involved in a homicide case involving Dr. Andy Timberlake, and a violent armed assault on Miguel Castro from GR&S." Griffin glanced at Roberson and Acardi, who both nodded.

Dino leaned back and watched everyone around him. Those who were familiar with the facts had a grim or scornful look on their faces. They were nodding or silently staring at the table in front of them. In contrast, those for whom the news came as a surprise gazed at Griffin, mouths open, dazed looks on their faces. Kuzminski touched his parted lips with his fingers. Sompy jerked his head back. Dino wondered what these nonverbal expressions meant. How much did they know, or to what extent were they involved?

"First of all," Griffin continued, "I have to thank Mr. Kuzminski for collaborating with the DEA and for letting Samanta Martinez work at GR&S for a short period of time." Griffin extended his hand toward Samanta. "As some of you may not know yet, Martinez, which is obviously not her real name, is both a scientist and a special agent working for the DEA."

"What!" one of the managers yelled.

"You gotta be kidding," someone else said.

"Special Agent Martinez has done a tremendous job," Griffin continued. "And she has successfully completed her mission."

Dino turned his head. Samanta appeared to have slightly red ears, but maybe it was his imagination.

"And I learned a lot about tomato farming," she threw in, releasing the tension and defusing the shock. A few people laughed.

"The key figure here in this company," Griffin continued, "has been Clayton Harrod. He's under arrest, but currently he's at North Collier County Hospital for treatment of a nasty gunshot wound to the arm."

"Huh? Clayton?" someone said.

"No shit." The man next to him shook his head.

Dino ogled Samanta, trying not to make it too obvious that she could have anything to do with the shooting. Samanta kept a stony face.

"Harrod is a brilliant scientist," Griffin continued, "as you all know. He was maybe a bit too brilliant. Using the most modern techniques that are being applied to the genetic manipulation of plants—please correct me if I'm not accurate," he looked at Samanta and then at Kuzminski, "he implanted genetic information into tomatoes so that they... uh..." He looked to Samanta for help.

"He used a genetic technique to introduce a foreign gene into the genome of an organism—to wrangle in a gene that encodes for a short cyclic peptide, that is, a small protein. This peptide has an extremely high affinity for one of the opioid receptors, the so-called μ receptor—" she pronounced it *mew*, "and has similar effects as some of the other opiates and opioids. But—" Samanta raised an index finger and her voice, "this peptide that they call Red-O, because they expressed it in tomatoes, is extremely potent, very toxic, and highly addictive."

"Excuse my ignorance," Griffin interjected, "what do you mean, expressed it?"

"Oh, science slang, sorry. It means the foreign DNA piece was transplanted into a tomato, and, because the plant cannot recognize that this gene is not one of its own genes, starts to use the foreign blueprint and produces the foreign gene product, the opioid, in huge amounts. Their problem was the plants *overexpressed* the protein—made too much of that toxic stuff. Something went flooey with their plan."

"But what I don't get is this: how on earth can someone design a new chemical, a previously unknown small protein like Red-O, and know that it will have such a powerful action?"

"Excellent question," Samanta said, "but I have no clue. Probably by serendipity, or by screening thousands of synthesized products. Maybe even with the help of artificial intelligence, and 3-D molecular modeling. Certainly doesn't happen overnight, and would definitely need a team of skilled scientists and highly sophisticated technology. And a whole lot of luck."

Griffin smiled. "Thank you—even novices in science like me are beginning to understand it. Wow, complicated stuff." He turned serious again. "What Harrod and the people around him did with this new opioid—let's call it Red-O too—was to extract it from the tomatoes, a special variety of tomatoes, genetically altered, of course, which they termed Grand Captiva. Then they purified it. And sold it." Griffin stopped and let the words sink in.

"They not only sneaked Red-O onto the illegal drug market through a secret back door, right here in the Naples area, but they also shipped the new and unknown drug across the entire state of Florida, and across the country. Packing and camouflaging it was the easiest thing in the world—the drug was packed in its natural envelope, the tomatoes. Nobody would be suspicious. No raid by the DEA would detect it."

Silence filled the room.

So, I wasn't totally nuts, Dino thought. That was exactly what he had imagined. He glanced across the table. Kuzminski's eyes were glued to Griffin's lips.

Sompy moved in his chair. Eventually he got up, muttered a brief excuse, and walked around the table to the exit.

Dino cringed and sat up straight in his chair. The cop who stood by the door backed off a few steps and let Sompy quietly open the door and leave the room. Dino's hands moved in jerks. "But... he can't just..." he stammered, glaring at Griffin.

"Pardon me?" Griffin said, with an astonished face.

Dino figured the detectives knew what they were doing, having Sompy on their radar. If Sompy was one of the bad guys too, he couldn't get very far. Dino focused his attention back on Griffin.

"Now, here's how it all started," Griffin continued, flashing a glance at Dino. "Dr. Timberlake, famous immunologist, had an idea, a clever idea. In order to treat some of his cancer patients with a new remedy, uh..." His look implied, please help me again with the technical terms.

"Therapeutic antibodies," Dino said, "to target cancer cells. Antibodies are proteins, too, by the way."

"Thanks," Griffin said. "Their conventional production is expensive and complicated, I am told. So Dr. Timberlake had the idea that he could use..." Griffin consulted his notebook for the exact reference, "a new technique called PMP, plant-made pharmaceuticals. His plan was to insert the blueprint of the antibody protein into tomatoes and let them produce the foreign product that he would extract, purify, and use on his patients."

"A '*plantibody*,'" Dino said. "Pun intended. That's what it's called."

Someone chuckled.

Griffin took a sip of water from the bottle. "Problem was— he didn't know how to do it. So he was seeking collaboration. Someone who was familiar with the technique and who could help him. GR&S was not too far away—and the logical way was to contact Mr. Kuzminski."

Kuzminski nodded in agreement. "And I put him in touch with Clayton Harrod."

"Right," Griffin continued. "Unfortunately—unfortunately both for the drug gang and the late Dr. Timberlake—Timberlake found out what Harrod was doing in his spare time, mostly at night. He documented the evidence and, over time, put everything on an external hard disk. Photos he took, documents, pictures of Harrod in the lab, experimental procedures. He should have come forward with it and contacted us. But he didn't, for reasons we don't know, and probably never will. Unfortunately, he had to pay a high price for keeping his secret. He was murdered."

"Do you know who killed him?" someone interrupted.

"I'll elaborate on that in a minute," Detective Roberson said. Griffin nodded.

"But then things turned really ugly for the drug team."

Dino looked up. Griffin would probably mention him now and explain how he had screwed up everything by butting in, but Griffin talked about someone else.

"Castro. Miguel Castro. He inadvertently put his hands on the wrong tomatoes. The deadly ones. He had no clue, was just doing his job—picking up tomatoes from the GR&S warehouse and transporting them to local farmers markets to sell," Griffin said. "The bad guys wanted to prevent the gene-manipulated Grand Captiva tomato from getting out into the public—at all costs. They didn't realize that it was too late. Seven people lost their lives."

Others almost did, Dino thought.

He looked across the table.

Sompy's chair was still empty.

78

DINO

Half an hour later, Detective Griffin ended the first part of the meeting. He had provided a comprehensive update on the busting of the opioid drug ring as related to GR&S with everybody present in the room. Everyone except for Sompy. Dino felt that Griffin's summary was much more accurate and coherent than the scattered pieces of sensational information the media had disseminated in the past few days. Now, in the subsequent part, the detectives had informed the group that they wanted to talk to everyone individually.

Dino sat opposite Detective Griffin in a separate, smaller conference room.

"Can I get you something—water, coffee?"

Dino felt nervous and feverish. Drinking something would probably help him fight his pounding headache. "Coffee would be great, thanks."

Inspector Acardi left the room and came back with a steaming Styrofoam cup.

"Can I ask you something?" Dino ventured.

Griffin smiled. "Sure."

"I've been in the crosshairs of the police, right? What made you think I was involved in this whole thing? I mean, involved on the wrong side."

Griffin looked at Acardi, then set his eyes on Dino. "To be frank, we were quite puzzled by the way you acted. You had access to a number of different opioids. You were hospitalized—twice, independently—because of an apparent opioid intoxication. You established contact with GR&S under a flimsy pretext. Worse, you broke into their research building, and you stole plants. They could easily press charges against you, but I'm not sure they want to. You had links to some key figures involved—Castro, Wattanapanit, Harrod, and, importantly, Goodlette, the drug mafia don. We found samples of tomatoes containing the Red-O opioid in your possession. How could we not have become interested in your activities? But then, toward the end, it became clear that you were a harmless citizen, totally innocent. Even naïve."

A harmless citizen? At times Dino had felt like a hero, or a secret service agent on a special mission. Naïve? Was the inspector trying to put him down?

"One more question, Detective, if I may."

"Go ahead."

"My house was wiretapped. Cameras installed. Who did that?"

"Our people," Griffin said dryly. "DEA and County Police."

"Don't tell me your people stole the tomatoes off my lanai? And took away all the frozen samples in my lab freezer..."

"Yup. Those were our people, including Special Agent Martinez."

Dino tried to tamp down his rising anger. "Is that legal? I mean videotaping me in my underwear in my own house?"

Both Griffin and Acardi flashed Dino a smile. "Did you forget that we're talking about a major crime here?"

Acardi jumped in. "Several people were killed, dozens injured by the illegal drugs, and an international drug ring was behind it. You really think anyone cares about the color of your underwear, Mr. Stampa? By the way," Acardi glanced at Griffin, "I'm pretty sure Special Agent Martinez has seen your underwear before, in real life, so—"

Dino inhaled sharply. His last remark was totally inappropriate. These damn cops seemed to see and know everything.

***

After half an hour of questioning by both Detective Griffin and Inspector Acardi, Dino was finally released, free to go. They'd simply wanted to clarify some points. They had nodded most of the times when he answered, like they already knew the answers, and never acted surprised or unwilling to believe him. Dino was convinced that his answers would match what other people were testifying to and fit into the big picture.

He knew he should go back to work and get in touch with Nate Herring as soon as he had a spare minute. The mere thought of it made his headache worse. Although Dino hadn't done anything wrong, he dreaded the confrontation. No doubt, the police would help him explain why he'd been away from his lab for several days.

He felt hot and his throat hurt. He wished he could go home and lie down, drink tea, swallow a couple of analgesics, something for the fever, and get over whatever was creeping up on him. But he couldn't. Not today.

In the men's room, he looked into the mirror above the wash basin. His face was pale, and his nose reddish, the dark circles under his eyes prominent. He hesitated—there was that fine fragrance in the air, pleasant, fresh, that he had encountered before somewhere. A faint whiff of that refined, tropical blend of... He got it. Sompy.

Sompy had been here. Before running off or hiding somewhere. He wondered why the cops hadn't arrested him yet. Sompy had sat there in the conference room as if nothing had happened, friendly and polite, shy, smiling as always, but seemingly nervous. Of course, he was nervous. Probably a thrill of horror running down his spine. Then he'd left, innocently, and nobody seemed to object. Sompy, the instigator, who was sitting in the dark, helping create highly toxic drugs, implant them into tomatoes. He was probably long gone by now.

Then it struck him. Maybe the reason the cops let Sompy walk was because they didn't know the connection. Maybe they had no clue that he was involved.

Dino let the cold water run, closed his eyes, and splashed it on his face. It felt good on his hot skin. Slowly he opened his eyes and looked in the mirror. He froze. Sompy stood right behind him.

Dino felt a sudden rush of adrenaline as his pulse quickened. He hadn't heard a sound. As usual, Sompy moved like a cat—a predator in the jungle.

Dino spun around and backed away from Sompy in quick, jerky steps. It dawned on him that Sompy stood between him and the exit door. No way Dino could reach the door without Sompy blocking him.

"Sorry for scaring you," Sompy said quietly. "You have a few minutes? I'd like to talk."

Dino pressed his back hard against the tiled wall. He felt trapped. What would Sompy do next?

"Outside," Sompy said. "I'll wait for you outside in the lobby." He turned around and was gone in an instant.

Dino checked the room. There were no windows. No way he could escape. He had no choice other than to confront the danger, to face the new challenge. His only chance was that there were certainly other people in the building. The police even. He could scream for help. He wasn't alone. That could be his lifesaver.

His whole body was trembling as he yanked open the door and bolted into the dim corridor and around a few corners into the wide lobby of the main building.

"Help! Police! Where's Griffin?" he shouted with a raspy voice. He saw the receptionist shoot up from her chair, eyes wide open, hand in front of her mouth.

Dino's head started to spin. His mouth felt dry as dust.

Then sheets of black dots appeared before his eyes...

79

DINO

"You just zonked out," Griffin said. "What happened?"

Dino saw an outstretched arm and a glass of water in front of his face. "You okay?" he heard the receptionist say.

"How long was I... where am I?" Dino said, confused. He was lying on his back on a sofa. The black sofa in the visitor corner. It all came back quickly.

"Just a few minutes. You collapsed on the floor, like in slow-mo."

"It could be his blood pressure," someone said. "You feel any pain?"

Dino propped on his elbow. He was staring into Sompy's face for the second time.

"Any pain, Dino?"

Dino was glad they were joined by Griffin. "I feel fine. Just a headache. Probably I have a cold and a fever. Nothing serious. Thank you for..."

Sompy took Dino's arm and helped him sit upright. "I only wanted to thank Mr. Stampa, that's all," Sompy said, looking at Griffin. His face was full of empathy. "But then he blacked out."

"Thank me? What for?" Dino said. He didn't feel dizzy anymore.

"For helping us unravel the mystery about the deadly tomatoes."

Dino gave him a blank look.

"You were the one, Dino, who caused us to hit on the idea that someone may have turned tomatoes into biofactories."

"Me? Why?" Dino looked from Sompy to Griffin and back.

"Because you analyzed them."

"Red-O," Dino said. Griffin nodded.

"A new kind of opioid, a small protein, made from a plant, designed by a crazy geneticist."

"I know. Tomatoes," Dino said. "But I never told anyone—"

Griffin raised his hand. "Don't underestimate the DEA."

"You... you hacked my computer?" Dino asked, dumbstruck.

"You know, in situations like these, anything is possible. We're talking about homicide and drug trafficking." Griffin let the words sink in. "Allow me to finish the story, Mr. Somporn. It was then easy to find evidence that Harrod extracted the Red-O from the Grand Captivas. Nobody had any idea. The stuff was sold and shipped to the customers. Somporn had no idea, initially. But then he documented the fraud—and you know the rest."

Dino swallowed. He had wrongfully suspected Sompy of fraudulent activities—how blind had he been? How needlessly terrified of this catlike creature?

"Needless to say, the whole story has done a lot of damage to our company," Sompy said. "But we'll recover. We have to buff up GR&S's image, but we'll get there."

Buffing up the image? Dino thought when everybody departed and after he'd insisted that he was fine. His own image at LCH was certainly not the best anymore either.

He fished for his cell and sent out a short text.

Laurie, how are things at the lab? Have been tied up... Will explain later. Thanks—D.

Thirty seconds later, Dino's cell phone chirped. New text message.

SNAFU. Total chaos. Dr. Herring here. Not happy.

80

DINO

Dino watched Mia doodling on her paper napkin. She stretched out her arm to pick some black olives from a plate in the middle of the table, checking whether anyone was watching, then devoured them with a smacking sound. She appeared normal and didn't seem to be too traumatized by her abduction. *Strong girl*, Dino thought.

They sat down for dinner.

"You look wonderful with your new necklace, Cat," Dino said casually. "Perfect match for you."

She touched it, smiling. "I love it."

The next piece of jewelry might be a ring, Dino mused. *Maybe even sooner than later*. But first he had to prove himself at the hospital, to stand his test, make sure he could retain his job.

As if Cat could read his mind, she asked, "How are things at LCH?"

"Nate Herring wanted to see me. He's an inscrutable person, hard to read. One moment he's nice, the next, he's a bear. First, he says he's not happy with my performance as supervisor of the analytical lab; two minutes later, he says I did an outstanding job helping unravel the mysteries about the phantom opioids."

"Frankly, I think they'd need a supervisor who shows up at work once in a while."

Dino grunted. "Are you in cahoots with Nate Herring? That's exactly what he said to me. Verbatim."

"You've been more of a sleuth than a scientist recently. Maybe they have a job for you at the DEA."

"Yeah, right." Dino's smile morphed into a pensive mien.

He was determined to make every effort to improve his work ethic, and to do a stellar job. You don't find a dream job like that every day, after all.

A new start.

***

MIGUEL

Miguel sat in his favorite armchair, a bowl of guacamole dip and a bag of tortilla chips in front of him, watching the news.

Wing News at six released a statement from the Collier County Sheriff. The media had been covering the opioid scandal for the past days and weeks, but renewed interest had kicked in over the past twenty-four hours.

"Maria! *Mira*," he shouted toward the kitchen.

"A major drug ring in Southwest Florida has been busted." The reporter was standing outside, microphone in one hand. Behind him several police vehicles with strobe lights on could be seen.

One of the masterminds of the organized group, one Jason Goodlette, had been arrested. He and several other members had been indicted for illegally producing and distributing a novel opioid drug that featured high potency and toxicity and which, until recently, could not be identified.

The opioid drug had been produced in tomatoes by genetically manipulating the plants. "This may sound like science fiction," the reporter added, "but, in fact, this technique, known as plant-made pharmaceuticals, has been in practice for a number of years with potential applications to biomedicine." Such altered tomatoes had likely been the cause of seven unexplained opioid overdose deaths and numerous hospitalizations in the past weeks.

"*Loco*," Miguel muttered. Crazy. He didn't understand the

details, but he got the gist of it.

"The secret activity blew up," the reporter continued, "when Miguel Castro, a vendor who worked with the large organic produce company in Sementina Springs, Green, Red & Sustainable, unknowingly sold some of the gene-altered tomatoes and was subsequently assaulted. A small batch of the fatal fruit that contained high quantities of the toxic opioid had inadvertently been distributed through the unlucky vendor. However, with Castro's help, his assailant was identified, which eventually led to the takedown of the major suspects."

Miguel balled a fist. "*Bastardo.*"

"The mysterious assault of Castro had been covered earlier by *Wing News*," the anchor said. He concluded by assuring the viewers that Mr. Castro's recovery was nearly complete.

Miguel thrust his chest out, inhaling a deep, satisfied breath.

He looked up to Maria, who stood next to him, and registered the gleam in her eye.

81

DINO

Cat pushed the large bowl of salsa that Miguel had brought for them into the middle of the table.

"So sweet of you," she said.

"The salsa is homemade," Miguel said, rocking back on his heels for emphasis. "My wife made it fresh with tomatoes and chili peppers from our own garden." His eyes twinkled. "All natural, not from the research lab."

Dino winced for a moment, looking up. "*Dead natural? Nothing artificial?*"

Cat put on a pensive look. "I wonder," she started, speaking slowly, deliberately, "if a tomato plant naturally produces a certain chemical compound whose blueprint has been artificially inserted into the genome of that tomato—will that new compound in the ripe tomato be considered a natural product or a man-made chemical?"

Miguel pushed back a strand of jet-black hair. His smile was infectious. "A sharp distinction between natural and artificial is more artificial than natural, I guess."

"Can't argue with you there," Dino said.

Acknowledgments

My sincere thanks go to Marsha Butler for being both an outstanding editor and a dedicated coach from day one of this project. Her optimism is contagious. I'm also indebted to Elaine Viets for her professional critique and encouragement.

I am extremely grateful to Christian Sengstag for being my first beta-reader and for his excellent feedback on aspects of molecular genetics and protein biochemistry.

Thanks also to the Florida Writers Association for their support and resources.

My thanks go to Alex Kale, Kyle McCord, Ronaldo Alves, Cameron Finch, the production managers, and the entire team at Atmosphere Press; they did a wonderful job in transforming a finalized manuscript into a real book. In particular, I want to thank Megan Turner and Chris Beale for their excellent editorial assistance; their expertise, dedication, and patience are invaluable.

I am also grateful to Silvana Pluss for her help with the Spanish phrases.

Last but not least, my deepest thanks go to my wife Carmen for sharing her thoughts on the story and putting up with me during the conception, lengthy gestation period, and accouchement of this book project.

If there are any errors in the story, they are entirely mine.

Author's Note

This novel is a story in which scientists are going rogue and where the science is jumping the tracks. In this and similar types of fiction, the science part plays a key role rather than being used merely as a side ingredient to spice up the plot. Despite this, I have taken great care to make sure that the science behind the story is easily understandable for everyone; there is no need for special knowledge in the field.

Science thrillers belong to the subgenre of *science-in-fiction* and should not be confounded with *science fiction*. Even though creativity and vivid imagination are a typical feature of science thrillers, there is no room for magic or anything supernatural, and there is no need to go extragalactic. Almost all the details and techniques are accurate and real—in fact, accuracy is of paramount importance. Nevertheless, fictitious events, emanating from the author's mind, can mingle with the real science, typically resulting in things not yet possible today but theoretically feasible and doable if extrapolated into the future (although some might sound a bit far-fetched).

Maybe surprising to many, several of the techniques described in this book have been used for quite some time in biomedical and agricultural research. For example, plant-made pharmaceuticals (PMP) have been widely used, and a variety of plants have been explored to generate "foreign" products, including certain antibodies. Also, cyclic peptides (cyclotides) do exist and have been explored for their potential use in biomedicine. On the other hand, drug discovery/development is an extremely complex, time- and resource-intensive process typically involving a large team; for individuals to find a novel chemical that features such dramatic biological activity as described in this book is virtually impossible and a figment of my imagination.

Sadly, the opioid crisis is more real than ever. The U.S. Department of Health and Human Services officially declared a public health emergency in 2017. From 1999 to 2021, nearly 645,000 people died from an overdose involving any opioid, including prescription and illicit opioids, in the U.S. (CDC, National Center for Health Statistics, 2021).

About Atmosphere Press

Founded in 2015, Atmosphere Press was built on the principles of Honesty, Transparency, Professionalism, Kindness, and Making Your Book Awesome. As an ethical and author-friendly hybrid press, we stay true to that founding mission today.

If you're a reader, enter our giveaway for a free book here:

SCAN TO ENTER
BOOK GIVEAWAY

If you're a writer, submit your manuscript for consideration here:

SCAN TO SUBMIT
MANUSCRIPT

And always feel free to visit Atmosphere Press and our authors online at atmospherepress.com. See you there soon!

About the Author

Swiss-born **URS A. BOELSTERLI** is an emeritus professor of toxicology who has published extensively in the field, including a popular-science book, *Why the Dose Matters*, aimed at a general readership. He spent many years in New England and Florida, which is where his novels are set. *Dead Natural* received the 2020 Royal Palm Literary Award (Silver) of the Florida Writers Association. He is retired and lives with his family in Switzerland.

Milton Keynes UK
Ingram Content Group UK Ltd.
UKHW012251110624
443988UK00006B/349

9 798891 322523